THE
BRIGHTEST
STARS

www.annatodd.com

ANNA TODD

NEW YORK TIMES AND #1 BESTSELLING AUTHOR

BOOKS BY
ANNA TODD

After
After We Collided
After We Fell
After Ever Happy
Imagines
Before
Nothing More
Nothing Less
The Spring Girls

Playlist

One Last Time — Ariana Grande

Psycho — Post Malone (feat. Ty Dolla $ign)

Let Me Down Slowly — Alec Benjamin

Waves — Mr. Probz

Fake Love — BTS

To Build A Home — The Cinematic Orchestra

You Oughta Know — Alanis Morissette

Ironic — Alanis Morissette

Bitter Sweet Symphony — The Verve

3AM — Matchbox Twenty

Call Out My Name — The Weekend

Try Me — The Weekend

Beautiful — Bazzi

Leave A Light On — Tom Walker

In the Dark — Camila Cabello

Legends — Kelsea Ballerini

Youngblood — 5 Seconds of Summer

Want You Back — 5 Seconds of Summer

To Hugues de Saint Vincent,
I hope you can feel the passion in this book
and I continue to make you proud.
I miss you terribly and I will try to drink more red wine,
just for you. ♥ RIP

Chapter ☆ One

THE WIND WHIPS around the coffee shop each time the old wooden door creaks open. It's unusually cold for September and I'm pretty sure it's some kind of punishment from the universe for agreeing to meet up with him, today of all days. What was I thinking?

I barely had time to put makeup over the swollen pockets under my eyes. And this outfit I'm wearing—when was the last time it saw the wash? Again, what was I thinking?

Right now I'm thinking that my head aches and I'm not sure if I have any ibuprofen in my purse. I'm also thinking that it was smart of me to choose the table closest to the door so I can get away quickly if I need to. This place in the middle of Edgewood? Neutral and not the least bit romantic. Another good choice. I've only been here a few times, but it's my favorite coffee house in Atlanta. The seating is pretty limited—just ten tables—so I guess they want to encourage a quick turnaround. There are a couple of Instagram-worthy features, like the succulent wall and that clean black and white tile behind the baristas, but overall, it's quite severe. Harsh gray and concrete everywhere. Loud blenders mixing kale and whatever fruit is trendy at the moment.

There is a single creaky door: one way in, one way out. I look down at my phone and wipe my palms on my black dress.

Will he hug me? Shake my hand?

I can't imagine such a formal gesture. Not from him. Damn. I'm working myself up again and he isn't even here yet. For about the fourth time today, I can feel the panic bubbling just below my chest and it dawns on me that every time I imagine our reunion, I see him the way I did the very first time I laid eyes on him. I have no idea which version of him I'll get. I haven't seen him since last winter and I have no idea who he is anymore. And really, did I ever know?

Maybe I only ever knew a version of him—a bright and hollow form of the man I'm waiting on now.

I suppose I could have avoided him for the rest of my life, but the thought of never seeing him again seems worse than sitting here now. At least I can admit that. Here I am warming my hands on a coffee cup, waiting for him to come through that that raspy door after swearing to him, to myself, to anyone who would listen for the last few months that I would never …

He's not due for another five minutes, but if he's anything like the man I remember, he'll strut in late with that scowl on his face.

When the door tears open, it's a woman who walks in. Her blond hair is a nest stuck to the top of her tiny head and she's holding a cell phone against her red cheek.

"I don't give a shit, Howie. Get it done," she snaps, pulling the phone away with a string of curse words.

I hate Atlanta. The people here are all like her, tetchy and forever in a hurry. It wasn't always like this. Well, maybe it was; I wasn't, though. But things change. I used to love this city, especially downtown. The dining options are out of this world and for a foodie living in a small town—well, that alone was reason enough to move here. There's always something to do in Atlanta and everything is open later than it is around Ft. Benning. But the biggest draw for me at the time was that I wasn't constantly reminded of military life. No camo everywhere you look. No ACUs on the men and women waiting in line for the movies, at the gas station, at Dunkin Donuts. People speak real words, not just acronyms. And there are plenty of non-military haircuts to admire.

I loved Atlanta, but he changed that.

We changed that.

We.

That was the closest I'd get to admitting any blame in what went down.

Chapter ✷ Two

"YOU'RE STARING."

Just a couple of words, but they pour into and over me, shocking every one of my senses and all of my sense. And yet, there's that calm too, the one that seems to be hardwired into me whenever he's around. I look up to make sure it's him, though I know it is. Sure enough, he's standing over me with his hickory eyes on my face, searching … reminiscing? I wish he wouldn't look at me like that. The small room is actually pretty packed, but it doesn't feel that way. I'd had this meeting all scripted, but he's disrupted everything and now I'm unnerved.

"How do you do that?" I ask him. "I didn't see you come in."

I worry that my voice sounds like I'm accusing him of something or that I'm nervous, and that's the last thing I want. But still I wonder—how does he do that? He was always so good at silence, at moving around undetected. Another skill honed in the army, I guess.

I gesture for him to sit down. He slides into the chair and that's when I realize he has a full beard. Sharp, precise lines graze his cheekbones and his jawline is covered in dark hair. This is new. Of course it is: he always had to keep up with regulations. Hair must be short and well groomed. Mustaches are allowed, but only if they're neatly trimmed and don't grow over the upper lip. He told me once that he was thinking of growing a mustache, but I talked him out of it. Even with a face like his, a mustache would look creepy.

He grabs the coffee menu from the table. Cappuccino. Macchiato. Latte. Flat white. Long black. When did everything get so complicated?

"You like coffee now?" I don't try to hide my surprise. He shakes his head. "No."

A half-smile crosses his stoic face, reminding me of the very reason I fell in love with him. A moment ago, it was easy to look away. Now it's impossible.

"Not coffee," he assures me. "Tea."

He isn't wearing a jacket, of course, and the sleeves of his denim shirt are rolled up above his elbows. The tattoo on his forearm peeks through and I know if I touch his skin right now, it will be burning up. I'm sure as hell not going to do that, so I look up and over his shoulder. Away from the tattoo. Away from the thought. It's safer that way. For both of us. I try to focus on the noises in the coffee shop so I can settle into his silence. I forgot how unnerving his presence can be.

That's a lie. I didn't forget. I wanted to, but couldn't.

I can hear the server approaching, her sneakers squeaking on the concrete floor. She has a mousy little voice and when she tells him that he should "so totally" try the new peppermint mocha I laugh, knowing that he hates all minty things, even toothpaste. I think about the way he'd leave those red globs of cinnamon gunk in the sink at my house and how many times we bickered over it. If only I had ignored those petty grievances. If only I had paid more attention to what was really happening, everything might have been different.

Maybe. Maybe not. I'm the kind of person who would take the blame for anything—except this. I can't be sure.

I don't want to know.

Another lie.

Kael tells the girl he would like a plain black tea and this time, I try not to laugh. He's so predictable.

"What's so funny?" he asks when the waitress leaves.

"Nothing." I change the subject. "So, how are you?"

I don't know what bullshit we're going to fill this coffee date with. What I do know is that we're going to see each other tomorrow, but since I had to be in the city today anyway, it had seemed like a good idea to get the first awkward encounter out of the way without an audience. A funeral is no place for that.

"Good. Given the circumstances." He clears his throat.

"Yeah." I sigh, trying not to think too much about tomorrow. I've always been good at pretending the world isn't burning around me. Okay, I've been slipping these past few months, but for years it was second nature, something I'd started doing sometime between my parents' divorce and my high school graduation. Sometimes I feel like my family is disappearing. We keep getting smaller and smaller.

"Are you all right?" he asks, his voice even lower than before.

I could hear it the same way I did those damp nights when we fell asleep with the window open—the whole room would be dewy the next morning, our bodies wet and sticky. I used to love the way his hot skin felt when my fingertips danced across the smooth contours of his jaw. Even his lips were warm, feverish at times. The southern Georgia air was so thick you could taste it and Kael's temperature always ran so hot.

"*Hmph.*" He clears his throat and I snap out of it.

I know what he's thinking, I can read his face as clearly as the neon *But First, Coffee* sign hanging on the wall behind him. I hate that those memories are the ones my brain associates with him. It doesn't make this any easier.

"Kare." His voice is soft as he reaches across the table to touch my hand. I jerk it away so fast you'd think it was on fire. It's strange to think about the way we were, the way I never knew where he ended and I began. We were so in tune. So ... just so different than the way things are now. There was a time when he'd say my name, and just like that, I'd give him anything he wanted. I consider this for a moment. How I'd give that man anything he wanted.

I thought I was further in my recovery of us, that whole *getting over him* thing. At least far enough along that I wouldn't be thinking about the way his voice sounded when I had to wake him up early for physical training, or the way he used to scream in the night. My head is starting to spin and if I don't shut my mind off now, the memories will split me apart, on this chair, in this little shop, right in front of him.

I force myself to nod and pick up my latte to buy some time, just a moment so I can find my voice. "Yeah. I mean, funerals are kind of my thing."

I don't dare look at his face. "There's nothing you could have done, regardless. Don't tell me you're thinking you could've—" He pauses and I stare harder at the small chip in my mug. I run my finger over the cracked ceramic.

"Karina. Look at me."

I shake my head, not even close to jumping down this rabbit hole with him. I don't have it in me. "I'm fine. Seriously." I pause and take in the expression on his face. "Don't look at me like that. I'm okay."

"You're always fine." He runs his hand over the hair on his face and sighs, his shoulders leaning into the back of the plastic chair.

It isn't so much a question or a statement, just the way it is. He's right. I will always be fine. That whole *fake it till you make it* thing? I own it.

What other choice do I have?

Chapter ☆ Three

I HAD HIT the job jackpot. I didn't have to open the massage parlor until ten, so most mornings I could sleep in. And being able to walk there from my house at the end of the street—bonus! I loved this street: the mattress shop, the ice cream place, the nail salon, and the old-fashioned candy store. I'd saved up my money and there I was, twenty years old, on my own street, in my own tiny house. My house. Not my dad's. Mine.

The walk to work was only five minutes—not long enough to be interesting. Mostly I just tried to stay out of the way of the cars. The alley was wide enough for one pedestrian and one car at a time. Well, a Prius or some kind of small car would be an easy fit; unfortunately, people around here usually went for big trucks, so most of the time I pinned myself up against the trees lining the alleyway until they passed.

Sometimes I'd create stories in my head, a little bit of

excitement before my shift started. That day's story featured Bradley, the bearded man who owned the mattress store on the corner. Bradley was a nice guy, and he wore what I came to think of as his nice guy uniform: a plaid shirt and khakis. He drove a white Ford something or other, and he worked even more than I did. I passed him every morning, already at his shop before I started at ten. Even when I worked a double or a night shift, I'd see that white truck parked in the back of the alley.

Bradley had to be single. Not because he wasn't sweet or cute, but because he was always alone. If he had a wife or children, surely I'd have seen them at least once in the six months since I'd moved to this side of town, but no. It didn't matter if it was during the day, at night, or on the weekends— Bradley was always alone.

The sun was shining, but not a single bird was chirping. No garbage truck was grumbling. Not one person was starting their car. It was eerily silent. Maybe that's why Bradley seemed a little more sinister that morning. I looked at him anew and wondered why he combed his white-blond hair down the middle, why he thought it was a good idea to expose such a harsh line of scalp. Really, what I wanted to know was where he was going with that rolled up rug in the back of his truck. Maybe I'd seen one too many episodes of CSI, but doesn't everyone know that's how you dispose of a body—roll it up in some old carpet and dump it on the edge of town? Just as my imagination was turning Bradley into a serial killer, he gave me the friendliest wave and a smile, a real one. Or maybe he was just that good at being charming and was actually going to—

I nearly peed myself when he called out to me.

"Hey, Karina! Water's out in the whole strip!"

His thin lips turned into a heavy frown as he waved

his arms around to show how upset he was. I stopped walking and lifted my hand to cover my eyes from the sun. It was harsh, shining its brightest, even though the air had a little bite to it. Georgia was just so hot. I thought I'd be used to it after a year, but nope. I longed for the cold of those northern California nights. "I've been tryin' to get the water company out here, but no luck so far." He shrugged his shoulders and held up his cell phone as proof.

"Oh no." I tried to mimic his tone of frustration over the water, but honestly, I kind of hoped Mali would shut down for the day. I had barely slept last night, so I could have used another hour, or twenty, of sleep.

"I'll keep tryin' to call them," he offered.

His fingers reached down and touched his longhorn belt buckle. He looked like he was already sweating and when he grabbed the massive rug from the bed of his truck, I almost wanted to help him.

"Thanks," I said. "I'll let Mali know."

Chapter ⭑ Four

THE DOOR WAS LOCKED, the lights were off—even the hallway light that we usually kept on—and it was freezing inside. I turned on the oil warmers and lit the candles in the lobby and in two of the rooms.

My first client wasn't until ten thirty. Elodie's wasn't scheduled until eleven thirty. She was still snoring when I left the house, which meant she'd rush through the door at ten past eleven and give her client a sweet smile and a quick apology in that cute little French accent of hers. Then she'd be on with her day.

Elodie was one of the few people in the world I'd do most anything for. That was especially true now that she was pregnant. She'd found out about the baby just two days after her husband's boots hit the dirt in Afghanistan. That kind of stuff was the norm around here. I saw it with my parents, with Elodie … pretty much everyone around these posts knew it was a possibility. Not just a possibility. More like the reality when you were married to the military.

I shook the thought off. I needed some music in here. I hated silence. I had recently convinced Mali to let me play more relevant music over the speakers while we worked. I couldn't handle another shift of "relaxing spa tunes" on repeat for hours. The sleepy sounds of waterfalls and waves got on my nerves like no other. Made me drowsy, too. I turned on the iPad and within seconds, Banks was washing away the memory of all that soft, dreamy babble. I walked to the front desk to switch the computer on. Not two minutes later, Mali came in with a couple of big tote bags hanging from her little arms.

"What's wrong?" she asked as I took the bags from her.

"Um, nothing? No, *hi*? No, *how's it going, Karina*?" I laughed and made my way to the back room.

The food in those bags smelled so good. Mali made the best homemade Thai food I'd ever tasted and she always made extra for Elodie and me. She graced us with it at least five days a week. The little avocado—that's what Elodie called her baby bump—only wanted spicy drunken noodles. It was the basil leaves. Elodie had become obsessed with them since getting pregnant, to the point where she'd pick them out of her noodles and chew on them. Babies made you do the strangest things.

"Karina," Mali said, smiling. "How are you? You look sad."

That was Mali for you. *What's wrong? You look sad.* If it was on her mind, it came out of her mouth.

"Hey—I'm fine," I said. "I'm just not wearing makeup." I rolled my eyes and she poked my cheek.

"That's not it," she said.

No, that wasn't it. But I wasn't sad. And I didn't like that my mask had slipped enough for Mali to notice. I didn't like it one bit.

Chapter ⭑ Five

TEN THIRTY CAME and my client was right on time. I was used to his punctuality, not to mention his soft skin. I could tell he used oil after his showers and that made my job easier, massaging already soft skin. His muscles were always so tight, especially around his shoulders, so I assumed he sat behind a desk all day. He wasn't military. I gathered that by his longer hair, curling at the tips.

Today his shoulders were so tense that my fingers hurt a little when they rubbed the patch of tissue at the top of his shoulders. He was a groaner—a lot of clients were—and he made these deep throaty sounds when I loosened the knots he held in his body. The hour went fast. I had to tap his shoulder to wake him when it was over.

My ten thirty client—his name was Toby, but I liked to call him ten thirty—was a good tipper and kept things simple. Except for that time he asked me out. Elodie freaked when I told her. She wanted me to tell Mali, but I didn't want it to become a thing when it didn't need to be. He was fine with my rejection—unusual with men, I know. Anyway, he hadn't even so much as hinted at any attraction toward me since, so I figured things were okay between us.

Forty-five minutes past eleven and there was still no Elodie. Usually she'd text if she was going to be more than fifteen minutes late. The man in the waiting area must have been new, because I didn't recognize him and I never forgot a face. He seemed patient enough. Not Mali, though. She was two minutes away from calling Elodie.

"I can take him if she's not here in five minutes. My next client can be moved an hour later, it's Tina," I told Mali. She knew most of the patrons who came in and out of her salon; she remembered names like I did faces.

"Fine, fine. But your friend is always late," she scolded. Mali was the nicest woman, but made of pure fire.

"She's pregnant," I said, defending my friend.

Mali rolled her eyes. "I have five children and I worked just fine."

"Touché."

I kept my laughter quiet and texted Tina to see if she could come in at one. She immediately responded with a *yes*, like I knew she would.

"Sir," I called to the man in the waiting room. "Your therapist is actually running late. I can start you now if you'd like. Or you could wait for Elodie." I didn't know if he was partial to her for some reason, or if he just wanted a massage. Now that we were on Yelp and booking online appointments, I never knew which clients wanted a specific therapist.

He stood up and walked to the desk without saying a word. "Is that okay?" I asked.

He hesitated for a second before he nodded. Okay …

"All right—" I looked at the schedule. *Kael.* What a

strange name. "Follow me, please."

We didn't have assigned rooms—not technically—but I had fixed up the second room on the left to perfectly fit my taste, so that was the one I used the most. No one else took it unless they had to.

I had brought in my own cabinet, my own decorations, and was in the process of convincing Mali to let me paint the walls. Anything would be better than this dark purple color. It wasn't exactly relaxing, plus it was dull and dated the room by about twenty years.

"You can leave your clothes on the hanger or the chair," I told him. "Go ahead and strip down to however you're comfortable. Lie facedown on the table, and I'll be back in two minutes."

The client didn't say a word; he just stood next to the chair and lifted his gray T-shirt over his head. He was definitely military. Between his solid build and his nearly-shaved head, he *screamed* soldier. I grew up inside army posts my entire life, so I knew. He folded his shirt and set it down on the chair. When his fingers tugged at his athletic pants, I left him alone to undress.

Chapter ✶ Six

I PULLED MY PHONE out of my scrub pocket and read the first line of a text from my dad: **See you tonight. Estelle is making one of her best recipes.**

I could name at least a thousand things I'd rather do, but this is what the three of us—sometimes four—did every single Tuesday. I'd missed only one family dinner since moving out a year ago, and that was when my dad drove Estelle in our family RV to the boot camp graduation of some distant relative, so technically I guess I wasn't the one who missed it. They still had it, on their little family vacay, while Elodie and I shoved our faces with Dominos.

I didn't respond to my dad because he knew I'd be there at seven. My "new" mom would be in the bathroom curling her hair and dinner wouldn't be started, but I'd be there on time. Like I always was.

It had been three minutes since I told Elodie's client I'd be back to start his treatment, so I pulled back the curtain and walked into the room. The lights were dimmed so everything was a shade of purple from the hideous walls. The candles had been burning long enough for the air to take on the clean smell of lemongrass. Even after my restless night, this room had the power to calm me.

He was on the table in the center of the room with the white blanket pulled up to his waist. I rubbed my hands together. My fingertips were still too cold to touch someone's skin, so I walked over to the sink to warm them. I turned on the faucet. Nothing. I had already forgotten Bradley's warning and for the last hour, I'd managed without water.

I rubbed my hands together and wrapped them around the oil warmer on the edge of the sink. It was a little too hot, but it did the trick. The oil would be warm on his skin and he probably wouldn't notice that the water wasn't working. It wasn't convenient, but it was manageable. I hoped that whoever worked the closing shift put clean towels in the warmer last night before they left.

"Do you have any specific areas of concern or tension that you'd like me to focus on?" I asked.

No answer. Had he already fallen asleep?

I waited a few beats before I asked again.

He shook his shaved head in the face cradle and said, "Don't touch my right leg. Please," he added the please at the end as an afterthought.

I had requests from people all the time not to touch certain parts of their bodies. They had all kinds of reasons, from medical conditions to insecurities. It wasn't my business to ask. My business was to make the client feel better and provide a healing experience. It seemed like every time I didn't have them fill out a treatment card, they had special request. Mali would scold me over this for sure.

"Will do. Would you like light, medium, or intense pressure?" I asked, grabbing the little bottle of oil off the cabinet shelf. The outside of the bottle was still really hot but I knew it would be the perfect temperature when it hit his skin.

Again, no answer. Maybe he was hard of hearing. I was used to this as well—one of the rougher things about army life.

"Kael?" I said his name, though I didn't know why.

His head popped up so quickly, I thought I frightened him. I jumped a little myself.

"Sorry, I just wanted to know what level of pressure you wanted?"

"Any?" He didn't sound like he knew what he wanted. Probably a first-timer. He put his head back into the cradle.

"Okay. Just tell me if the pressure is too light or too firm and I'll adjust my touch," I told him.

I could be a little heavy-handed and most of my clients liked that, but I'd never worked on this guy before.

Who knew if he'd ever come back? I'd say only about four of out of ten first-timers actually returned and only one or two become regulars. We weren't a big salon, but we had a steady clientele.

"This is peppermint oil." I dotted the little bottle against my forefinger. "I'm going to rub some into your temples. It helps with—"

He lifted his head up, lightly shaking it. "No," he said. His voice wasn't harsh, but it let me know he absolutely did not want me to use peppermint oil. Okay …

"Okay." I screwed the lid back on the bottle and

turned the faucet. Damn it. The water. I knelt down and opened the towel warmer. Empty. Of course it was.

"Um, just a second," I told him. He laid his head back into the cradle and I shut the warmer door a little too hard. I hoped he didn't hear it over the music. This wasn't turning out to be the smoothest session...

Chapter ★ Seven

MALI WAS IN THE HALLWAY when I pushed through the thin curtain to search for towels. "I need water. Or warm towels."

She put her fingers to her lips to tell me to hush. "There's no water. I have towels. Who didn't stock?"

I shrugged. I didn't know and didn't really care; I just wanted a towel. "He's been in my room for five minutes and I haven't started yet."

At that she moved faster, disappearing into the room across the hall and popping back up with a few hot towels. I grabbed them from her, shifting the steaming bundles from palm to palm to cool them off.

When I got back into the room, I waved the towel through the air one last time and rubbed it across the bottom of his bare feet. His skin was so hot to the touch that I pulled the towel away and touched the back of my hand to the top of his foot to make sure he didn't have a fever or anything. I couldn't afford to be sick.

Literally. The days on my dad's Tricare were coming

to an end and I couldn't afford health insurance on my own.

His skin felt so hot. I lifted the blanket a little and realized he was still wearing his pants. That was just … strange. I didn't know how I was going to rub his other leg, the one I was supposed to massage.

"Did you want me to avoid your legs altogether?" I quietly asked him.

He nodded his head in the cradle. I continued to run the hot towel across the bottoms of his feet, something I did to clean off any oil and dirt. The hygiene of clients … well, let's just say it varied. Some people came in wearing sandals after walking around all day. Not this guy, though. He must have showered before he came in. I appreciated that. These were the things you thought about as a masseuse. I started on the balls of his feet, applying pressure there and moving to the arch of his left foot. There was a soft, bubbly line across the bottom of his left foot, but I couldn't see the scar in the dark. I slid my thumb slowly along the arch and he jerked a little.

I was used to timing my hour sessions perfectly, about five minutes per leg, so I took the extra time to work on his shoulders. A lot of people carried tension in their shoulders, but this guy—if these weren't the stiffest shoulders I'd ever worked on, they sure came close. I had to stop myself from making up a story about his life.

I continued, keeping his legs covered by the blanket and working on his neck, his shoulders, his back. His muscles were defined, but not bulky or hard under my moving fingers. I imagined his young body had been carrying the weight of something for a long time—a rucksack, maybe. Or just life itself. He didn't express enough of himself for me to make up a life for him the way I did with Bradley and most of the other strangers around me. There was something about this guy that kept my imagination at bay.

His scalp was the last part I worked on. The soft pressure release usually made people moan or at least sigh, but nothing came from his lips. He didn't make a peep. I thought maybe he'd fallen asleep. That happened often and I loved when it did. It meant I did a good job. When the time was up, I felt like it had just started. I usually drifted in and out of thought—my dad, my brother, work, my house. But there was something about working on this guy. I came up with nothing.

"Thank you, was everything okay?" Sometimes I asked, sometimes I didn't. This guy was so quiet that I wasn't sure if he'd enjoyed it or not.

He kept his face in the cradle so I barely heard him when he said, "Yeah."

Okay ...

"Okay, well I'm going to step out and let you get dressed. I'll see you in the lobby when you're finished. Take your time."

He nodded and I left the room, pretty sure I wouldn't be getting a tip.

Chapter ⋆ Eight

I HEARD ELODIE in the lobby. She was talking to Mali, who was giving her a hard time for being late.

"I took your client—he's dressing now," I told my friend. It didn't hurt to let Mali know that everything was covered, no harm done. Elodie smiled at me and tilted her head to the side. She had this thing about her where she could get away with just about anything.

"I'm so sorry, Karina. Thank you." She kissed both of my cheeks. That was something I got used to the first week she moved in. I wasn't really fond of excess touching but with her, it was hard to recoil the way I normally would.

"I couldn't fall asleep last night. The avocado started kicking." Her smile grew wide, but I could tell by her eyes that she wasn't rested. I could relate.

Mali put her hand on Elodie's stomach and started talking to the baby. I half expected her to ask the bump *what's wrong, why aren't you smiling?* but Mali was soft and kind around children, even the ones who hadn't been born yet. It made me a little uncomfortable, the way she was touching Elodie like that, but the idea of the baby kicking was exciting, so I smiled. I really was happy for my friend. It worried me that she was so alone here with her family and most of her friends across the Atlantic Ocean. She was young. So young. I wondered if she'd had the chance to tell Phillip that she thought she felt the baby move yesterday, or if he would even get to check his email today. The time zones made it so hard for them to talk as often as Elodie or anyone with a soldier in their life would want, but she was handling it with grace, as she did everything. It scared the hell out of me, though—the fact that she was going to have a baby in a few months.

Elodie's eyes snapped to the curtain behind me and she lit up like a Christmas tree, pushing past me to the client. She said a name that I couldn't hear completely, but it didn't sound anything like Kael. She double kissed his cheeks and hugged him.

"You're here! I can't believe you're here! How did you know?" She squealed and hugged him again.

Mali nodded to my next client who was walking through the front door. "Back to work for you," she said.

Chapter ⋆ Nine

TINA WAS ONE of my favorite clients. She worked from home as a family therapist and more than once let me use her massage session as *my* therapy. I wasn't open with too many people, but Tina had no one to tell my secrets to. It made me sad for her, though, thinking about how lonely she must be in her big, empty house, eating dinner alone in front of the TV. Then again, that's what my life consisted of, so I guess I shouldn't feel too sad for her. I felt slightly guilty about the way a strike of fear slapped against me—was Tina's life my future?

Today's session with her felt like it was never going to end. I checked the clock again: ten minutes left.

"So, how are things with your brother?" she asked. I moved her hair to the side so I could focus on the tight muscles in her neck. Tina had recently cut her hair—The Demi, she called it—but hated it and immediately started wearing hats to cover her dark strands. It still wasn't long enough to put into a ponytail.

I didn't really want to talk about my brother. Actually, I didn't want to feel the way I would feel if we talked about my brother.

"The same. I've barely heard from him since he's been staying with my uncle. Who knows when he's coming back?" I sighed, gliding my fingers down Tina's neckline.

"Is he in school there yet?" she asked.

"No. They keep saying they're going to sign him up, but haven't." I tried not to think much about it, but my brain didn't work that way. Once I cracked the door open, the wood snapped off of the hinges and everything rushed in.

"It sounds like they don't plan on it," Tina said.

"Yeah. I figured as much. He won't talk to me about it, and his scholarship to the community college expired last month."

Little pokes of stress rapped at my shoulders and down my spine. I understood that Austin couldn't bear to live with our dad any longer, but I was conflicted; he was my twin, twenty and headed nowhere. He shouldn't be living in the next state over with our thirty-year-old uncle who smelled like Cheetos and watched online porn all day, but I also didn't want him to live in my house with me. It was complicated. I still couldn't believe my dad had let him leave in the first place. But I really couldn't blame my brother. Again, complicated.

"Honestly, Karina, you can't take on full responsibility for this. It's not good for you and at the end of the day, your brother is the same age as you. Or five minutes younger, if I remember?"

"Six." I smiled and moved my hands down to her shoulder blades.

I knew she was right, but that didn't make it any easier.

I moved my hands along her skin, using a compression stroke. "You have to decide what's best for you," she said. "You're starting a new chapter and you should have the most de-cluttered life possible."

Easier said than done.

"I'll ask my dad if he's heard anything from him."

Tina didn't say anything after that. She must have known that talking about the dinner with my "family" would be too much for me that early in the day, so she just enjoyed the rest of her treatment while my thoughts boiled inside my brain.

Chapter ☆ Ten

IT WAS ALMOST SIX when I finished for the day. I had three more clients after Tina, and each of them occupied my mind in different ways. Stewart—I called her by the last name stitched into her ACUs—was an army medic who had the most beautiful eyes I had ever seen. She kept me busy talking about her next post, about how, with her job, she could be stationed almost anywhere in the world, so being posted to Hawaii was like hitting the jackpot. It was nice to see her so happy.

Some people loved to move around in the military and Stewart was one of them. She was only a year older than me, but she'd already been deployed to Iraq—twice. And man, did she have stories. At twenty-one, she'd had experiences most people couldn't dream of. But when those experiences turned into memories...well, they started playing through her mind on a constant loop. Never waning, never quiet, those memories became background noise that eventually took up residence in her head—tolerable, but always there. I knew all about it. My dad's brain was full of that clamor. With six tours between Iraq and Afghanistan, his background noise blared throughout our house. His house.

I thought about all of this while Stewart lay on my table. I was glad she could open up to me, that she could unburden herself by talking and releasing a bit of her background noise. I knew better than most that it wasn't just the physical aspect of massage that reduced stress, that helped a body come alive.

It was almost poetry the way Stewart talked about her life. I felt every word when she spoke. I thought about things I tried hard not to. She connected me to something and when she told me everything she had been through and everything she knew, she opened me up to a different perspective.

For instance, Stewart talked a lot about how, in the United States, less than eight percent of living citizens had ever served in the military. That included all the branches— every veteran who had ever served, even for one term. Out of over three hundred million people, less than eight percent. It was hard for me to realize that the way I grew up, moving from post to post, trying to make new friends, trying to adapt to strangers every few years, wasn't the reality for most people. For most Americans, anyway.

Less than eight percent? It seemed impossible to me, that small of a number. From my great-grandfather to my dad, my uncles and cousins who were scattered across the country (except that loser uncle my brother was living with), everyone around me wore a uniform or lived with someone who did. The world had never felt so big until Stewart and her statistics.

She talked a lot during our sessions, like Tina. But unlike Tina, Stewart didn't expect me to share. I could hide behind her experiences, many of which forced me to bite back my tears. Maybe that's why her sessions went so fast.

Chapter * Eleven

THE WATER CAME BACK ON right after Stewart left. I washed the sheets and towels, and while I was waiting for my next client or a walk-in to arrive, I worked on a new playlist.

Elodie managed to be busy with a client each time I finished with mine. I was dying to ask her how she knew that soldier with the strange name, but we kept missing each other. I usually didn't get involved in other people's drama—I had enough of my own—but Elodie didn't know many people here. The only other army wives she talked to were on Facebook. My next client was a sleeper. He usually conked out within five minutes, which left me with the entire hour to think about my brother. Oh—and how much I was dreading tonight's dinner. I was slightly envious of Austin for being so far away in South Carolina, sleeping past noon and working part-time at Kmart.

I also thought about Elodie's friend, how he wore pants throughout his treatment and how the amount of tension he held in his body wasn't healthy for such a young guy. He couldn't have been older than twenty-two. If that.

My last client of the day was a walk-in who left me a big tip for a thirty-minute pre-natal massage. Her belly was so full and she seemed so tired. I almost asked her if she was okay, but I didn't want to be rude.

I walked by Elodie's room again. The door was closed and for a second, I even imagined that her soldier friend might be in the room with her. My imagination sure ran wild.

Before I went home, I helped Mali restock the back room and the towel warmers, and folded the laundry. I wasn't in a rush to get home, especially on so-called family dinner night.

When I finally left for the day, I took Mali's delicious leftovers home with me. That whole thing about pregnant women eating for two might be an old wives' tale, but it was still important for Elodie to have nutritious meals. I carried the food in one hand and tried to call my brother with the other. Voicemail.

"Hey, it's me. I was just calling to check on you. I haven't heard from you in a few days. Call me back. I'm going to Dad's for Tuesday dinner. You suck for not being here."

I hung up and put my phone in my front pocket. Around me, the sky looked like the sun couldn't decide to set or not, staying an orange color that made everything look just a little nicer. The parking spots in the alley were all full. Bradley's white truck was there—parked sideways, taking up two spots—and the truck bed was so full of mattresses it reminded me of that fairy-tale about the princess and the pea. He walked out the back door and tossed a pillow into the pile.

"Water's back!" he shouted, waving his hand.

"Yeah …" I said, smiling. "Thanks for being on the water company!" I added.

Okay, that was awkward. I could feel it and I knew

that conversation would mull over inside my head later tonight. My brain usually worked that way. Bradley didn't seem to notice or overthink my words the way I did—he just told me to have a good night, locked the door to his shop, and climbed inside his truck.

Doors slammed, tires crunched over branches, and voices filled the rest of my short walk home. I thought about dinner tonight and what forced conversation we would have during at least three courses.

I had to be at my dad's by seven, which meant I had to be ready to leave my house by six forty. I needed to shower and put actual clothes on, even if I was just giving my appearance minimal effort. My dad's wife had stopped commenting on my looks once I lost enough "extra pounds" to please her. Small mercies, I guess.

I really wanted to stay home and eat leftovers with Elodie. I'd had variations of that same thought every single week since I moved out. I thought it would go away, that I'd get used to the routine. But nope. I hadn't and didn't think I ever would. Sure, dinner once a week was better than living there—by far. But, I hated the task of it, hated that my entire week revolved around Tuesday at seven. When I did my laundry, when I washed my hair, when I could work. It all revolved around this dinner. I guess I wasn't as much of a grown-up as I thought.

Chapter ☆ Twelve

I WAS STARTING to hate Facebook. Every single time I opened the app, there was either a newborn baby, a proposal, or a death. If it wasn't that, it was politics, with everyone shouting so loudly they couldn't hear what the other was saying. The whole thing was exhausting and I had barely posted anything in months. I never felt like I had anything to share with people I hardly knew. And unlike Sarah Chessman, who had moved away my senior year, I didn't feel like every Crockpot meal or selfie was social media worthy.

But out of slightly bitchy curiosity, and because I had another few minutes to waste on my walk home, I went to Sarah Chessman's page to scroll through her boring life. Maybe it was the fact that I was walking through the noisy alley and my feet hurt like hell, or that I'd be knocking on my dad's door in an hour, but Sarah's life actually looked okay today. She had a husband—a newly minted soldier stationed in Texas—and she was pregnant. I watched a ten-second video of her opening a box full of pink balloons, revealing the gender of her upcoming baby. She didn't look terrified the way I would if I were her.

I started to feel like a hypocrite for judging her, so I clicked back to my main feed. My dad had posted a picture of himself holding a fish in one hand and a beer in the other. He loved to hunt and fish; my brother and I couldn't stomach it. Austin more than me. He would go on hunting trips with Dad until we got to high school and started dating. My brother, who I had talked to every day up until a few months ago but now could barely get on the phone, had already liked my dad's post. So did someone with a golden retriever as their profile picture. The golden retriever friend had commented that my dad was "looking happier than ever."

It stung. It really stung. I had been hearing that phrase since he got remarried three years ago. From the neighbors to the cashiers at the PX, everyone thought it was okay to congratulate my dad on how happy he was. No one seemed to consider that I might be in earshot, that telling him how happy he was *now* implied that he had been really unhappy before. No one seemed to consider me. That's when I started clinging to people, boys mostly. Some at my high school, some older. I was searching for something I wasn't getting at home, but I couldn't tell you what it was.

Mostly, I clung to Austin. Maybe it was the twin thing, maybe it was the fact that our parents were never around when we needed them most, when their guidance would have mattered. Staying close to my six-minutes younger brother seemed to help for a while, but once we were out of high school, I started to consider that maybe Austin wasn't the person I had built him up to be. One of the weirdest parts about growing up was the way memories changed.

Like when Austin took me to that party in Chesapeake

Manor, where all the officers' kids were partying. He told me that everyone our age was drinking, that I should just relax. Then he passed out in one of the bedrooms with some girl from a high school across town and I was forced to sleep there, surrounded by loud, belligerent boys. That's when one of them, the one who called me "Austin's sister" and had too deep a voice for a high school kid, swore I had a crush on him and shoved his tongue down my throat—repeatedly. Until I started crying and he got "weirded out."

Funny how my telling him to stop, my constant *no no no, please no* didn't do it.

Nope, it was the salty, hot tears streaming down my face that finally got him to go away. Eventually I fell asleep on a couch listening to some war video game being played in the other room. Austin never apologized the next morning. He never asked how I had slept or where. He just kissed that random girl on the cheek and made a joke that she and I both laughed at, and then we Ubered home like nothing ever happened. Our dad yelled at me, not him, and we both got grounded for a week.

I clicked on Austin's profile and thought about calling him again, but then Elodie opened the front door and surprised me. I hadn't even realized I was on my front porch.

Chapter * Thirteen

MY HOUSE IS SMALL, so when you go through the front door, you're already in the living room. That's one of the things I liked about it, the way it was all cozy and warm, everything there waiting. The lights and TV were on when I got home that night, the room filled with the voice of Olivia Pope. And there was Elodie, standing at the door, greeting me with a nervous smile. Something was up.

I hadn't known Elodie that long, but I felt I knew her well. I'm not sure how much we had in common, other than being the same age. And even that, well, I felt older somehow. I looked older, too. Elodie had this way about her that made her appear younger than she was, especially when she smiled. And when she was nervous or sad, she looked about sixteen. Younger even. That brought out the protector in me.

Elodie tried her best to be the perfect young army wife, but she was already at the center of so many petty rumors. The wives in Phillip's platoon made little jokes about her accent and called her a "mail-order bride." She was hardly the only one. Tons of soldiers met their wives online, but that didn't seem to matter to these women. Maybe they should talk to Stewart. I bet she had some statistics about how many members of the military met their spouses on sites like MilitaryCupid.

Anyway, that's how a lot of military posts were—everyone bickering and jostling for position. Elodie's neighbors were bitches who spent their days selling pyramid schemes on Facebook and bullying her over her grass being an inch too long. That's not an exaggeration. I was with her once when the "mayor" of her housing department pulled up, tires screeching, and scolded Elodie for letting her grass grow half an inch too long.

Yes, the "mayor" measured.

No, she didn't have anything better to do.

That's why Elodie preferred to spend her nights on my couch, or in my bed, depending on where she fell asleep. I got the feeling she liked the couch the most. She didn't wake up asking for Phillip when she was on the couch.

I planned on asking Elodie about the guy from earlier. Obviously she knew him—but how? She didn't have many friends, as far as I was aware, and she didn't spend much time socializing. Maybe Phillip had buddies outside of his platoon. It wasn't too common, but it wasn't impossible either.

Elodie sat down on the couch and tucked her feet under her. Her petite body was changing, her belly starting to swell. I wondered where the baby would sleep in my little house.

Elodie's favorite American show at the moment was *Scandal*. She was binge-watching it for the first time.

"What season are you on now?" I asked her.

"Two," she said softly.

She was being so quiet. I pulled my shoes off and it wasn't until I dropped one on the floor and something moved in my peripheral vision that I realized another person was in my house.

A noise, a little like a shriek, flew from my mouth when I saw him. He was staring at me, the one-syllable client from earlier. He was sitting in my chair—the dark pink, used-to-be-red one that my nana gave me before we moved to Georgia.

"Um, hey?" I said when my heart stopped doing little flips from the aftershock of surprise. How did I not see a whole human in my living room? I had been feeling spacey a lot the last few weeks, but that day was another level.

"How was work?" Elodie asked, looking at the TV while her fingers picked at the fabric on her pants, and then back to me.

"Good …"

I stared at this Kael guy and he stared back at me. When I would recall this later, the first time he was inside my little white house, the memory would change from a burning pain to pure bliss and back—again and again and again. But when it happened in real life, it happened fast. Before he was anything to me—before he was everything—he was just a quiet stranger with a blank face and distant eyes. There was something indomitable about him, something so closed, that I couldn't even begin to make up a life for him. He hated peppermint oil and hadn't wanted me to touch his leg—those were the only clues I had to who he was.

I smelled the popcorn right before the popping actually started. "I'm making popcorn," Elodie announced. She was nervous. What was going on here?

"Okay …" I started. "I'm going to take a shower. I have to be at my dad's at seven."

I walked down the hallway. Elodie followed, chewing on her bottom lip.

"Well?" I asked.

"He just got home last night. He was with Phillip." Her voice was low and I could tell she was gearing herself up to ask me something. My mom was like this too, when she wanted something. "Can he stay here for a day until he can get ahold of his ..." She trailed off, stopping for a second. "Until he can get into his place. Sorry to ask like this, I—"

I held up my hand. "How do you know this guy?" I wanted to make sure this was on the up and up.

"Oh—I met him right before they left. He's a good guy, Karina. Honest. He's Phillip's closest friend over there."

"What's he doing back?" I asked her.

She shook her head. "I didn't ask. Should I ask?" She peered into the living room.

"I wouldn't," I told her. "He can stay here, but if he ends up being a creep, he's out. So are you," I teased her.

She smiled at that and touched my arm. She was always so affectionate. Me, not so much.

"Thank you. You're the—"

"I know, I know. I'm the best. Now I have to shower so I'm not late to my dad's."

She rolled her eyes. "Yeah, you should thank me."

We both laughed and I shut the bathroom door in her face.

Chapter ★ Fourteen

MY LITTLE HOUSE was in dire need of a few … ish, repairs.
It'd been that way since I'd moved in a few months ago. Every
day it was the same dance, bouncing from foot to foot on the
cold tile, completely naked, waiting for the water to heat up.
That wasn't even the worst of it. Once the water got hot, it
didn't stay that way—not for long anyway.

The water went from hot, to cold, to hot again. I
could barely stand it. I loved my slightly shabby little house,
but there were a lot of things that needed fixing and it was
going to take a while to get through them all. I tried some of
the smaller renovations myself. Like the shower tiles I bought
during an over-adventurous Saturday afternoon at Home
Depot. I bought cans of paint, little tubes of white gunk to
patch the holes in the hallway walls, some knobs to replace
the ones on the kitchen cabinets, and some tiles for the
bathroom. The knobs found their way onto the cabinets. I
had to admit they really did update the cabinetry just like
HGTV told me they would. Great!

I painted the kitchen walls. Also great. Then I started the bathroom shower tiles. As in, I removed about half of them and replaced maybe ... six.

I counted them.

Okay, so eight.

As convenient as it was to use the "remodel" as a way to discourage my dad's random drop-ins, I really needed to stop procrastinating. This house was my way to prove that I could take care of myself. I didn't know who I was trying to prove that to more, myself or my dad. And did it really matter?

The water was finally warm enough to wash my hair. It only shorted out on me a couple of times. When I turned it off, the shower still dripped behind me as I rough-dried my hair. I thought of Elodie's friend again, the stranger in my house. He seemed nice enough, but so quiet. I wrapped a hand towel around the leaking bath faucet. I wondered if Phillip was the kind of guy to mind his friend staying with his pregnant wife.

I started to feel uneasy as I blow-dried the tips of my hair. It was impossible to blow-dry in less than thirty minutes and I only had about ten before I had to leave. That would have to do.

I had to do laundry—and soon. I didn't need to be super dressed up for my dad and his wife, but I knew my outfit would be the topic of conversation at the dinner table. Outside of each of our outfits and the typical, "Have you seen any movies lately?" question, my stepmom had nothing to talk to me about. To be fair, I had even less to say to her.

I barely had any clothes left in my dresser, so I shoved my hand in the Forever 21 bag next to my nightstand. Would I be Forever 21? I guess I'd find out next month on my birthday. There wasn't much of use in the bag: a pair of jeans one size too big and a brown shirt that fit me but looked like it would make me itch.

I could hear Elodie's voice as I got dressed. It sounded like she was trying to explain *Scandal* to her soldier friend and it made me laugh because she was the absolute worst at explaining movies or shows to anyone. She always got everyone's names confused and would spoil the ending without even meaning to. As someone who hated spoilers, I now knew better than to ask her about anything she had already seen.

I finally made it out to the living room with about five minutes to spare before I had to leave. Kael was sitting in the same spot, his eyes looking like they were going to close any minute, his T-shirt clinging to his broad shoulders. It was funny the way the chair looked so small when he was in it.

Elodie popped out of the kitchen with a big bowl of popcorn. "Leaving?" she asked.

I nodded, digging my hand into the bowl. I was starving. "I'm going to be late," I said, groaning.

"What would happen if you didn't go?" Elodie and I joked about my Tuesday date often. Every single Tuesday to be exact.

"They would disown me." I looked at Kael. He wasn't looking our way, but somehow, I knew he was listening. He was a soldier, after all.

"So, wouldn't be so bad, yeah?" She wiped her buttery fingers across her shorts and then licked them. Just to be sure, I guess.

"Not bad at all. Hey." I pulled open the fridge door to grab a drink. Elodie went a little far on the salt in the popcorn. "Do you want me to bring you home dessert?"

She nodded, smiling with a mouth full of popcorn.

"I'll be back around nine. Maybe later but hopefully not," I told both of my houseguests. I found myself wondering what they would be doing after I left. The images in my head bothered me a little, but I wasn't sure why. Before I could even contemplate that, his voice surprised me just as I reached the front door.

Chapter ✴ Fifteen

"CAN I USE your shower?" His voice was soft as rain, and he looked at me patiently, as if he expected something. It was a look I would come to know well.

Kael was familiar in the way that only a stranger could be. I hadn't seen him before today, but already I had memorized his face. The thick draw of his brow, the little scar above his eye. It was like I had come across him somewhere, or sometime, before. Maybe I had seen him in passing, at a store or on the street, on line for a coffee or donut. Or maybe he just had one of those faces that felt familiar. There were people like that.

"Can I?" he asked again.

I fumbled a little. "Um, yeah. Of course. Of course, you can shower. And maybe you want something to eat? There's not much in there, but make yourself at home."

I could tell that Elodie was waiting for Kael to leave the room so she could start talking, but I didn't have time for even five minutes of adorable small talk. I knew my dad and if I was just five minutes late, he'd spend twice that time lecturing me. I needed to leave.

"Thanks," Kael muttered and stood up.

He looked so big next to my little leather couch. Actually, he looked so big next to everything in my house, even the china cabinet I bought off Craigslist, before I realized how dangerous it was to meet strangers in the back of the Walmart parking lot. I had a lot of stuff in my house, most of it old and previously owned, and I had a thought for a second, an insecure one, about this guy in my home. Did he notice the pile of dirty clothes desperately waiting to be washed, the stack of dirty dishes in the sink?

And why did I care?

"If there's that one pie … how do you say …" Elodie struggled for the English word. "The one with the little rouge …" She held up her fingers and I finished her thought for her.

"Cherries?" *Rouge* was one of the very few words I remembered from high school French class. Elodie nodded, but she didn't have to. I knew she could eat an entire cherry pie in one sitting—I'd seen her do it. And who could blame her? My dad's wife Estelle was a decent cook. If I liked her more, I would admit that I actually loved her food. But I didn't, so I wouldn't.

"Yes, yes! Cherries." Elodie licked her lips. I had to laugh because she was feeding into every stereotype of a pregnant woman I'd ever heard.

I told her goodbye again, and Kael nodded at me, barely looking in my direction before heading down the hallway. I found myself waiting for the bathroom door to shut.

"Is he always this quiet?" I asked Elodie. Then I shouted, "Towels are in the closet behind the bathroom door!" loud enough that he would hear me.

She shrugged. "I don't know ..." She winced a little.

I sighed. "Yeah, don't remind me."

She chewed on her lip the way she always did, and I gave her a somewhat reassuring smile. I left before another minute could pass.

Chapter ☆ Sixteen

I WAS LATE. Not a fender bender holding up traffic late, or my dad called last minute and asked me to grab some pop on my way late. This was big late, the kind of late that would end with my dad's dramatic sighs and a lecture about how Estelle had to keep the oven on to warm the food, but now the chicken was all dried up, and did I ever think of anyone but myself? I was supposed to be at my dad's house in ten minutes and I was still sitting in my driveway. As I said, *late.*

I wasn't sure what I was doing, sitting in my car and staring out the windshield in silence. All I knew was that I hated Tuesdays and that I dreaded starting the car. I hated any and all obligations that I had no control over. I didn't like to be told what to do and where to be, and yet I let my dad put that burden on me. He'd applied that kind of pressure my whole life—and I did nothing to stop it.

I checked my phone again: a missed call from a random number. When I tried to call it back, it said it was a collect call. Did those even exist anymore?

I went on Instagram, for no reason really, and scrolled through pictures of girls I had known in high school and were now away in college or in the military themselves. Not a ton of people I went to high school with ended up going to college. For money or whatever reason, it just wasn't the norm like it was in movies. I stopped scrolling when I saw a picture of a coast, bright blue water, and white sands. This was the backdrop to a couple of lounge chairs shaded by beach umbrellas, and in the corner of the photo, two hands clinking glasses of what I guessed were piña coladas. The caption read, "OMG if you think this view is nice wait till we post pics tonight!!! The sky here is sooooo beautiful!" with a bunch of heart-eye emojis. The girl whose account it was, Josie Spooner, was a complete social narcissist who posted every time she left the house. Her daily coffee cup with a quote about how she's "ready to kick Monday's ass!" or "Ugh, people suck. So bad. Don't feel like talking about it!" filled my feed often. I didn't know why I didn't just delete her. I hadn't spoken to her since we moved from North Carolina. Then again, if I deleted everyone who annoyed me on social media, I would have zero friends.

I was mid eye-roll when I caught something out of the corner of my peripheral vision. It was Kael, dressed in his tan camouflage ACU uniform, striding down the grass and onto the sidewalk.

I rolled my window down and called to him. "Hey!"

He walked toward my car, ducking a little so he could see me.

"Where are you going?" I asked, before I realized how nosy that sounded.

"On post." That soft voice again.

"Right now? You're walking?" Like it was any of my damn business.

He shrugged his shoulders. "Yeah. My car's there." He looked down at his uniform. "And my clothes."

"But it's so far."

He shrugged again.

Was he really going to walk three miles?

I looked at the little digital clock on my dash: seven o'clock. I should be knocking on my dad's door right now, but here I was, sitting in my driveway, debating with myself whether or not to offer him a ride. We were both going to the same place after all ...

Well, maybe we were. Ft. Benning wasn't as big as say, Ft. Hood, but it was big enough.

Kael stood up straight, his upper body disappearing from view as he walked away. I called out for him again, almost by instinct.

"Do you want a ride? I'm going through the West Gate—where's your company?"

He leaned down again. "Near Patton, same gate."

"That's right by me—I mean my dad's. Get in."

I noticed the way he was fiddling with his fingers. It reminded me of how Austin used to get so antsy when we had to go to our mom's. He would sit in the backseat with me, picking at the skin around his nails until they bled.

I repeated my offer. It was going to be the last one.

Kael nodded, no words, just walked to the passenger door—actually he went for the back seat.

"This isn't an Uber," I told him, only half joking.

He sat down next to me. This was different. Usually my only passenger was pint-sized Elodie, but here was this big guy sitting next to me with his knees touching the dashboard, smelling like my coconut body wash.

"You can adjust the seat," I told him.

I put the car in reverse and my gear shift stuck for a

second. It had been doing that lately. My reliable 1990 Lumina had been my one constant since I bought it for five hundred dollars—almost entirely in singles from tips I made at La Rosa's pizza, where I had worked after school and on the weekends.

I was the only one of my friends to have a job in high school. My small group of friends would complain, trying to pull me away from work to go to parties, to the lake, to smoke weed in the parking lot of the elementary school we hung out at. Yes, elementary school. We were mildly delinquent, but at least I could pay for my own delinquency.

"Ugh," I groaned and jiggled the gear.

Kael stayed silent in the seat next to me but I swear I saw his hand lift from his lap like he was going to reach over and help me if I didn't get it. But I did. My tires crunched down the gravel driveway and we were on our way.

I didn't text my dad that I was going to be late. Why would I, when I knew he'd lecture me by text and then again in person, just so he could be sure I got the point. He was that kind of guy.

Yay for Tuesdays.

Chapter ☆ Seventeen

THE ALLEYWAY LOOKED DESERTED. It was like everyone had cleared out in the last hour, which I supposed they had. Kael buckled his seatbelt across his chest. I ignored the little ding my car gave, the one that reminded me to put my seatbelt on, like I always did. Luckily it was an old car so it would only ding once, sometimes twice.

I thought about starting a conversation, but from what little I knew about this guy, it wasn't really his thing. I glanced over at him and quickly turned on the radio. I had never been around anyone who made me feel this prickly awkwardness before. I couldn't explain what it was like—couldn't even be sure that I disliked it—but I just felt like I should talk. What was that, the urge to pierce the air, the need to fill the space with words? Maybe Kael had it right and the rest of us had it wrong.

The radio was playing a song I hadn't heard before, but I recognized Shawn Mendes' voice. I turned the music up a little and we drove in silence until we got closer to the post.

I hoped his company was as close as I thought it was. I tried not to come on post unless I had to, or to go to the doctor. Which was often one and the same.

My gas indicator light was on, a bright reminder of how irresponsible I was. When the Shawn Mendes song finished, it was time for a commercial break. I listened to the ads: a testimonial for a weight loss clinic, an offer for low interest car loans. "Huge Military discounts!" the voice promised with a borderline shout.

"You can change the station if you want," I told him, ever the cordial host. "What kind of music do you like?"

"This is fine."

"Okay."

I exited the highway and was glad to see there wasn't a line to enter the base. I loved living on my side of town, close enough to the post, but far enough from my dad that I could breathe.

"Here we are," I said, as if he couldn't see the bright lights ahead of us.

He shifted his hips and pulled out a dog-eared wallet from the pocket of his ACU pants. He dropped his military ID into my open hand. The tips of his warm fingers grazed my skin and I jerked my hand away. His ID fell between the seats.

"Damn it." I shoved my fingers into the slim slot and managed to grab the card just as it was my turn to approach the guards.

"Welcome to The Great Place," the soldier working the gate said.

"Really?" I couldn't help but tease him.

Ever since the soldiers were required to recite that ridiculous motto, I gave them shit about it. I couldn't help it.

"Yes, really," he said, his tone neutral. He inspected

our ID cards and the standard decal stuck to my windshield.

"Have a good night," the soldier told us, though I knew he didn't care about our night.

He probably thought we were together, that I was some barracks whore driving us to this guy's small room where we'd have sex while his roommate slept in the other bed.

"I don't know where I'm going," I told Kael.

He switched off the radio. "Turn right," he mumbled, just as I was passing a street on the right.

"Right *now?*" I jerked the wheel to make the turn in time.

He nodded.

"Next light. Turn left there. There!"

As if it wasn't bad enough that I would get to my dad's late as hell and that the car was running on empty, I could feel my palms getting clammy on the steering wheel. Kael looked over just in time to see me wipe them on my jeans.

"They're up here on the right. It's a big brown building," he told me.

The buildings were all nearly identical. The only thing differentiating one from the other was the number painted on the side.

"Yeah, they're all big brown buildings here at The Great Place."

I swear I heard the tiniest hint of a laugh, just a small puff of smoke, enough to show that he was at least mildly amused by my comment. Sure enough, when I looked over, there it was—a sliver of a smile spread across his lips.

"Just here." He pointed to a massive parking lot. Kael kept his finger pointed at a navy blue truck parked in the back of the mostly empty lot. I pulled up next to the truck, about a car's length away.

"Thanks ..." He looked at me like he was searching

for something.

"Karina," I told him and he nodded.

"Thanks, *Karina*."

My stomach flipped a little and I told myself it was just nerves, that it didn't have anything to do with the way he said my name. I tried to calm the swarm of bees in my stomach as he climbed out of my car without another word.

Chapter * Eighteen

I DON'T KNOW what I expected him to drive, but this beast of a truck wasn't it. Despite his size, I figured he'd drive something small and sleek, not this old blue thing with rust circling the wheel well. That's the problem with pretending— people's real lives are never like you imagine. He had typical Georgia plates, with peaches and the cheesy slogan, and Clayton County printed across the bottom. I had no idea where that was. I wondered if he was pissed that he joined the army and somehow ended up in his home state.

He was Elodie's friend, so it was only right that I made sure he got into his truck okay. I didn't want him to have to trek three miles back to my house if he couldn't get it to start. I knew all about cars not starting. I watched as he stuck his hand under the metal sheet just above his front tire and felt along the surface. He repeated this with all four tires before he pulled his phone from his pocket.

His expression changed from concerned to upset. He wiped one hand over his face; the other still held his phone. I couldn't make out what he was saying, but I avoided the temptation to roll down my window to hear. There was just something about him that I needed to figure out.

The more I watched him, standing there in the dark, pacing around with his iPhone going back and forth from his pocket to his cheek, the more I needed to know who he was.

I was just about to Google Clayton County, Georgia when he opened the car door and leaned down.

"You can go," he told me.

Almost rude. If he wasn't locked out of his car, I would have been snarky back, but I couldn't find it in me.

I looked at his truck and back to him. "Are you sure? Can you not get in?"

He sighed heavily and shook his head. "My keys are supposed to be here. I'll find my way back, it's cool."

"I'm so late to this thing I have to do."

"The dinner," he told me.

So he was paying attention.

"Yeah, the dinner. I can't take you back before … but maybe I can call my dad and just cancel. It's not like—"

Kael interrupted me. "It's cool, for real."

I couldn't just leave him there. I told him so.

"Why?"

I opened my door and got out of the car. "I don't know?" I replied honestly. "It's a long walk back. Do you have another set of keys somewhere? Or a friend who can come help you?"

"All my friends are in Afghanistan," he said.

My chest burned.

"Sorry," I said, leaning my back against my car.

"For what?"

We kept eye contact until he blinked. I quickly

looked away.

"I don't know? The war?" It sounded so stupid coming from my mouth. An army brat apologizing to a soldier for a war that started before either of them were born. "Most people wouldn't have asked me why just now."

Kael's tongue grazed his bottom lip; he tucked it between his teeth. The parking lot lights above us clacked on, buzzing, breaking our silence.

"I'm not most people."

"I can tell."

The lights shone through the windows of the barracks across the street, but it didn't seem like he lived there. That meant he was either married, or higher ranking than his age would suggest. Soldiers below a certain rank could only live off post if they were married, but I couldn't imagine that a married man would be sleeping on my chair right after a deployment. Besides, he wasn't wearing a ring.

I was checking out his ACU jacket for his rank patch when I saw his eyes on me.

"Are you coming with me, Sergeant, or are you going to make me stand in this parking lot until you call a locksmith for your car?" I looked at the patch on his chest, his last name stitched in capital letters: Martin. He was so young to be a sergeant.

"Come on." I put my hands up, begging. "You don't know me, but this is what will happen if I leave you here knowing you will walk back to my house. Two seconds after I drive away, I'll feel guilty and I'll obsess over it the entire way to my dad's, the entire dinner," I explained. "I'm talking apology texts to Elodie, who'll be stressed because she worries about everyone, and then I'll feel even more guilty about stressing out a pregnant woman, so I'll have to drive around trying to find you if you haven't made it back yet. It's messy, Kael, and honestly easier if you just—"

"Okay, okay." He held up his hands in mock defeat. I nodded, smiling in my victory, and you know what? He almost smiled back.

Chapter ☆ Nineteen

NO MATTER WHERE we were stationed, my dad always chose to live in post housing, from Texas, to South Carolina, down to Georgia. I didn't mind it so much when I was young, because all of my friends lived by me, but as we moved, then moved again, and again, it got old fast. I started to hate the groomed cul-de-sacs and the lines of cars at each gate. My dad loved being so close to the PX, the grocery store without tax, and to the company where he worked every day. He felt safe, but as Austin and I grew up, we started to feel trapped.

I remember my mom pacing around the houses, each one of them, during the summer days. There were these hours of madness for her where the curtains were always closed and the couch turned into her bed. At first, the shift was subtle, only lasting while dad was at work. She had two personas and could switch gears within seconds. But sometime over the summer before eighth grade, the mania took over. She woke up later, took fewer showers, stopped dancing, and even stopped pacing.

Dinner was late, then hardly at all, and our parents' voices at night got louder and louder.

"Uh, Karina?" Kael's voice drew me out of my memories.

He was eyeing the green light above us. I pressed the gas.

"Sorry," I faltered, clearing my throat.

My chest was aching as I drove my thoughts into reality.

"Okay, so we're going to my dad's house and he's kind of…" I exhaled, trying to pinpoint such a complicated man with one word. "He's sort of—"

"Racist?" Kael asked.

"What? No!" I felt a little defensive over his question until I turned toward him and saw the look on his face. It said that he genuinely figured that's what I was going to say.

I didn't know what to think about that.

"He's not racist," I told Kael as we drove. I couldn't think of anything he'd ever said or done to make me believe he was. "He's just kind of an asshole."

Kael nodded and leaned back in his seat.

"It's usually like a two-hour thing. Too much food for three people. Too much talking."

I turned onto the main road, really the only one I could navigate on the entirety of Ft. Benning. We were less than five minutes from my dad's house. We were twenty-six minutes late. It would be fine. I was an adult and something came up. They would get over it. I repeated that to myself again and began to concoct my excuse that didn't necessarily involve a stranger staying at my house.

My phone started vibrating in the cup holder between us, and I reached for it the moment I saw that it was Austin calling. I grabbed the phone. I couldn't even remember the last time he actually returned my calls.

"I'm going to get this, it's—" I didn't finish explaining to Kael.

"Hello?" I spoke into the phone, but only got silence.

I lifted it from my cheek. "Damn it." I'd missed the call. I tried to call him back but he didn't pick up.

"If you see that light up, tell me? The sound only works sometimes." I looked down at my phone and Kael agreed with a nod.

I turned onto my dad's street and tried to spend the last two minutes of the drive conjuring up an achievement, or something I could stretch to sound like one. I would need something to talk about after the scolding for my extreme tardiness. My dad always asked the same questions. To me, to his darling wife. The difference was, it only took her planting a flower bed or going to someone else's kid's birthday party to get praise, when I could save a small village and he would be like, "That's great Kare, but it was a *small* village. Austin once saved a slightly larger village and Estelle created two villages."

It wasn't healthy to compare myself to his wife, or to my brother. I was self-aware enough to know that, but the way I felt she was positioned against me still bugged the hell out of me. And then there was the fact that Austin was always my dad's, and I was my mom's. This worked out better for my brother than it did for me.

"We're almost there. My dad's been in the army a long time," I told him. Kael was a soldier, he wouldn't need more of an explanation.

He nodded beside me and looked out the passenger window.

"How long have you been in?" I asked.

I heard him swallow before he spoke. "Little over

two years."

I almost asked him if he liked it, but we were pulling up in front of my dad's house.

"We're here," I warned him. "It's like a whole fiasco, three courses. Lots of small talk and coffee after. Two hours, minimum."

"Two hours?" He blinked.

"I know. I know. You can wait in the car if you want?"

Kael opened the passenger door and leaned down to talk to me while I was still in my seat.

I checked my hair in the mirror. It was almost dry. The air was thick with humidity and it showed.

I grabbed my phone. Austin hadn't called me back. "Just saying, however awful you think it's going to be, it will be worse than that."

"Mhm," I thought I heard him say. I looked up as the passenger door shut. The reality of just how bad an idea it was to bring a stranger to Tuesday dinner was sinking in.

Chapter ✳ Twenty

I WAS FIDGETY, wiping my hands on my legs. I always did that when I was nervous. "I'll do the talking," I said to Kael as we approached the door. "Let me explain why we're late. Why *I'm* late." Then it dawned on me who I was talking to. Soldier wouldn't have a problem being quiet.

We walked into the kitchen, which was filled with the aroma of honey and cinnamon, and what might have been ham. It smelled like a holiday.

"Sorry I'm late," I said. "I had to stay behind a little at work, um … and then I was helping Elodie's friend." I turned behind me to introduce Kael.

My dad was seated at the head of the table when we came in. No reading the paper, no listening to the radio. Just waiting. I looked at him sitting there with his craggy face and his sparse white hair. It was really thinning now. So was his papery skin. Everyone on my dad's side turned to snow early. It looked beautiful on the women—

at least it did in photographs—but I always hoped I would take after my mom. I guess we'd see.

My dad moved his eyes off me and looked at Kael, who took a step back. Instinct or nervousness—who knew? Despite being just a tad over five feet tall, my dad was intimidating. He could be soft when he wanted to. And when he didn't want to, he could cut life a knife.

"Martin, nice to—"

My dad shook Kael's hand. I was waiting for the fall-out about being late when Estelle walked into the kitchen, carrying a bowl with a big wooden spoon sticking out of it.

"Hey!" She greeted me like she usually did. Excited. Fake.

Estelle always wore slightly different versions of the same outfit: jeans with a little flare at the bottom and a buttoned-down shirt with a pattern. Always. Today's top was striped blue and red. Like all of the others, this one had darts at the waist and bust to, as she put it, "create a streamlined silhouette." I couldn't be less interested in the fit of Estelle's clothes—or anything about her for that matter—but she told me one day how she liked to buy these fitted shirts because of the way they flattered her shape. She twisted her torso like a model when she said it, as if she was having fun bonding with her then-boyfriend's daughter. It had been excruciating.

It was weird that Estelle never changed her style. I loved consistency, but not from her. I didn't want anything from her.

"Oh, well ... hey. Hi! I'm Estelle." She wasn't doing the best job at hiding her surprise over the extra body in the room.

Kael waited for her to put the dish down before

extending his hand.

"So, um, Kael is Elodie's husband's friend. He just got back from deployment yesterday." I avoided looking at my dad. "He's going to eat with us, ok? He's locked out of his car."

Estelle motioned for Kael to sit next to my dad in his King chair, but I sat there first so Kael could sit beside me. No need for him to occupy the hot seat.

"I'm assuming you've heard from your brother?" my dad asked.

I pulled out my phone. "I missed a call from him."

"He's on his way."

"What?"

My dad took a long, slow drink of water.

"He was arrested last night."

I stood up from my chair. "What? For what?"

My dad's eyes were a carbon copy of my brother's. He was like him. I was like her. We had heard it all our lives. That didn't mean it was true. Example: this arrest.

"I don't know, exactly. The precinct won't tell me. If it had been on government property I could easily have found out," he huffed. My dad was in knots—frustrated and disappointed. I could see it all roll off him and I knew he was feeling as if he had failed as a parent. Couldn't disagree with him there.

"And how is he getting here?" I asked.

"Driving. He should be here in a couple hours."

Kael sat there staring at the table, strumming his fingers, trying to be discrete.

"Where is he going to stay?"

"Here," he answered with certainty.

I sighed. "Does he know that?" I picked up my phone and dialed my brother, but it went straight to voicemail. I didn't bother leaving a message.

My dad furrowed his thick eyebrows. "Does it matter? He's getting himself in real trouble. This isn't child's play anymore, Karina. You two are adults now."

"Us two?" I scoffed. "I'm not the one who was arrested. And Austin's not even here to defend himself, so that's hardly fair either."

Estelle clucked around my dad as we fought. She did this every time. She was literally making my dad's plate as we discussed his only son's failing future. He and I raised our voices, but she was her normal, perky self. Kael shifted uncomfortably in his seat.

"Would you like some ham?" Estelle asked Kael.

She was exactly what my dad needed. Someone who could ignore the chaos and play the role of the obliging wife in the second half of his life. My mom was a hurricane and Estelle wasn't even a drizzle.

"The glaze is a family recipe. Here take some." She held up a little plantation-style gravy boat full of dark, syrupy liquid. When she bought the thing off eBay, she literally told me it was "from a real plantation," like that wasn't a gross thing to say and own.

Kael thanked her for helping him make his plate. I told my dad that I knew he shouldn't have sent my brother away, that this was his fault. He told me the fault was all mine.

"I'm not hungry," I told Estelle when she passed me the ham. My stomach gurgled, proving me a liar.

"Don't be a child," my dad told me. He smiled at me, a sorry attempt to soften his words.

"You just said I was an adult. Now you say I'm being a child. Which is it?" I hated bickering like this, but my father brought out the worst in me. Especially when the subject was my brother. "I'm just confused why you're acting like it's not a big deal," I said. "Because it is. It's a very big deal."

"I know, Karina, but this isn't the first time."

"It's only the second," I snapped. "It's not like he's a career criminal."

"Let's not worry about him until he's here, okay? There's nothing either of us can do from here. He's a twenty-year-old man." My dad's response to my brother's second arrest was rational, almost to the extreme.

I wished I could just push my emotions away like that. It took me a while to shift gears. My dad could bounce back and forth between extreme emotions, just like my mom. She was worse at it. Or better. I guess it all depended on how you looked at it.

My stomach rumbled again and I gave in and started making myself a plate. Kael had a forkful of mashed potatoes moving up to his mouth. I figured he could sense we were calming down and getting into our regular motion. We would be back bickering soon enough.

I put my phone on the table, screen up, just in case Austin texted or something. And then I tried hard not to think of him, driving all the way here by himself, scared about being arrested, scared about facing our dad.

"So Kael, are you home for good?" Estelle was the stage director, moving the conversation away from our family dramatics. This time I was almost grateful.

"I think so. Not quite sure yet, ma'am."

His manners were impeccable. I wanted to know more about this man. I bet his mother was kind. I couldn't remember the last time I heard someone my age call someone ma'am.

I watched him as he politely answered every question she threw at him. What battalion was he assigned to? Where in Afghanistan was his camp? His answers were short but sincere and his lips wrapped around every word he said. I wished he enjoyed talking more than he seemed to.

By the time we were eating dessert, I'd forgotten that we were even late. Austin's arrest took the attention off of me. Not the first time that had worked in my favor.

Chapter ★ Twenty-One

"WELL, THAT WAS NICE," Estelle said. She stood awkwardly, waiting for me to hug her. Sometimes I did. Sometimes I didn't.

"Let me know when Austin gets here. I'd stay and wait, but I have to work in the morning."

My dad nodded.

Kael stood in the doorway, half-in, half-out.

My dad hugged me. "What are your plans for the weekend? We're going up to Atlanta if you want to—"

"I'm working." I loved Atlanta, but no way was I going with them. And wouldn't their plans change with Austin coming to town?

"It was so nice to meet you, Kael. Drive safe." Estelle smiled. I wondered if she thought he was my boyfriend. I would never introduce him in that way, but she was awfully smiley and more than a little nosy the way she looked at us when I nudged him to open the door.

I didn't give anyone else a chance to speak before I

stepped onto the porch and practically ran down the driveway.

"God, I hate those dinners."

Even after all we had endured, Kael didn't have a word to say.

"Do you have a family?" I assumed he wouldn't answer, but anything was better than silence.

"Do I have a family?" he repeated.

"I mean, obviously you have a family, otherwise you literally wouldn't exist. But are they like that?" I nodded toward the house.

"Nope," he said, staring out the windshield of my car. "Not at all."

"In a good way or a bad way?" I asked.

"Both." He shrugged, buckling his seat belt.

"I think it just bothers me this much because Estelle is so different from my mom. She was really fun when I was young. My mom, not Estelle," I clarified, though he didn't ask. "She used to laugh and listen to music. She would dance around the living room listening to Van Morrison, waving her arms around like a bird or a butterfly. It feels like a lifetime ago."

I was thinking back to that other version of my mom, the one who had long, flowing hair that moved in the wind. She was just as carefree now, but not even close to the same way.

"She used to lift her hands up and push them through her hair, letting it fall around her. It always tickled my face and I would laugh and she would shake her hair and dance around me."

The thrum of my engine cutting through the thick Georgia air was all I could hear. I'd never noticed the sounds before; I'd never had time to.

"And my birthday parties! She used to go all out for

them. It was this huge thing, more like a birthday week. We didn't have a ton of money or anything, but she was creative. One year she decorated the whole house in those lights from Spencer's, do you remember that store?"

He nodded.

"They had these disco lights and my mom put them all around our living room and kitchen. All of our friends came over. I mean, I only had like three friends, most of the kids came for Austin. We always had a packed house. I had this boyfriend—I think his name was Josh? And he brought me cornbread. That was my birthday gift."

I didn't know why I was going into such detail, but I was so lost in my own memories that I just kept going.

"I don't know why he brought me cornbread. Maybe his mom just had it lying around? I don't know. But I remember getting this karaoke machine and thinking it was the coolest present ever and my mom went into her room and locked the door so we could feel older than we were and not be chaperoned the entire time. Of course, we ended up playing one of those stupid party games and I had to kiss a boy named Joseph, who actually just overdosed on heroine a few months ago ..."

I could feel Kael looking at me, but it was the weirdest thing—I couldn't stop myself from talking. We were at a red light. The sky was pitch-black and the red lights were reflecting off his dark skin.

"Wow, I'm talking a lot," I told him.

He looked over at me.

"It's cool." His voice was so soft.

Who *was* this guy? So patient, so quiet, yet so in touch with the moment. I tried to imagine Elodie's husband having a conversation with him. Phillip was buoyant and friendly and Kael ... well, I didn't know what the hell to think of him.

It had been a long time since I'd had this type of conversation with someone, if I ever had. My brother was the only person I reminisced about my parents with. But even he had stopped wanting to relive our childhood with me.

"My mom raised me and my sister up in Riverdale." Kael's voice was sudden and sharp, drowning out the purring engine, the sound of the wind.

"I love that show," I told him and he smiled. I caught it before it vanished. I filed it away.

"It's all right."

"The show or the town?" I asked.

"Both." He didn't smile.

"How old is your sister?" I figured I'd better pounce while he was feeling uncharacteristically chatty.

"Younger than me."

"My brother, too." I wanted to ask him her exact age, but we were coming up to my little white house. "By about six minutes."

Most people laughed when I told them this. Kael didn't say anything but again, I knew he was looking at me.

The wind blew dirt over my windshield as I pulled into my driveway. Paving my driveway was rapidly moving up my to-do list. I parked and apologized again for fighting with my dad in front of him. He nodded, muttering his version of, "It's cool."

I reached between us to grab my purse from the floorboard behind my seat. "At least you won't have to go through that again. As for me, I'll be back there next Tuesday at seven p.m. sharp." I said "sharp" as much as for myself as for Kael. If I was late for next week's dinner, I would never hear the end of it.

The alley was so dark on moonless nights like this that it was hard to see the porch. A beam came from Kael's phone and he shined it onto the porch.

"I need to get some lights out here."

Kael's body kept moving next to me and I saw him looking around the yard, down the driveway, down the alley to the side of the yard. His neck was sort of jerking. It wasn't an alarming movement, just a quiet survey of his surroundings. I tried to imagine him in Afghanistan, a heavy gun strapped to his body and the weight of the free world on his shoulders.

"My sister is fifteen, by the way," he said, as he walked past me into the house.

Chapter ✦ Twenty-Two

ELODIE WAS ASLEEP on the couch, her small body sprawled out at awkward angles. I sat my purse down on the floor, kicked my shoes off, and covered her with her favorite blanket. Her grandmother had made it for her when she was a kid. It was really worn now, almost threadbare, but she slept with it every day. Her grandma had passed a few years back; Elodie cried every time she talked about it.

I wondered if she missed her family. She was so far from them and pregnant, with a husband away at war. She didn't talk about her parents much, but I got the impression they weren't very keen on her running away to the U.S with a young soldier she'd met on the Internet.

I couldn't say I blamed them. Elodie moved a little when I turned off the TV.

"Did you want to watch that?" I asked Kael. I forgot that he would be sleeping out here and considered waking Elodie up to come to my bed.

"No, it's cool."

Oh, this man of many words.

I continued, "Well, I'm going to put this pie in the fridge and go to bed. I have to work in the morning. And if you need anything from the store write it on my list stuck on the fridge," I offered.

Kael nodded and sat down in my red chair. Was he going to sleep there?

"Do you need a blanket?" I asked.

He shrugged and said, "If you have one," almost under his breath.

I grabbed an old comforter from the hallway closet and brought it to him. He thanked me and I told him goodnight again. I felt wide awake when I got to my bed. Through the night, I thought about how Kael had been with my dad and Estelle, how he somehow managed to make the dinner more bearable. I thought about the kind and unexpected way he filled up my gas tank on the way to my Dad's and then, of course, because I overthink everything, I thought about how I should pay him back for the gas, even if he didn't want me to.

I felt so restless. I turned over, grabbed a pillow, and put it between my legs, hugging it close. I thought about how it would be really nice to have a warm body in bed next to me. At least then I'd have someone to talk to when I couldn't sleep. Unless it was Kael. I smiled at the thought, thinking how if it was him in my bed …

I caught myself before I went any further.

What the hell was wrong with me that I was picturing Kael in my bed? I needed physical contact, that had to be the reason that no matter how much I tried to think about anything else—anyone else—I couldn't help but imagine him lying next to me, staring up at the ceiling the way he'd stared out the windshield the whole ride home.

It had been almost a year since I had human contact

that wasn't work related outside of my family and Elodie. Not that I was used to having it in large or consecutive doses, but Kael was making me daydream about him and I. People my age usually met guys at clubs or school or through friends, but I didn't have much experience with any of the above.

Brien and I had gone back and forth a little, still making out in his car after I promised myself I would never speak to him again. The last time I let it happen was in his barracks room, when I rolled over and something jabbed my side.

An earring. I'd felt like I was in a movie because, one, who loses an earring while hooking up and doesn't notice? And, two, I had been playing the part of the lonely, desperate-for-attention girl who knew her guy was hooking up with other girls, but it took a hideous hoop earring to make her admit it to herself.

We fought about it. He said it must have been his roommate's girlfriend's earring and had nothing to say when I reminded him that I had seen his roommate hook up with multiple people, not one of whom was female.

I grabbed my phone to scroll through social media to get Brien out of my head. I typed Kael's name in Elodie's friends list but nothing came up, so I searched for him again. I found a profile with less than one hundred friends, which seemed odd to me. I didn't talk to ninety-nine percent of the people I was "friends" with, but I still had almost a thousand. That seemed excessive, having a thousand people I didn't talk to have access to me.

His profile picture was a group shot of Kael with three other soldiers. They were all dressed in ACUs and standing next to a tank. Kael was grinning in the picture, maybe even laughing, that's how bright his smile was. It was weird to see him like that, his arm around one of the guys. But apart from his profile picture, I couldn't get any information from his page at all. Everything was private. I almost requested to be his friend, but it felt stalker-ish to send him a Facebook request while he was sleeping on my chair in the living room

I clicked out of his profile and started scrolling through my Facebook friends, unfriending people who I barely knew. I removed about a hundred before I fell asleep.

Chapter ✦ Twenty-Three

I WOKE UP fully clothed, with my cell phone on my chest. It felt like the heat was on and I never turned the heat on. I checked the time: almost four in the morning. I had to be up at eight so I could run to the grocery store before work at ten. I plugged my phone into the charger and sat up. I kept my T-shirt on, but unclasped my bra and slid my jeans off. It was so hot in my room and my throat was dry. I could feel the sweat on the back of my neck when I tied up my thick, curly hair.

I thought about putting pants on before I went to the kitchen for water, but it was four a.m. and Kael and Elodie would undoubtedly be sleeping. It was so hot, I couldn't think about sliding thick pajamas over my thighs right then, so I made sure I was quiet when I walked down the hallway and into the kitchen. I kept the hallway light off and relied on the little nightlights plugged into my kitchen outlets to see.

I grabbed the jug of water out of my fridge and chugged it until I couldn't anymore. I closed the fridge and almost screamed when I saw Kael sitting at the kitchen table.

"Shit, you scared me." I wiped my mouth with the back of my hand. Then I felt bad because I knew I had made him feel bad. "Sorry if I woke you. It's so hot in here," I told him.

"I was up."

I took a step closer to him and it took his eyes raking down my body, down my bare thighs, to remember that I was only in my panties. I tried to use my hands to cover my ass, but there was no use. I should have just thrown on pants. Or panties that half my ass didn't hang out of.

"Why are you up? Were you just sitting here in the dark? Sorry I don't have any clothes on. I thought you would be asleep."

Kael's head tilted just a bit, like he was confused by what I was saying, and he looked down at my legs. I immediately felt a wave of insecurity, thinking about the dips of cellulite peppered across my thighs. He looked back up at my face.

"Can I have some of that water?" he asked me.

I flushed, not only because I was still half naked, but because he had obviously watched me chug water out of a gallon jug.

I nodded and opened the fridge. "It's just tap water. I buy one of these"—I held up the jug labeled Spring Water—"every once in a while, and just refill it with tap water. So, it's not actually spring water."

Why was I rambling?

"I've been in Afghanistan for months, I think I can handle some Georgia tap water."

His sarcasm surprised me. I smiled at him and he smiled back—another surprise. He took the jug from my hand and lifted it to his mouth without touching his lips.

"So why are you up? Getting used to the time difference?" I asked.

He handed back the jug and I took another swig. I was still hot, but the kitchen was much cooler than my bedroom. The cold tile felt good under my feet.

"I don't sleep much," Kael finally answered.

"Ever?"

"Never."

I sat across from him at the little table.

"Because of where you were?"

My stomach started to ache from my navel to my throat, thinking about him, this quiet young man, being woken up in a war zone from shells or rockets or whatever terror he went through.

He nodded. "It's weird being back here."

Between his honesty and the vulnerability shadowing his face, I thought I could be dreaming.

"Do you have to go back?" I asked, hoping he would say no.

In the back of my head, an alarm was blaring, screeching to warn me, or maybe Kael, of how I was starting to feel toward him. I had known him less than twenty-four hours, yet I wanted to protect him, to keep him from going back there.

"I don't know," he responded and we both fell silent.

"I hope you don't." The words were out before I could care how they sounded.

Part of me felt like I was betraying my childhood, my family lineage of soldiers and airmen, but I guess I wasn't as patriotic as I was expected to be. Not if this is what it meant.

When Kael laid his head down on his crossed arms and said, "Me too," my whole body heaved. This military life was so unfair sometimes. I wanted to ask Kael if he thought about what he signed up for, or if, like most of the young soldiers I knew, he had been persuaded to join by the poverty around him and the promise of a steady paycheck and health insurance.

"I'm sor—" I started to say, but his eyes were closed. I stared at him in the dark for a few seconds before a small snore fell from his full lips.

Chapter ⋆ Twenty-Four

"DO YOU ALWAYS wear your uniform?" I asked him in the cereal aisle. The cart we had chosen had a creaky wheel that liked to get stuck on turns. I'd handed Kael my grocery list in the parking lot, assigning him to hold onto it. He didn't say anything, so I took it as a yes.

"No," he said, surprising me.

I looked at him, pressing him to say more. "Seems like it." I attempted to soften my words by smiling at him, but he didn't look down at me.

"I don't have any of my clothes."

Shit. "Oh. Sorry. I didn't think about that. Where are they? Do you need a ride to get them?"

He grabbed a box of Cinnamon Toast Crunch. At least he had good taste in cereal. He was keeping his items in the basket in the front of the cart where kids usually sat while parents tried to keep them entertained and cooperative.

"I don't know where they are." He looked confused. I was getting better at reading him every day. Granted, it had only been two days, but still. I was cracking him open, slowly but surely. His face was actually pretty expressive.

"Was going to go to the mall later. Or Kohl's. Wherever."

We passed an older man who kept his eyes on Kael and me just a beat too long. I noticed his lingering stare, shifting back and forth between us, and the hairs on my neck prickled. The man disappeared around the corner. When I went to mention it to Kael, I started wondering if I was just paranoid and decided not to give the grumpy old man any more attention than I already had.

"I work until four, but I could run you to get clothes after?" I offered.

The Commissary was crowded as always. The low prices on groceries and the zero tax were barely worth bracing the crowd for. I would rather work an extra shift than wait behind shopping carts stuffed to their brims.

Kael pointed down the next aisle, the beginning of the freezer section. "You know there's Uber and cabs and stuff, right?"

I glared at him. "I was trying to be nice."

"I know. I'm just fucking with you." His voice was light, a different tone than I had ever heard come from his lips. It made my skin tingle. I looked away.

"Ha. Ha," I teased back.

My throat was aching. I would always remember that, the way he made parts of me ache that I had never felt before. I would always be thankful for that.

"So, should I take you or not? Can you grab those little pizzas? The red box." I pointed behind him.

"If you want? I mean, I'm already staying on your couch, imposing on your family dinners, eating your granola bars."

"You ate my granola bars?"

He laughed. If I hadn't turned around, I would have missed it. It was that quick.

"I'm buying you another box." He was definitely not into owing people things.

"I would normally say it's fine just to be polite, but my electric bill is high as hell this month, so go ahead." I nudged his shoulder. He tensed up beside me. It was a shift as small as a pinprick, but I felt it down my spine.

Kael took a step away from me as we continued to walk. The music overhead was louder, it had to be. I felt uncomfortable. Embarrassed. It was as if something had cracked open last night. I guess a three a.m. chat in your panties would do that. Kael was different today. More open. Almost talkative. Still, I wondered. Did I think he was flirting with me? I hadn't actually thought of it that way, but it felt something like it.

"Sorry," I ended up saying a silent minute later. We were standing in the chip aisle. I was deciding between flavored pretzels and Doritos Cool Ranch chips when Kael grabbed a bag of Funyuns and tossed it into the cart.

"I used to love those when I was younger," I told him. "My best friend Sammy and I ate them all the time. Oh my god, that and Mountain Dew. My mom wouldn't let me drink it, but Sammy's mom always had the Kroger brand version that was actually better."

I was totally rambling.

Kael seemed to be more relaxed than he was a few seconds ago. I didn't look at him as long as I wanted to, or tell him how much I missed Sammy since she got married and moved across the country, like I wanted to. Not the married part, just the move the hell away from here part.

We didn't talk again until we checked out separately.

We both had to show our ID cards, his Active Duty and mine a dependent ID. He was a gentleman and helped me load my car, carry the bags into my house, and he even asked if he could help unpack them. I hated that my brain was trying to figure out why he was so nice. It was like I couldn't just accept kind gestures or compliments from people, like I wasn't worthy of them.

But as much as he made me feel flustered and a little bit paranoid, I was starting to kind of like the way I felt around him. As long as he didn't think we were going to end up hooking up. He hadn't mentioned a girlfriend or anyone in his life at all—though, he hadn't exactly been forthcoming. But we weren't doing anything wrong. Nothing. Just grocery shopping and sharing a living space for a few days.

If I was his girlfriend, I wouldn't be too happy about him staying with two women. Regardless if one was pregnant or not.

Why was I back to assuming he had a girlfriend? Or that he would even like me?

Hell, I didn't even know him enough to like him that way, and he looked like the kind of man that every woman was drawn to. I realized that I was a little more interested in him than I had admitted to myself. I was sort of freaking out and he was in the seat next to me. I could feel his eyes on my face.

"Everything okay?" he asked after all the groceries were put away. It took half the time with him helping and I didn't have to tell him to recycle the paper and plastics.

We were both sitting at the table now. He was scrolling through his cell phone and I was eating my second granola bar and getting ready to leave for work. I could hear the shower from down the hall so I knew Elodie was up. Thank God. I couldn't imagine telling Mali that Elodie was going to be late again.

Through my lashes, I tried to watch Kael without him noticing. He noticed immediately, like the good soldier I was sure he was. I felt the words building in my throat and didn't want to stop them. I had to know. "Do you have a girlfriend?" I blurted out.

"No. Do you? Have a boyfriend, I mean, or a girlfriend?"

I shook my head. My fingers felt like they were shaking against the cold back of the chair.

"No. Neither."

He let out a breath and stood up. My eyes followed his movement from the fridge, to the cabinet to grab a glass, and back to the fridge. He poured himself some milk, splashing a little onto the floor. If I could have had one thing in that moment, it would have been for him to say something, anything. My throat felt like it was on fire. My whole body felt like it was on fire.

"So, we'll be gone until later, but we always have our phones on at work. If my brother comes by, let him in?"

Kael nodded. I watched as he cleaned up the splashed milk that I'd assumed would dry on the floor with the rest of the random spillage that had accumulated since I'd mopped about two weeks ago.

Elodie came walking down the hallway with her short hair soaked, staining the shoulders of her gray t-shirt. "The shower is finally fixed!"

"What do you mean?" I made my way down the hallway toward the bathroom.

"The temperature! You had it fixed right?" she asked. I passed her, shaking my head. Sure enough, when I went into the bathroom and turned the shower on, it was immediately warm. I turned it to cold. Immediately cold. The pressure was even stronger, like a normal shower. Such luxury.

"I have no idea how it's fixed. I'm glad it is though, because ..." I started to say. My eyes landed on Kael's and he licked his lips, turning his cheek slightly away from me.

"You!" It dawned on me. "Did you fix it?" Somehow I knew he did, even though it was such a foreign concept to me.

Kael nodded sheepishly. "It wasn't a big thing. It was just a loose pipe. It took me less than five minutes."

Elodie walked toward him, her hair dripping as she moved. "You are so nice. Oh, I can't wait to tell Phillip. Thank you, thank you," she told him, hugging one of his arms.

First the gas, now fixing my shower. Of course I thought it was nice of him, but it also made me feel helpless.

"What she said." I was annoyed and they both picked up on it. "Okay, gotta go, I'm going to be late. See you at eleven." I hugged Elodie and walked to the front door.

I didn't look back at Kael as I walked out. I knew I would feel guilty if I did. He did something nice for me. It was not only thoughtful, but practical. I appreciated it, I did, but I also didn't want him treat me like I needed help fixing things. I bought that house to prove that I was no damsel.

Chapter ✫ Twenty-Five

MY MORNING WAS the same as always: two elderly retirees and one married soldier who came in the same time almost every week. He never made an appointment, but I always kept the spot open for him. He was nice and easy, tipped well, and didn't groan and moan while I did my job.

I now had "free time" to help clean up around the spa and avoid walk-ins—as much as they could be avoided. I didn't like the uncertainty of them. They were always uncomfortable and they hardly ever came back. Even the fittest of bodies let their insecurities shine in my room. It was comforting and disheartening to know that other people thought of their bodies in the same harmful way that I did.

I was pulling out my second round of towels from the dryer when I thought of how I used to have to roll silverware when I waitressed at a steakhouse. I guess all jobs come with add-on chores.

"That guy came here for you," Mali told me while we folded towels.

"What guy?"

"The one you used to like," she said. The way she wrapped "like" around her tongue made me feel like a child.

Oh. Brien. Great.

"When?"

"About ten minutes before you got here."

I dropped a towel onto the pile before I folded it. "What? Why didn't you tell me?"

She snickered. "Because I was afraid you would call him and we can't have that." She shrugged her shoulders. I gaped at her, grabbed the towel, and threw it at her.

"I would not call him, by the way." I may have been a little defensive. Anyway, I didn't think I'd call, even if I was curious to know why he came by. I know I didn't leave *my* earring in his bed, that's for sure. I guess I could call him after my lunch break.

Okay so, maybe Mali was right.

"Mhmm." She nodded *yes* with her lips jutted out sarcastically. The deep wrinkles on her bronzed skin made her look extra serious, though I knew she was mostly teasing. She'd never liked Brien and even cut off the electricity in the lobby when he came to see me the first time after our breakup. In her defense, I was crying and he was accusing me of something that I couldn't even remember anymore. That must've meant I was innocent, right?

Truth was, I wasn't as sad as everyone thought I should be after we broke up. And, truth was, I'd used him to fill something broken inside of me. That's what most relationships actually boiled down to.

Mali interrupted my sour memories of Brien. "We have a walk-in," she said.

Her back was hunched so she could see the little security television screen. I couldn't make out whether it was a man or a woman, but I knew Elodie had just started on her two-thirty appointment and we were the only two in until four, when three more therapists came in for the night shift.

"I'll take it. I don't have any more appointments today."

Honestly, I was hoping there wouldn't be any walk-ins and that I would be able to do laundry, clean my room, and help Mali with the bookkeeping, instead of giving a massage, but this was my job. This is what I chose. That's what I told myself every time my fingers ached or my head pounded from the smell of bleach on the towels just after they'd been washed.

I pushed through the curtain in the lobby to find Kael walking around the small space, almost pacing. There were only a few chairs in the lobby, but between them and the front desk, they took up so much space. I watched him walk back and forth before I pushed all the way through the curtain.

"Hey?" I greeted Kael, my stomach tied in a knot.

"Hey."

We stood there, standing in the thick smell of incense and the dim lights in the room. The old PC tower on the floor hummed between us.

"Is everything okay?" As I asked, it dawned on me that he might be there for a reason.

"Yeah, yeah. I came to get a massage, actually." He held up his hands.

"Really?"

"Yeah. Is that okay?" His voice was soft, an unsure question.

I nodded and brought my hand up to my mouth. I didn't know why I was smiling, but I was and I couldn't stop.

Chapter * Twenty-Six

I PULLED BACK the curtain to my room.

"I'll give you two minutes or so to undress and I'll be back," I told him.

Kael stood by the table with his arms crossed. His sweats hung on his hips and his skin glowed in the candlelight. I couldn't remember the last time I liked looking at someone as much as I did Kael. It fascinated me. He fascinated me. I didn't know what it was about him, but he got more attractive every time I looked at him.

I moved out into the dark hallway and took a deep breath. I told myself that it wouldn't be weird. I did this all day, every day. He was just a regular client, a stranger really. I barely knew him and on top of that, I had already given him a massage. I pulled my phone from my pocket to see if Austin had called me back yet. Nothing. I texted my dad. Anything to distract myself.

I could hear Mali talking to her husband down the hall. Something about extending a hot stone promotion we had going this month. She was always trying to come up with new promotions and semi-free marketing for their small business. It was impressive to watch her keep this place full of steady clientele, even though there were parlors on every nearly every block outside of each gate. Most were about thirty bucks, some more, some less. Some shady, some not.

A text from my dad popped up on my screen.

Austin is okay. He's asleep right now.

I shoved my phone into the pocket of my uniform. It had to have been two minutes. If not longer.

"Can I come in?" I touched the curtain.

"Yeah."

He was face down on the massage table, his head in the cradle, the white sheet resting right at his waistline.

"Do you remember what you liked and didn't like last time?" I asked, mostly just for my own consumption.

"Everything was good."

"Okay, so I'll apply the same pressure and see where we go from there?" I asked him. He nodded.

I grabbed the towel and went through the motions. The warm towel glided easily across the bottoms of his feet. He was wearing his sweats on the table again, the black fabric peeking out of the bottom of the white sheet. I almost pushed them up a little so I could rub his ankles more thoroughly, but something told me not to. He was wearing the pants for a reason and though I could admit to myself that I was dying to know what that reason was, I didn't want to make him uncomfortable or cross any boundaries.

I pressed my thumb into the pad of flesh right under the line of his toes and he groaned. I eased up and his tense body relaxed. He rolled his ankle to get rid of the feeling. It was a sore spot for a lot of people.

"Sorry. It usually releases tension."

I walked back around to the top of the table where his head was and reached for my oils.

"No peppermint, right?" I asked him.

"No, thanks. I hate the smell."

Okay then.

"I'll use one without a smell. Will that work?"

His head nodded in the cradle.

I rubbed the warm oil between my hands and started at the base of his neck. The cords of his muscles were thick around his neckline and down his shoulders. In a way, he looked like someone built to fight, to protect, but sometimes he seemed so boyish, silly even, someone who should be kept out of harm's way.

"Elodie is here," I told him. He stayed quiet as I moved my hands across his soft skin. His shoulders held a little less tension than yesterday. Holy shit, it had literally only been a day since he came in for Elodie!

"I met her in training for my therapist license. She had just gotten here from France after researching programs for military spouses."

I remember how thick her beautiful accent used to feel to me. "She was so determined and was taking the first day so seriously. I was drawn to her almost immediately." I explained.

He laughed a little. His shoulders danced with slight amusement.

"Phillip's as nice as I think he is, yeah?" I asked Kael while we were on the subject. He stayed quiet for a few seconds.

"He's a good guy."

"Promise? Because he brought her here from another country with no family and no friends here. I worry about her."

"He's a good guy," he said again.

I needed to stop grilling him and just do my job. I kept thinking about more and more to say to him. But he didn't come here to talk to me. He came here to get a treatment for his aching body.

I moved down his back and up his arms, settling into my normal groove. I did the same thing most treatments, medium pressure, a little more oil than most therapists use. The song playing was an older Beyoncé song and I let the music fill the quiet air until about twenty minutes later, when I asked him to roll onto his back.

He closed his eyes when he turned over and I took the liberty of studying his face. His sharp jawline, the light stubble under his chin. He took a deep breath when I tucked my hands under his back and raked them up his skin, pressing and stretching the muscles in his back.

I opened my mouth to ask Kael about shopping tonight. Then closed it.

Seconds later, I almost asked him what sounded good for dinner. Then I almost told him that I loved the song that was playing and in my head I was telling him how Mali let me have my own music playing in my room. Something about him just made me want to speak. Almost.

I wasn't sure what to make of it.

I sighed.

I couldn't chit and chat to him the whole time he was on my table. It was unprofessional. I repeated that to myself a few times.

I checked the time. Only two minutes had gone by since I'd had him roll over. Fuck my life. I wanted to tell him that time was going so slow. Or ask him if he could smell the caramel cake candle I'd had burning since I opened.

"Everything good?" I asked finally.

He nodded. "How's your brother?" His question

surprised me.

"I thought he'd have come to my house as soon as he arrived to town, but I guess not," I said. "He's asleep at my dad's now. I still haven't gotten to talk to him alone. It's so frustrating. We used to be so close."

Kael kept his eyes closed. I was kneading my closed fists down his shoulders and arms. His eyes clenched shut.

"Sorry I'm talking so much. I seem to do that a lot." I laughed but it sounded so fake. Probably because it was.

Kael's eyes opened for a second and he leaned his head up, forcing eye contact. "It's fine. I don't mind it."

I looked away and he laid his head back down. "Thanks, I think," I teased and my stomach flipped when his face broke into the biggest smile I had seen on him yet.

Chapter * Twenty-Seven

I WAS WAITING for Kael when I got Elodie's text with the Buzzfeed link. She was the queen of "Is It Your Fault You're Single?" quizzes, and "Are Women Taking Over the Self-Employment Industry?" articles. This one was "25 Things You Need To Know About Target" I was one click away from finding out something new about Pringles and Tide PODS, or maybe how to spot the quickest checkout line, when Kael appeared in the lobby.

"Hi," I said. "Hope everything was okay."

"Yeah, thanks," he answered. I rang him up and handed over the credit card slip to sign. I'd never felt anxious seeing a client scribble his name across that little black line before, so this was new. And, of course, Kael wasn't giving anything up, which left room for me to fill in the blanks. First I wondered if he'd come back for another massage. Then it was, *What's going to happen after he stops crashing on my couch?*

He left me a twelve dollar tip on a forty-five dollar massage. It was more than generous. Certainly it was more than I usually got. I felt a little weird about it, like he was giving me charity or something. Or paying for my time, which I guess he was. But I did need the money, so I took it with a smile. Ok, the smile was mostly forced, but he couldn't tell. At least, I didn't think he could.

I thought about how I had talked through half of his massage. It probably didn't make for the most relaxing experience.

"Sorry I talked so—"

Kael cut me off before I could finish. "No," he said, and offered me a friendly shrug of his shoulders. "It's cool."

I was learning him, but I still couldn't tell whether he was lying or not. Wouldn't he be at least a little annoyed by all my nervous chatter? Ok, he asked me a question or two, but I was the one who talked about my shifts and how my brother was causing me major stress over his second arrest. I almost spent the next few minutes talking about my brother and how I was worried about him, but for once, I didn't want this to be about Austin. Maybe I wanted to seem more mature than I was, or maybe I wanted to protect Austin from a stranger's opinion. Whatever the reason, I moved on to something else.

"What color should I paint the walls in here?" I had asked him.

"What color do you want to paint them?" he'd answered.

And ...

"Is it overly decorated in here?" I'd asked.

"I didn't notice," he'd answered.

And ...

"Do you feel like you're in an expensive spa in a big city, instead of here, in this strip mall?"

Shrug.

Kael answered with a word or two now and then, but mostly it was my voice that filled the room. We were in the lobby now—not exactly a therapeutic space—but he was still playing the strong, silent type.

"Do you want a receipt?" I read the prompt from the credit card machine.

"Of course." He held out his hand.

"Of course? Such certainty over a credit card receipt?" I teased him. I was beginning to love doing that. He reacted differently nearly every time. It was fascinating.

"Responsible," he said. He almost smiled as he tucked the receipt into his wallet. It was leather, light brown and obviously well-used.

"Sure," I snorted. "Whatever you say."

"Better hope you don't get audited." No smile this time, but he did give me a raised eyebrow.

Mali was watching everything closely. When Kael came out into the lobby after his session, she had been busy nearby, humming to herself while wiping the fingerprints from the glass door. Now she'd given up even the pretense of cleaning.

"See you tonight?" I asked.

"Yeah. For sure."

He waved to me and said a polite goodbye to Mali, calling her ma'am and all. The door closed and she turned her attention to me.

"Mhm?" I knew what she was thinking.

"What *mhm*?" I closed the cash register and stuck the tip in my pocket.

Her eyes fell on the door again and a Cheshire-cat grin spread across her face. "Oh, nothing."

"Stop gossiping," I told her as I disappeared down the hallway.

Chapter * Twenty-Eight

I WAS KEEN to go home while the sun was shining—for once. That's why I didn't stay to clean as thoroughly as I usually did. I still put a load of towels into the dryer and opened a couple of boxes of product and put everything away, but my coworkers could do a little more to pick up the slack around here. I was okay with that.

The alley was busy when I left. Bradley was helping a customer load a king-size mattress into the back of a truck when he waved to me, friendly as ever.

I pulled out my phone to open Instagram when my brother's name popped up on the screen.

"Austin, what the hell is going on? Are you okay?" I didn't bother with *hello*. I had no time for formalities.

"I'm fine. It's fine. Really, Kare, it's not that big of a deal. It was just a fight."

"A fight? With who?"

He sighed for a second. "Some guy. I don't know. I was out somewhere and this guy was giving a girl at the bar shit."

I rolled my eyes and pressed my body against the trees lining the alleyway so a van full of kids could pass.

"So, you're telling me that this whole thing stemmed from your chivalry?"

Austin was good at spinning things. He would make a wonderful publicist for a messy celebrity—or a horrible husband.

"Yes. That's exactly what I'm saying," he said, laughing.

His voice was calming, it was like hearing an old song you had forgotten you loved. I'd really missed him.

"Right. So how much trouble are you in?"

"I don't know." He paused.

I thought I heard the flick of a lighter. "Dad bailed me out ... which sucks, because now I'm going to owe him money."

Unbelievable. I wish I had his ability to look the other way and not worry about things. He knew he would figure it out—or someone would figure it out for him—before it got too serious.

"Yeah, because owing dad money is your biggest problem."

"I didn't kill anyone, ok? It was your standard bar fight."

I laughed. I could *feel* his magic working. I was starting to feel almost-ok about his arrest, and the ink on his discharge papers wasn't even dry yet.

"How did you even get into a bar? We're not twenty-one for another month."

This time, it was his turn to be amused. "You're not serious."

"Yes, I am!" But I was joking, sort of.

There was this thin line between me worrying about

my brother and just wanting to have fun with him. I was by no means a stickler, or super responsible; I was just light years ahead of my twin. The difference was incredibly noticeable.

I knew my loser uncle was taking Austin to bars with his gross older friends, probably introducing him to women who downed too much alcohol, wore too much makeup, had too much experience … too much everything.

"You're a worrier. You and Dad."

I groaned. I didn't want to worry. I didn't want to be the nagging older-by-six-minutes sister. And I certainly didn't want to be anything like my dad.

"Don't lump me in with Dad. Come on. I just don't want you to be in trouble. That's all."

I was almost home.

"Yeah, wouldn't want to mess up this bright future of mine." It was meant to be funny, but a hint of sadness filtered through.

"Do you want to come over tonight? I miss you."

"I can't tonight. I'm meeting up with someone. But tomorrow? Dad and Estelle are going to Atlanta this weekend, so I'll have the house to myself."

"House party!" I laughed at the memory of Austin's streak of failed house parties throughout high school. Most of the kids our age had been too afraid of the military police to go to a party on post, but fewer people actually made the parties more fun.

"Totally."

"And I was totally joking. You're not going to have a party at Dad's house."

"Uh, yeah. I am."

He could not be serious. Our dad would lose his mind if Austin had a party at his house. I couldn't bear to think of the consequences.

"You are not. I mean, throwing a party a couple of days after you get arrested? What is wrong with you? We aren't in high school anymore!"

It was stuff like this that made me return to my family theory, which was that Austin was the one who got all our mother's charm. My little brother was always so good with people. He could be thrust into any situation and people would flock to him. What's that saying, *like flies to honey?* He had all the honey. Me—I was just the opposite. I fluttered around people like Austin, easily charmed, like my father.

"Speak for yourself."

"How do you even know enough people here to have a party? I mean—"

"Look, I gotta go. See you sometime tomorrow. You should come over. Love you."

He hung up before I could get in another word.

Oh, Austin. *I love you, but sometimes you make some really shitty life choices.*

Chapter ✶ Twenty-Nine

I WAS A LITTLE SURPRISED to find my front door locked. I dug for my key and let myself in, grabbing my mail from the box on the way. My little mailbox was falling off my house. Another thing to fix. As I slid through envelopes, a realtor's brochure of fancy, expensive houses in Atlanta was on top. I searched for the smiley realtor, Sandra Dee, it said her name was. The price for a house in Buckhead, with a sparkling swimming pool was two-million-dollars. Yeah, I freaking wish, Sandra.

Until I hit the lottery or my random ideas of opening up a chain of high-end but fair priced spa experiences takes off, it's my little house with the dangling red mailbox for me. When I got inside, the house was heavy with silence. I went through the rest of my mail—nothing interesting, mainly bills and flyers—and because the entire house smelled of Elodie's popcorn and it made my stomach growl, I grabbed some pretzels from my pantry.

My house felt different with no sound. It felt strange

not hearing the name Olivia Pope every few minutes. I was completely alone. No Elodie. No Kael. We didn't agree on a time or anything, but I guess I'd just assumed that he would be at my house when I got off work.

Where else would he go?

I microwaved the last of the leftovers from Mali. I washed a load of dishes. Sat at my kitchen table. Grabbed the paperback I was reading and tried to pick up where I had left off. I kept thinking about Kael, wondering how he would be when we went shopping. Would he be more talkative or would it be a silent excursion?

I loved to torture myself with second thoughts, so now I was thinking that maybe I had misconstrued the whole situation and that Kael was under the impression I would be dropping him off to shop by himself. Then I convinced myself that I had invited myself to shop with him, and that he probably thought I was weird or pushy. Or both.

Ten minutes later, I was back to reality. No way would Kael be sitting around overthinking our conversation—wherever he was. I was totally overreacting.

Overthinking. Overreacting. Not exactly skills I could put on my resume. I put the book down without having read a word, then picked up my phone and went through Facebook, typing *Kael Martin* in the search box. No change in his profile. And I still couldn't bring myself to send him a friend request.

I clicked out of his page and went to my inbox, as if I was expecting an important email or something. I was pacing around my room before I knew it, going in circles, getting myself worked up. I stopped dead in my tracks when I caught a glimpse of myself in the mirror. With my dark hair pulled back, my eyes wild, I looked like my mother. Frighteningly like my mother.

I lay on my bed and grabbed my book again, but soon felt like I needed a change of scenery, so I went to the living room and flopped on the couch. I checked the time on my phone. Almost seven. I picked up where I left off on my last dog-eared page—I had never been a bookmark kind of girl—and let Hemingway's brutal tale take me to the first World War. It wasn't the distraction I had hoped for, though. The closer I got to sleep, the more Kael's face appeared on multiple characters. He was a drill sergeant. A wounded soldier. An ambulance driver. And he looked at me like he recognized my eyes.

I woke up on the couch, the sun bright on my face. I looked around the living room, gathering my thoughts.

Kael hadn't come back.

Chapter ✶ Thirty

IT WOULD BE THREE DAYS before I saw him again. When we finally crossed paths again, I was sitting on my front porch, trying to get my feet into a new pair of shoes I had seen on Instagram. I knew that the IG model I followed had most likely been paid to wear them, but I still had to have them. Per the caption, they were "The Best!" and "SOO comfy!!! *heart-eye emoji*" Maybe for her. I could barely get the first one on. I mean, the damn thing just wouldn't go over my heel. I was tugging on the shoe, leaning back on the porch like some kind of idiot, when Kael pulled up in his gigantic jeep-truck-thing. Nice timing.

He must have gone shopping after all, since he was head-to-toe in civilian clothes. Black jeans, a rip on one knee, and a white cotton shirt with gray sleeves that looked almost identical to one that I had. The only difference was that mine said "Tomahawks" on it and had a picture of an actual tomahawk.

My best friend from South Carolina gave it to me. It

was from her old high school in Indiana somewhere. I wondered if her Midwestern home had been like the place where my mom grew up, a little town that was hit hard by the advances of technology, causing factory after factory to close down completely. I also knew horror stories from the place, like when the hyper schoolchildren had gone on field trips to sacred Native American burial grounds—what they called "Indian Mounds"—and stomped all over them while being taught a false history of dangerous savages. No mention that these people were victims of genocide or that we had taken their land and forced them into poverty today.

Come to think of it, I didn't really want to wear that shirt anymore.

Kael stopped just short of my porch.

"Hey stranger," I said to him.

He tucked his lips in and shook his head, then nodded. I guess that was his way of saying hello.

"Looking for Elodie?"

Little Mama was spending her Friday night at the monthly family readiness group meeting for Phillip's brigade. She was determined to make the other wives like her before the baby came. I didn't blame her. She needed all the support she could get.

"I'll tell her you stopped by."

"No, actually. I just—" Kael paused. "I went to get a massage but you weren't working." He looked down the alleyway toward the shop.

"Oh." Now that was a surprise.

I scooted over on the porch and made room next to me. Sort of. I had been blowing the seeds off dandelions in between my Cinderella act, so Kael had to move a pile of bald weeds before he could sit down. He dropped them softly into the palm of my hand.

"I could use some wishes for sure," he said.

"There's more if you want." I pointed to my weed garden. I hadn't meant to harbor all those dandelions, wild daisies, and creeping something or other, but there they were by the corners of my concrete porch. Surrounded.

"I'm good," he told me.

He looked so different in regular clothes.

"I see you went shopping?" He was obviously okay sitting in silence, but I wanted some conversation. Plus, I wanted to know where he'd disappeared to.

Kael pulled at his T-shirt. "Yeah, sorry about that. It's been kind of a crazy few days."

I had to ask. "Crazy? How?"

He sighed, picking up a dandelion stem from the steps. "Long story."

I leaned back on my palms. "Yeah."

"When do you work again?" he asked a moment later.

A plane flew overhead right as I started to answer. "Tomorrow. But only for two hours. I'm filling in for someone."

"Do you have any openings?"

He was looking at me, his dark eyes hooded by his long lashes. "Maybe."

"Maybe?" He raised his brows and I laughed. He was soft today. I liked this relaxed version of him. Kael the civilian.

"I'm going to a party tonight," I told him. "It's at my dad's house." He made a face. "Yes. Exactly. Only worse because my brother is being an idiot and throwing it while my dad and his wife are off in Atlanta at the Marriott, eating lobster tails and boozing with expensive wine." I rolled my eyes.

My dad never took my mom anywhere like that. They never had adult time without my brother and me. One of the many reasons they didn't work out. That and the fact that they were the two least compatible people on earth.

"Your dad doesn't seem like the kind of guy who wants a party thrown at his house," Kael observed. "Especially when he's not there."

If only he knew. "Oh, he's not. That's why I'm going to chaperone."

He made a noise—something between a grunt and a laugh. He was actually amused. I was really liking this, the way I was starting to read his face and guess what he was thinking.

"Aren't you a little young to be chaperoning?"

"Ha. Ha." I stuck my tongue out at him ... then snapped my mouth shut as soon as I realized what I'd done. I was flirting with him!

And I didn't know how to stop. Who was this person, sticking her tongue out a a boy?

"How old are you, Mr. Expert-on-Ageism?"

"That's not what ageism means," he corrected me with a smile.

I scoffed. I was equal parts charmed and surprised.

"Okay Mr. Know-it-All, how old are you?"

He smiled again.

So soft.

"I'm twenty."

I shot up. "Really? I could be older than you?"

"How old are you?" he asked.

"Twenty-one next month."

He licked his pink lips and bit on the bottom one. It was a habit of his, I'd noticed.

"I turn twenty-one tomorrow. I win."

I opened my mouth in an O. "No way. Show me your ID."

"Really?" he questioned.

"Yes, really. Prove it." And then, because I couldn't help myself, I added, "I want receipts."

He pulled his wallet out from the back pocket of his jeans and handed it to me. The first thing I saw was a picture of two women. One was older than the other by a couple decades or so, but the resemblance was there.

I looked up at him, apologizing for the lack of privacy. The picture was obviously old and important, otherwise it wouldn't be in his wallet. Across from the picture of the women was his military ID card. I read his birthday. Sure as sin, his birthday was tomorrow.

"So you're older than me by like a month," I gave in.

"I told you."

"Don't brag."

I leaned into Kael and repeated the awkward grocery store shoulder-bumping. Only this time, he didn't move away from me, or freeze up. This time, on my sunny porch, in ripped jeans and with soft eyes, he pressed his shoulder back into mine.

Chapter ✦ Thirty-One

"I HAVEN'T SAT on my porch in so long. This is nice."

It was just me and Kael, with the occasional passing car for company.

"I'd sit out here almost every day when I first moved in. I couldn't believe it. My porch. My place." I paused for a moment. "It feels good, you know? The street in front of you, the house behind you."

Talking to Kael was like writing in a diary, sort of.

"I've always loved sitting out front. Not just here. Did you notice that swing on my dad's porch? I'm not sure if you even saw it, but we moved that swing with us when we were growing up. It came from base to base, from house to house—just like my dad's recliner."

I could feel Kael listening, encouraging me to go on.

"When we first moved to Texas, we didn't have a big enough porch, so we kept it in the shed. It's heavy wood … you can see where it's splintered in a few places and where it's worn down on the arms a little. It's not like that plastic outdoor furniture you get now. What's it called—rosin?"

"Resin," he said, helping me out.

"That's it—resin." I was thinking about my mom now, how she would sit out front in the dark and stare up at the sky. "My mom practically lived on our porch, all year round. She told me once that she believed God was made up of all of the stars and that when one burned out, a little bit of the good in the world died with it."

Kael's eyes were on me and I was aware of how the heat was spreading on my cheeks. The way I was talking ... well, it was like I was thinking out loud. I barely realized it. I knew that it sounded cheesy. I'd read things like that in books sometimes or had seen it in movies, and it just didn't seem possible. What a cliché. Yet there I was, being opened by a stranger.

"I mean it was way more complicated than that, obviously. That was the quick version. There were actually civilizations whose entire religions were based on the whole galaxy of planets and stars. My mom used to tell me all about them. I mean, it makes sense, doesn't it? They were here first."

Kael spoke up. "Were they?"

His words seemed important, there were so few of them. I guess that's why when he asked me questions, I wanted to really think about my answers.

"I'm not entirely sure," I finally said. "What about you?"

He shook his head.

"I think that's okay," I told him. "There are so many different religions ... too many people to get to agree on one thing. I think it's okay to take a little time, learn a little more. Don't you?" Such a heavy question, and wrapped in the most casual bow.

He sighed, blowing out a puff of air. I could hear the

whisper of his words coming together, but couldn't quite make them out. The longer he sat on his opinion, licking slowly at his lips, chewing on his cheek, the more I anticipated his answer. Time melted as I waited.

"I think so," he said at long last. "I just want to be a good person. I know a lot of people inside and outside the church who are both bad and good. There's so much out there that's bigger than us ... I'd rather focus on how to make things better than wonder how we got here in the first place. For now, at least." He sounded so sure.

He kept talking. This was the most he had shared since we met. Usually I was the one going on and on. "I don't know what I believe yet," he said.

There was a long pause before he continued. A car door slammed and my phone buzzed with a text from Elodie. She was going to someone's house—someone named Julie— so everyone except her could have a few drinks. I dimmed my screen and put my phone facedown on the concrete porch.

"I don't know," he repeated. "But I do know that I have a lot of shit to make up for."

His voice slipped a little at the end and my brain took a bite of his words. The gravity of what he was saying ate at me. My throat burned and I swallowed, trying to dilute it, but it didn't work. It was physically painful to think about the kinds of things Kael had seen at his age—at *our* age. It was easier not to feel anything at all, but I couldn't do that.

I'd always felt so much, ever since I was a child. I was always either burning or floating, moving from one extreme to another. "Karina feels things deeply," my mother said of me. "She takes things to heart."

Kael cleared his throat. I wanted so badly to ask him what he had to make up for, but I knew he wouldn't want that. I could feel him next to me, brewing, but I kept my eyes on the sky. I blinked, watching as blue swirled into orange. I pictured him with a gun strapped to his chest, a boyish smile. I didn't know what he'd experienced over there, but that blank stare on his face ... I had to say something.

"I don't think it works like that. I think you're safe."

My words were weak when said, but if he could feel what I felt for him in that moment, he would know it couldn't be further from the truth.

"Safe?" he asked, as the clouds drifted over us. "From who?"

Chapter ✳ Thirty-Two

I DIDN'T HEAR loud music or see bright lights when I pulled up. And nobody had spilled onto the lawn. That had to be a good sign.

"Doesn't seem too bad," I said.

The bungalow was in the far corner of a quiet cul-de-sac, with a field at the back and houses all around. I had to park on the street because three cars were already in the driveway—two of which I didn't recognize. Plus there was my dad's van, an ugly white thing he hadn't touched in at least a year. I'd come to hate that van. It wasn't always that way, but pleasant memories of our one Disney road trip had long ago been replaced by ugly arguments and resentments that spilled over from the front seat.

My parents didn't have typical husband and wife shouting matches. Even as a child I remember wishing for some of the honest anger I had heard in other families. Theirs was worse. My mom would use a cold, flat voice to deliver her punches. She hit hard, and she knew instinctively where to strike, how to make it hurt the most. I was a needy girl and wanted her anger to reassure me that she cared. I think my dad wanted it too, but she either couldn't or wouldn't give us that. My dad and I both navigated our losses differently.

Kael's phone lit up in his hand. He glanced down and put it into his pocket. I felt important. Prideful as it was, I still felt it.

We were walking up the grass when someone I didn't recognize came out of the house and walked towards the street. I saw Kael watch him until we were safely inside. It wasn't anything obvious, just a tilt of the head, an almost imperceptible scan of where this other guy was and what he was doing. It made me wonder what Kael had experienced, and what he might fear. I tried not to let it affect my mood, thinking about what he had seen in Afghanistan. I was sure that was the last thing he wanted to talk about the night before his birthday.

I led Kael into my dad's house for the second time in a week. Brien had only been there a total of maybe three times our entire four months of dating. He liked my dad … well, he liked trying to impress him while staring at Estelle's boobs. She was new back then, her boobs too.

Ugh. Brien was the last person I should be thinking of. I looked back at Kael to edge him back into my mind, and also to make sure he was still behind me.

Someone's music was playing on the TV screen. It was a Halsey song, so I knew I'd like at least one of these random people. I was relaxing a little now. Austin had been right about the party, so far anyway. There were only about ten people there and everyone seemed to be out of high school, thank God. And there was no sign of Sarina or any of her other friends and as far as I knew, she was Austin's only high school hook up. No sign of Austin either, which meant he was either outside smoking, or in some room with a girl. As long as it wasn't my old room, and the girl was of age, I didn't care.

Five or six people were dotted around the living room. The rest were in the kitchen, crowding the booze counter. There wasn't much to speak of: a bottle of vodka, a much bigger bottle of whiskey, and tons of beer. We stayed in the kitchen, moving around a guy and a girl who seemed to be mid-argument, and passing a man wearing a gray beanie. I couldn't see his hair, but I suspected he was a soldier, based on his build. My brother always seemed to gravitate toward people in service, even when we were in high school.

Austin and I made a pact from a young age that neither of us would ever enlist, but he still had a natural draw to army life. Whether it was out of habit or comfort—the pull of the familiar and all that—I didn't know. His curiosity scared me sometimes.

Kael stood near me by the kitchen sink, not touching or speaking, but close enough that I could smell the cologne on his shirt. The smell was sweet and it made me wonder if he had other plans tonight. I wasn't naïve. I knew the local clubs like Lone Star and Tempra were flooded with singles and single-for-the-night's. But I didn't want to think about Kael at either of those places. I grabbed a plastic cup from the stack and poured in a little bit of vodka and a lot of cranberry juice.

"Want one?" I asked Kael.

He shook his head, *no*. He seemed tense. Whether he was more tense than usual, I couldn't say. He looked at me as if he wanted to say something, but couldn't. His eyes leveled on the cup in my hand.

"I'm only having one since I'm driving," I explained, slightly defensive. Guilt didn't really feel appropriate, since I could crash upstairs in my old bed if I needed to.

"I don't like liquor much." I didn't need an explanation, but it did make me wonder what it was that was making him seem so on edge.

It was like he wanted to be present, but his mind was wandering back and forth between the kitchen and somewhere else. I tried to guess where, and even considered straight up asking him, but the idea made my heart pound.

"I'll just take a beer," Kael said.

I handed him a can from the bin in front of me, next to the partition between the living room and kitchen. Shelves full of eight-by-tens of my dad and Estelle, and me and Austin when we were young, stared back at us. My mom had long since been erased from the record.

Kael studied the beer for a moment, rolling it in his hand before popping open the tab.

"Natural Light, huh?" He raised his brows. They were so thick, they shaded his deep-set eyes and helped hide him from the world. Like he needed help with that.

"Yep. The best of the best." I took a gulp of my vodka mixture. I felt it fast, my cheeks and tummy warming up.

Kael took a drink of the watery beer. I lifted my cup to touch his can. "Happy birthday! You'll be drinking legally in about three hours," I joked.

"And you in a month," he said, taking a swig of the beer and making a face. I didn't blame him. I much preferred vodka over heavy bubbles of beer. It was my go-to when I drank. Drink less, feel more.

Another plus with vodka: I knew exactly how much to drink before I would get too drunk. I'd pretty much mastered vodka. I'd been drinking it since Austin and I had gone to that Seniors Only party back in South Carolina.

Austin and I were probably the only freshmen there. We scanned the place when we arrived, but it didn't take long until Casey, a popular seventeen-year-old, made a beeline for Austin. She was one of the popular seniors. *Popular.* I hated that word. Austin didn't, though. He knew it was his way in. The moment he complimented Casey's eyelashes—it was something lame like, *You have the longest eyelashes*—well, that was it. Five minutes later, they were tongue-to-tongue and I was left to wander the party by myself.

The only person who talked to me was a boy who had a mustard stain on his shirt. He had sharp canines, like a wolf, and he smelled like orange Lysol. I left him in the hallway by the bathroom and found the vodka bottle in the freezer. It was cool going down. That's probably why I drank so much so fast. Too much. Too fast. I ran to the bathroom with my hand covering my mouth, holding in the vomit. Unfortunately, I ran into Lysol guy again, and he looked at me like I was the pathetic one. Maybe I was? I mean, I *was* the one pushing people out of the way to get the toilet.

But that was then and this was now. That party was different. I was different. I had learned to hold my liquor. And I was no longer the girl who couldn't walk away from a scary guy without second guessing herself. I felt safe with Kael. Interested and interesting. Like I was the senior at this party.

Chapter ✶ Thirty-Three

KAEL WAS TAKING everything in. He wasn't obvious about it, but he was watching. Analyzing. Paying attention.

We made eye contact and he surprised me by being the one to break the silence between us.

"Just how I thought I would spend my twenty-first birthday," he said, taking another gulp of beer. And another.

Someone turned on an old Usher song and I smiled into my cup. People were definitely trying to set the mood if they were playing old school Usher. I was liking this group, even though I tried not to. I was a sucker for nostalgia.

"Wow. Usher. Well, take all the sarcasm out of what I just said." Kael smiled.

I hadn't known this guy long, but wow, I loved it when he was this way. Unguarded and funny. I laughed at him and he took me in—my mouth, my eyes, my mouth again. He wasn't subtle about it.

Was he aware of the way he was looking at me?

He had to be aware of the way he was looking at me.

My head felt fuzzy and it had nothing to do with the vodka.

"Kare!" Austin's voice boomed over everyone and everything, including the blender being used to make some sort of neon mixed drink that I hoped wouldn't be splattered all over my dad's bathroom floor later.

"There you are!" He wrapped both arms around me. He smelled like beer himself.

The thought passed just as quickly as it came. He hugged me tight and kissed my hair.

"Look at you," he said, holding his plastic cup in the air. I knew he was drunk. He wasn't wild. He wasn't belligerent. But buzzed for sure.

"Did you get a drink?" Austin's green eyes were bloodshot. I reminded myself that he had just gotten out of jail, that he probably needed the drink.

The fact that jail was a part of my vocabulary was something in itself, but I refused to be anything but chill the entire night. I was there to blend and now that Kael was there, I wanted him to have fun.

"Yes." I held up my cup and Austin nodded his head as if to say *good*.

"Did you meet everyone?" His words were slightly slurred. His hair was messy, tousled, hitting the middle of his forehead.

"Not yet. I just got here."

"You look happy. Are you happy?" my twin asked me.

His cheeks were flushed. I put both of my hands on his shoulders.

"You look drunk. Are you drunk?" I taunted him. In a loving way, of course. But I taunted him nonetheless. He was drunk. I was happy. But I wasn't going to talk about it in front of an arguing couple and Kael.

"I am. As you should be," Austin told me with conviction. "It's so good to be back." He raised his hands in the air. His happiness was contagious, giving me a burst of energy I hadn't felt in a while.

Austin raised his cup to mine and then moved to Kael's. It took a second for him to register that Kael wasn't someone he had invited.

"Hi." Austin extended his hand to Kael. I cringed, wishing I had poured double the vodka into my drink.

"Hey, I'm Kael. Nice to meet you." The two guys shook hands like they had just made a billion-dollar deal.

"Kael." Austin let that one sit for a second. "Nice to meet you, man. We have drinks in here, pizza on the way. She knows where everything is," he said, pointing at me with his cup. "You guys should come out to the living room with me."

Kael looked at me and I shrugged. I knew it was either the best, or worst, idea to follow Austin back to the living room.

"Here, refill your drinks and come with me."

I tried to make eye contact with Kael, but he was looking at Austin, who was asking how long he had been in the army. Austin could tell. Even without being told, he could tell.

I knew that Austin wouldn't embarrass me by asking too many questions in front of Kael, but I also knew by the way he was looking at me that he was going to ask a hell of a lot questions later. The arguing couple disappeared down the hallway, probably to have make-up sex in the downstairs bathroom.

"I'm glad you came," Austin said to me, leading us into the living room.

He looked at Kael again and I rolled my eyes. Austin and I mostly stayed out of each other's dating lives. Not that there was much on my end to be nosy about. I had only had one serious boyfriend who I had decided not to think about for the night and as months passed, I realized we weren't as serious as I thought we were. I had been told I love you by someone who meant it. Austin was different, falling in love every week. He somehow managed to stay honest about it, channeling his need and loneliness into physical contact. If it was the thing that made his life just a little better, who was I to judge? I had that same itch, just no one to scratch it.

Chapter ★ Thirty-Four

KAEL AND I WERE smushed together on one end of the couch. Not squished. Not smashed. *Smushed.* Austin and a guy who had introduced himself as Lawson were on one cushion; Kael and I were on the other.

"You look so familiar," Lawson said to Kael after a few minutes.

Kael reeled off a few things that sounded like army lingo and Lawson shook his head. "No, that's not it."

"You say that to everyone," Austin said. Then he grabbed a video game controller from a basket under the entertainment center. "Who's ready to play?"

"Not me," Lawson said. "Time to go. I have to be up at five for duty." He and Austin stood up and did that handshake thing guys do where they slap their palms together and make a fist.

Once there was more room, I moved over a little on the couch. We weren't smushed anymore, but my thigh was still touching Kael's.

"Do you want to play?" Austin lifted a controller to Kael, who shook his head.

"No, I don't really play."

Oh, thank God.

"Who wants to play?" Austin asked again, holding up a controller to see if he had any takers.

The front door opened and a familiar face walked in. I couldn't remember his name off the top of my head, but I knew he and Austin used to hang out before he went to our uncle's house to *keep out of trouble.* Yeah, because that worked out so well.

"Mendoza!" Austin rushed to the door to greet the guy in the Raiders shirt. Austin always collected people around him. He was good at it.

The guy, presumably Mendoza, hugged Austin. His eyes landed on me as I stared him down. My cheeks flushed. He looked next to me, to Kael.

"Martin!" he said, pulling away from my brother. He walked over to the couch and Kael stuck his hand out between us. It took me longer than it should've to realize that they knew each other and that Martin was Kael's last name.

"Thought you were staying in tonight." Mendoza's honey-colored eyes were on me.

"I was going to," Kael said.

Mendoza looked at me again, then back at Kael. "Right," he said, smiling.

"You two know each other?" Austin pointed between them. I sat there, observing. Confused. Austin was just as surprised as I was.

"Yeah, we were in basic together. And we deployed—"

"Mendoza, this is Karina," Kael interrupted, looked at me.

"My sister," Austin said to both boys.

"We met before. I don't know if you remember," I said. It shouldn't have rattled me that Kael and this guy knew each other, but it did. Military bases always seemed so small, but they were really little cities with hundreds of thousands of people. When someone said, "Oh, your dad's in the army. I bet he knows my cousin Jeff, he's in the army, too!" it didn't really work that way. So, Mendoza knowing Kael *and* Austin, and sort of knowing me, was a coincidence to say the least.

"I do. We met a couple times." Mendoza cocked his head to the side. "Didn't we go to the castle one night? What was that, like two summers ago?" I thought back to the end of summer, riding in my dad's van, which had been too full of Austin's friends. Definitely squished.

"We did," I told him. "I forgot all about that." Brien was there too. We had just met, in fact. I didn't mention that.

"Your brother and that damn castle." He laughed, and Austin flipped him off.

Kael was looking at us both like we were crazy. "Have you heard about it? Dracula's castle?" I asked. It sounded ridiculous out loud.

He shook his head and I continued to explain. "It's not really a castle, but it's this big stone tower that everyone says was haunted."

"IS haunted!" Austin argued.

"*Is* haunted," I said, rolling my eyes. I had gone to Dracula's castle at least five times with Austin since we'd moved here. I didn't know if the story about the kid getting electrocuted at the top was really true, but the old tower had earned a reputation for being haunted by ghosts. "Actual ghosts!" is what everyone said. There were all kinds of stories.

"Anyway, so it's a tower and people drive up there at night to drink and try not to get caught," I explained to Kael.

"She's acting like she's cool now, but she's always the

first one to run back to the car." Austin held up his drink to Kael and Mendoza, laughing.

"Oh, fuck off." I shot him a look—more laughter followed.

Mendoza started to taunt Austin. "Oooh, looks like sis has grown up since I saw her last," he said, picking up the bottle of dark liquor from the table.

"Shots, anyone?" he asked the room.

Chapter ☆ Thirty-Five

EVERYONE TOOK A SHOT of warm liquor. Everyone except Kael, that was. There were shouts of "To Austin!" and "Welcome Back Bro!" Austin gave a mock bow to acknowledge his friends as they celebrated his return. I wasn't sure if any of them knew that he had been arrested. Looking around at these guys ... well, I wasn't sure if any of them would even concern themselves with something as trivial as a night in jail. But maybe I was being hard on them.

We all migrated back to the kitchen to cheers Austin's return to Ft. Benning. I put my shot glass in the sink and gathered up a few more. A guy in a bright blue T-shirt that said *Bottoms Up!* grabbed his glass back from me and went for a refill. Definitely a soldier. He was with a younger-looking guy wearing a brown MURPH tee. Also a soldier. I kept forgetting just how distant I had become from life on post. Sure, I still saw soldiers at work and at the grocery store. I still smiled at them while going through the gate to The Great Place, but I didn't have any friends who were soldiers. Not one.

Not unless you counted Stewart. She was the closest thing I had to an army friend. But even though I liked and respected her, even though I felt close to her, I couldn't really claim her as a friend. As Mali liked to remind us, clients were not our friends.

I turned on the hot water and rinsed out a few shot glasses just for something to do. I was glad Austin didn't see me. He would have made some crack about my being *responsible.* It wouldn't have been a compliment. God, it was so weird having him back, being at my dad's, being surrounded by all these people. No doubt about it: This was Austin's world and I was just visiting.

I wasn't the same person as I was before he left, though. It felt good to remind myself of that. And Austin, as much as he gathered people around him, he latched onto them, too. Which was risky in his case, because he was often the one to run, like our mother. And he often left broken hearts behind, also like her.

I walked over to Kael, Austin, and Mendoza.

"Another?" Mendoza asked.

"No way." I shook my head and held up my hand, the universal symbol for *no, thanks.*

My stomach still burned as the tequila settled inside of me. The flavor was strong—pretty good, but so strong compared to the cheap vodka diluted with orange juice that I usually drank.

"Come on. Anyone?"

Austin's eyes were on Kael, who was also saying no. He didn't need to put his hand up or shake his head. Apparently "no" is all the answer you need when it comes from a guy.

Austin turned to Mendoza and refilled his glass. "He's trying to get as many shots in as possible before his wife calls for bedtime," Austin heckled him.

By the way Mendoza smiled when my brother teased him, I could see their bond. He was a nice guy, this Mendoza. I could feel it. It was never easy to predict the people I would meet through my twin, because he never had a type. Soldiers were usually involved, but that could be more of a geographical thing. Mostly strays. Mostly friendly. But every pack had a few wild cards.

"Well, she did let him come out this week," another male voice taunted. I turned around to see the guy in the *Bottom's Up!* T-shirt holding his shot glass in a way that was slightly menacing. He had a square face, tiny lips, and a bad crew cut.

Mendoza laughed still, but it didn't reach his eyes. Not like it did when he had joked with Austin. The guy in the T-shirt snickered, pointing a Bud Light bottle at Mendoza. "How many kids you got now anyway?" This question was delivered with a straight face.

"Three," Mendoza replied, humorless now. Something shifted in the room. I could feel it. Kael stiffened next to me. Austin inched closer to the two jerks.

"Three? That's it? I thought I saw you driving out of the commissary with like ten—"

"You're not funny, Jones. Neither you, Dubrowski. Comedy's not your thing. Now, move along, or get out," Austin snapped, pointing his chin towards the door. His eyes may have been glassy, but he was fully present. He wasn't having any of their shit.

The room was silent, except the obnoxious intro music to the video game that was playing on a loop in the background.

"Chill, we're leaving anyway," *Bottom's Up!* said.

No one made a sound as Jones and Dubrowski sat their beers on the counter, opened the back door, and left. Mendoza and Austin stared at each other for a second. I tried not to look, but I caught a glimpse of it.

"Who were those guys?" I asked Austin when the door shut.

"They're in my new company," Mendoza answered. "I thought they were cool and felt bad because they're so young and just got home and don't have any family here, you know?"

"Quit being so fucking nice!" Austin slapped Mendoza on the back and we all laughed. "See where it gets you? Now let's have a drink and not waste any more time or tequila on those pricks."

"This isn't just any tequila my friends." Mendoza held up the bottle. "It's an Anejo, aged to perfection. Smooth as butter." He showed me the label and I nodded, reading what I could as he watched me, before moving it to Kael.

Anejo or not, I knew I shouldn't drink much more. Even with my mother's tolerance for all vices, I could tell the alcohol was settling into my bloodstream. My cheeks were red—I could feel them.

But Kael was less blurry somehow.

You know those moments when someone just looks different to you? Like you swipe and a filter covers the picture? Everything about them becomes a little deeper in color, a little more vibrant?

Kael was leaning against the counter in my dad's

kitchen of all places, answering trivial questions from my
brother, when it happened. There was something about
watching him with there with Austin, the way the way he
was standing with his back straight, his eyes a little more
wild than usual. He was still the definition of composure,
but there was something emanating from him in that
moment.

Something strong and dark. I had to see more.

Chapter * Thirty-Six

"WHERE ARE YOU FROM?"

"Atlanta area. You?" Kael took a drink of his beer. And then another. I remembered that he said he was from Riverdale. Easier to say Atlanta, I supposed. I liked knowing that, as if I was in on one of his secrets.

Austin crossed his arms. "All over. Ft. Bragg, Texas, and a couple others. You know, army brat."

Kael nodded. "Yeah. I can't imagine, man."

The doorbell rang. "Pizza? I hope so. I haven't eaten all day," Austin said, disappearing from the kitchen.

"Are you hungry?" I asked Kael.

"Kind of. You?"

I nodded.

"Shall we?" I gestured toward the living room.

He nodded, smiled at me, and tossed his beer into the trash.

"Do you want another one?" I asked, looking into my almost empty cup and debating on a refill.

"I'm good. One of us has to drive," he said.

"Ah," I said, biting on my lower lip. Kael's shoulder brushed against mine. He was standing so close to me. "I can stay here."

His eyes widened a little. "You can too. There's plenty of room."

We had stopped walking, but I couldn't remember when. He was looking down at me and I was looking up at him. I remember the curve of his lashes shading his brown eyes. The way he smelled like cinnamon. For the first time, the scent didn't remind me of anything except for him. My brain was short-circuiting, not connecting thought with my tongue.

"I mean, you don't have to stay here. You can use my car, or an Uber. Whatever, I was just suggesting because I'm obviously not driving and your car—" Kael leaned toward me. I had to work hard to catch my breath.

"I'll get another beer," he told me in a whisper. He paused there, so close to my mouth, that the bottom of my stomach ached.

He moved away, casually, and grabbed for another beer. I swallowed, blinking.

Did I think he was going to kiss me?

I *so* did.

That had to be why I was breathing like I had just run up a flight of stairs.

I gathered myself as quickly as I could.

"Uh, yeah. Me too," I said, voice hoarse and audibly awkward. I pulled open the freezer door to grab some ice. The cold air felt so good against my hot face. I let it roll over me for a few seconds before I filled up my cup.

Kael was waiting for me by the wall, sipping his new beer. My insides wouldn't settle. Gah, he made me feel so on edge one second, yet so calm the next.

We were both quiet as we walked into the living room. There seemed to be the same number of people in the house—minus the two assholes—but the crowd felt dense now that everyone was crammed into the living room. It didn't help that my heart was pounding in its cage, no matter how hard I tried to calm myself.

Austin was talking to the pizza delivery man. I watched as he handed over some cash, shoving a wad back into his pocket. As far as I knew, Austin had only been working a few hours a week at Kmart, which he supplemented by asking my dad for money here and there. My brother was never good with money. Even when he worked summer jobs, he'd spend his check the day he got it. I wasn't much better, so I wasn't judging, but where did that cash come from? It didn't make sense.

"Kare! Grab some plates?" Austin yelled to me, passing out pizza boxes to the group.

I didn't know what was going on, but my brain couldn't handle any more tonight. I just wanted to have fun, to not worry about things that I couldn't control. I had been trying that for years—maybe tonight would be the night that I actually followed through with it?

Chapter ✦ Thirty-Seven

BLACK JEANS WERE a girl's best friend. They stood out from the usual indigo. They made your legs look longer. And that dark wash was great when you were out on a date and needed to do something about greasy pizza fingers. Not that I was on a date. Was I on a date?

There was just this way that Kael was looking at me that made me wonder. The fact that he agreed to come to the party at all made me wonder. But as with everything with Kael, I couldn't be sure.

We were still sitting next to each other on the couch. Kael's empty plate rested on a napkin on his lap. The plate was clean and the napkin was spotless. My plate had a splinter of hard crust on it and a bit of stray pepperoni. My white paper napkin was splotched with pizza sauce. My black jeans didn't show my greasy handprints, though. Small mercies. I wasn't neat and tidy. Not like Kael. And certainly not like Estelle, the perfect housewife whose picture was hanging in a thick black frame above us. A black cloud was more like it. I couldn't see her face, but I could feel her bearing down on me. I knew that picture well—it had been taken on one of their many vacations. My dad was next to her wearing a big smile and a Florida tan. A beachfront American gothic.

Kael leaned up to grab a pizza box. "Can you hand me a napkin?" I asked.

Another guy might have made a crack about the red sauce massacre I had going on, but he didn't say anything, just grabbed some pizza and napkins, then leaned back into the couch cushion. I could feel the heat rising off him. My imagination was playing with that. My body, too.

"Want some?" he asked. He offered his plate, which had two thick slices, glistening with cheese.

I shook my head, thanking him.

"I see you have a new twin." Austin pointed to Kael and mostly everyone looked at him, then me. His shirt and jeans were practically identical to mine. I thought back to the photograph of my dad and Estelle, standing side-by-side in their matching Hawaiian shirts from Old Navy, and burned with embarrassment. Kael cracked a smile, though. A very small smile, but it was there, all right.

"Ha ha," I said, rolling my eyes. "You were gone a while, sooo—"

Laughter bounced around the room.

"Fair enough." Austin took a bite of pepperoni pizza. Cheese slid down the slice and he caught it with his tongue. He was so much like a teenage boy sometimes, as if he had stopped maturing after tenth grade. It was part of his draw, I guess—the innocence of him. He really did have a good soul and it was easy to see. He was the kind of boy who would start a fire and then save you from it.

I wondered if this new girl understood what she was in for, if she knew she was playing in the brush on a hot day.

A pretty brunette with a smattering of freckles across her cheeks, she had deep blue—almost navy—eyes. Her shirt set off her coloring, and the style of her loose peasant top resembled her hair—ruffled sleeves falling in waves down her arms, just like the ones curled into her long tresses. She was sitting on the floor by Austin's feet, looking up, a flower tilted to the sun. The attraction she had to him was clear as day. The way she almost willed him to turn his face to hers, to say something, anything, to her. The way her shoulders were angled toward him, pulled back to expose her long, graceful neck. She wasn't sitting cross-legged like the others on the floor. The awkward child's pose was not for her. She had folded one leg on top of the other, ankle to knee, and she was tilted sideways so that her legs formed an arrow pointing toward my brother. This girl was vulnerable and open. Calculating, too.

Body language could be so obvious.

Did Austin know that she was planning their first kiss, their first date?

The paper plate in his hand slipped a little and she lifted the corner for him. He looked at her, smiling, thanking her, and then she did this pouty thing with her lips, and a flippy thing with her hair. It was impressive as hell, even to me, and I wasn't the intended target. I looked away from my brother and the girl. I'd seen this movie before.

Chapter ✶ Thirty-Eight

"MENDOZA SEEMS NICE," I said to Kael.

"Yeah. He is." Kael looked at his friend, who was offering his special tequila to someone who had just come in. I thought I had seen the guy before. In the kitchen, maybe. I remembered his black-and-white checked T-shirt. From the way he reeked of cigarette smoke, it was clear that he had just been outside for a smoke break. At least this group of friends was respectful enough not to smoke inside the house, unlike some Austin had had in the past.

"He's married?" I asked.

Kael's forehead scrunched up a little and he nodded.

"Cool." I was about out of small talk. I could have talked about the weather or the Falcons, but that would have seemed desperate. I was buzzed from the drinks and getting paranoid about Kael's silence, and while I may have been anxious, I wasn't desperate. I wasn't going to be the needy girl at a party. A party at my dad's house, of all places.

Kael nodded and then … nothing. I should have been

used to the barriers he put up, the distance between us, but he had let down his guard a little since coming to the party, so much so that I was beginning to forget it had even existed. But there it was, brewing next to me.

And that was why I didn't like dating. Or whatever this was.

I knew I was being ridiculous. I mean, it had only been about twenty minutes since I'd decided to admit to myself that I was attracted to him. We had been standing side-by-side in the kitchen and I could feel that heat of his. It didn't matter that we weren't touching. I could feel myself being drawn toward him. It was strong, this pull. Almost animal in its intensity. I lost myself in the physical for a moment, and then my brain took over and started to dissect the reasons he wouldn't like me, or why this couldn't— wouldn't—work. I was such a romantic.

I looked around the room, to friendly Mendoza pouring Austin and the ruffly brunette a shot. To the three guys sitting on the floor, and the voices coming from the kitchen. Everyone was alive in their own way, talking, listening, drinking, laughing, playing with their phones. Everyone except the one person I really wanted to connect with.

My frustration grew and grew inside my head and by the time Austin and the girl were making out (which took less than five more minutes), I couldn't sit there anymore. I needed some air.

I got up from the couch and if Kael noticed, he didn't care to show it.

Chapter ☆ Thirty-Nine

I SAT DOWN on my mom's swing, feeling the heaviness of the situation with Kael. Not for the first time, I thought of it as a mood swing. My own little joke. Only it wasn't funny.

I'd lost track of the number of times I'd made my way out to the porch. If I was feeling anxious and alone, if I wanted to think something through or just daydream, I'd head to the swing. I was out there a lot after my mom left, sometimes I thought maybe she would be sitting there. And when Dad was talking about shipping Austin off to live with our porn king uncle, you'd find me on the swing. There was just something soothing about the gentle back and forth as the seat pushed into its arc and then returned. I could be close to full-on panic, but after a few minutes on the swing, my breathing would slow and I'd feel myself calm down. Most of the time, anyway.

When Brien and I were on the rocks, I'd planted myself out here, trying to get some perspective. But more than once, Estelle had followed me out to see how she could help.

She'd give me this look that I could tell she thought was sympathetic, but I just thought was creepy. It was like she was trying to sell me something. A used car, maybe. A used stepmother was more like it.

She'd say things like, "I was young once, too, you know." That was my cue to say, "Oh, but you're still young," and, "You're so pretty." But I wasn't going there. I wouldn't have given her what she wanted even if it had been true. Then she'd tell me that everything was going to be okay, that what I was going through was tough, but she understood how I was feeling. That bothered me the most. How could she possibly understand what I was feeling when she didn't know me and I didn't know myself?

And there I was again, sitting on my dad's porch, not really knowing what I was feeling. I wanted to get closer to Kael, but I felt stung by his silence. I wanted to ask him to join me on the swing, but I felt too timid. I wanted … whatever it was I wanted, I wasn't getting it, so I had sulked off like a little kid.

I was kicking my feet a bit and just starting to move the swing when the front door creaked open and Kael stepped out onto the porch. He leaned against the railing, watching me with glassy eyes. He looked older, somehow. I wasn't sure if I liked it.

The streetlight hummed as it cast a dim glow over my dad's yard. I could make out cars, trees, houses—but just the outlines. I wasn't sure if this was because it was getting dark or because I was getting buzzed. I didn't particularly care. It had been a while since I had had anything to drink other than a little wine and I felt this hazy glow. Actually, I felt pretty damn good.

Rocking gently back and forth, I was aware that my breathing was syncing to the rhythm of the swing, and that made it easier to pretend that I hadn't noticed Kael. No way was I going to be the first one to say something. I kept my mouth shut and my thoughts to myself. God, this guy was tough to figure out.

Maybe it was the way he was with me—observing, non-judgmental. That was rare. So often you could feel people sizing you up, trying to figure you out. *Who are you and what do you have that I want?* Not Kael. He just noticed. I liked that. But it didn't seem fair, somehow. He knew a lot about me and I hardly knew anything about him. The things I did know I could count on one hand. Almost reflexively, that's what I did.

One: He was charming in that strong, silent way.

Two: He had this almost magnetic draw that attracted people to him.

Three: He made you want to know what he thought of you. (Or was that just me?)

Four: He acted as if he had something really important to say.

Five: There was no five. That's how little I knew about him.

Everything about Kael seemed so complex, but uncomplicated at the same time. He hadn't said much to me while we were inside, other than to ask if I wanted a slice of pizza, but he had clearly followed me out. So why was he just standing there with that force field around him, shifting his weight from one foot to the other and looking at me as if words were a burden too heavy to carry? I started to say something to break the tension, but stopped myself just in time. No way was I going to make this easy on him. I'd give him a taste of his own medicine and see how he liked it.

*Chapter * Forty*

DUSK WAS GIVING WAY to night. The sky was darkening now, filling with the most gorgeous stars. I knew everyone thought they were magical, diamonds hung aloft in the sky and all that, but I found them sad. Stars seemed so fierce and bright, but by the time they got to us, they were dying, almost gone. And the biggest stars? They burned the fastest, as if their intense radiance was too much for them to hold onto. Damn. There I was getting sappy. I always thought of how fragile things were when I drank. I could move from beauty to despair in the blink of an eye. Or the twinkle of a star. As I said, *damn*.

"Can I sit with you?" Kael finally asked. Had he seen the shadow cross my face?

I nodded *yes* and moved over to make some room.

"This is *the* swing?" he asked.

I nodded again. I still had a dose or two of his own medicine to give him. Not really. I was just trying to stay cool. If I was going second-guess myself, I might as well be cool about it.

"She didn't take it with her?" he asked into the night air.

I jerked my head, looking at his face. "What?"

"When she…" He could see that he had struck a nerve, but he couldn't exactly backtrack.

I blinked. He was referring to my mom, of course. For all his reserved nature, he sure liked to ask questions that packed a punch.

"Left?" I finished for him. "No, she didn't take anything."

Not even us.

Not even me.

I didn't really feel like talking about my mom, but I was happy he asked—happy that he had remembered the swing. He was a good listener; I'd give him that. We sat with nothing but the stars between us for a while, which was fine by me. I just wanted to sit next to Kael, to know he was there. In that moment, it was enough.

The peace didn't last long, though.

"Oh, man, you wiped out!"

"No, hey, Austin—watch!"

"Dude! You are crazy. I mean what the fuck!"

It was just some lame video game, but it had put Kael on high alert. It was hard not to notice how hyperaware he was of his surroundings. I couldn't imagine how tough that must be, to never be able to relax. It must've been exhausting. He turned to say something, but was interrupted by wild shouts from inside the house.

"You got him, man. Killed him with one shot!"

"Fuck yeah! Dead as a fucking doornail, man!"

I shook my head. Kael clenched his jaw.

At least we agreed on something.

Chapter ☆ Forty-One

"I'M BEING WEIRD, aren't I?" Kael asked, picking at his fingers.

How the heck was I supposed to respond to that?

"Do *you* think you're being weird?" The best way to avoid answering a question was to repeat it. I had learned that from my dad.

He let out a breath. "Yeah, probably?" he said, cracking a smile. I loved the way his whole face changed when he smiled.

I couldn't help but laugh. "Well, I wouldn't say weird. But one minute you're ignoring me and the—"

"Ignoring you?" he asked, startled.

"Yeah," I explained. "You were kind of blowing me off."

He seemed genuinely surprised. Almost hurt. "I wasn't trying to." He hesitated. "It's kind of hard to adjust to being back here. It's been like a week and it's just so … different? It's hard to explain. I don't remember it feeling this weird last time I came back."

"I can't even imagine," I told him. Because I couldn't.

"It's the small things. Like those coffee makers with the little pods, or being able to shower every day and wash my clothes in an actual machine with those little pods."

"I'm guessing there aren't any tide pods in the army," I said. My dad always hated them, so even when he returned and could use them, he refused. He liked old school powder and it grossed me out.

"Sometimes. Wives would send packages to their husbands and we would all get the hook up," he said.

I wondered if anyone sent him packages, but didn't ask. Besides, it was my turn to laugh now, but I didn't. If I wanted to connect with this guy, to find out who he was, then maybe I should make the first step. Stop deflecting. Build a bridge. Find some common ground and all that. "You know," I started, "my dad always came back acting like he just got home from *Survivor*. It was kind of a joke in our house. Not that it was funny." I was so bad at this. I was overthinking every single word that came out of my mouth.

"It's fine." He smiled, obviously amused by my ramblings. He looked at me straight on. "Honestly, Karina. It's fine. You're fine."

I kept going, more relaxed now—reassured. "He would crave the weirdest things, and eat Taco Bell for a week straight after coming home."

Kael nodded slowly, sucking on his lips. "How many times has he gone?"

"Four."

"Wow." Kael blew out a breath. "I'm over here complaining about two," he said, laughing weakly.

"That's a lot, though. And you're my age. I'm over here complaining about zero."

"Did you ever think about joining?"

I shook my head so quickly.

"The army? Nope. No way. Austin and I always said we wouldn't."

I sounded like those creepy twins you read about in sappy books where they make weird promises to each other. One lives in the shadows and the other has to live out their twin's legacy. I didn't want to think about which role I played in that saga.

"Why not? Just not your thing?" Kael asked me.

"I don't know," I started. *Careful, Karina,* I warned myself. I didn't want to offend him, but my mouth was known for spitting out words without my brain's approval.

"We just agreed one day. I don't remember what even triggered it, but my dad was deep into his third deployment and ..."

I could picture the smoke as it billowed through the hallways. I smelled the fire before I saw it.

"And my mom made ... well, let's just say she made a mess in the living room. A charred mess."

Kael looked at me, puzzled.

"She said it was from a glue gun, like for crafts? But it was a cigarette. She fell asleep on the couch with a lit cigarette in her hand, and had barely woken up when I came rushing down the stairs to find the room filled with smoke. It was crazy," I told him.

A few people came out of the house. A few people went in. Party traffic. I stopped talking. The last guy to come out was wearing a plain white T-shirt with a red stain on the chest. I stopped my imagination from turning a pizza sauce stain into anything else. Kael kept his eyes on me the whole time. It was intense, the way he looked at me. The bottom of my tummy ached and eventually, I had to break eye contact with him. Pizza stain guy walked down the steps and got into his car. I recognized him from the kitchen. He was one of Austin's quiet friends. The quiet guys always left first.

"And then?" Kael encouraged.

"She was walking toward the door, just straight forward, headed for the door like she was going out to buy milk or some orange juice. She didn't yell for us. She didn't look for us. No ... nothing."

Kael cleared his throat. I gauged his expression to make sure he wasn't uncomfortable with the details.

"So ... you know those quizzes where they ask you what you would save if your house was on fire?"

"Not really," he said.

"I guess it's like a Facebook thing. They ask what possessions you would save if your house was burning down and your answer is supposed to reveal your personality. If you say you'd save your wedding album, that says one thing about you. But if your choice is to save your vinyl collection, that says something else."

Kael raised his eyebrows, as if he hadn't ever heard of anything so absurd.

"I know, right?" I continued with my story. "Anyway, it's so insane, but the smoke was growing and as I rushed up the stairs to get Austin, I remember thinking, *that quiz is the most ridiculous thing ever. Who would even think about possessions at a time like this* ... But then I was thinking about that stupid quiz so what does that say about me."

"I think it says that your mind was keeping you from panicking. I think it says that you have good instincts."

I let that sink in for a moment before continuing. "So, I ran up to Austin's room and shook him awake. We ran downstairs together—he was leading now, squeezing my wrist, so hard, and when we got outside to the lawn, our mother was standing there just watching the smoke. It wasn't like she had tried to set the house on fire, nothing like that. More like she didn't even realize what was going on."

"Karina ..."

"It was like one of those old movies, you know, where the madwoman starts the fire and just gets mesmerized by it, like she just goes into a trance—" I laughed a little, not wanting to be awkward. "Sorry, all of my stories are over the top."

"Karina ..." God, I loved the way he said my name.

"Oh, it's—" I was going to say, *it's okay.* That's what I always said when I told this story. Not that I told it often. But the thing was, sitting in the dark with Kael beside me, urging me on, listening, not judging ... Well, I knew that it wasn't okay. It wasn't okay at all. I could have been killed. Austin could have been killed. It was so not okay. But what was not okay was usually my reality.

Chapter ☆ Forty-Two

"YOU'RE A GOOD STORYTELLER."

That was a kind thing to say. Not, *God, your mom sounds like a wack job.* I was a good storyteller. I liked the sound of that. I liked the certainty with which he said it.

"So yeah, I don't know what I was even talking about..." I did that a lot, told long tales with lots of sidetracking and other mini-stories in between.

"You not wanting to join the military," Kael reminded me.

"Oh yeah." I pulled myself together. "I mean, it was basically my dad being gone so long and coming home and then having to train so much still. He was always gone and he was always so unhappy. My mom, too. The lifestyle basically broke her, you know?"

He nodded.

"So, my brother and I promised after that fire that we wouldn't live our whole lives this way."

"Makes sense," Kael said, looking around the yard,

then back to me. "Wanna hear my side?"

I shook my head, teasing. He smiled.

"I get that. For real, I do. But to me, a black kid from Riverdale, joining the army changed the trajectory of my life. It was the thing that changed my whole family. My great-grandpa's dad was a slave, and here I am, you know? The only job I'd ever had was bagging groceries at Kroger and now I drive a decent car, can help my mom—" He stopped abruptly.

"Don't stop-" I urged him.

That earned me a big smile. "All the shit like that. It's hard, yeah. Really fucking hard sometimes, but it's the only way I was ever going to be able to afford to go to college. Live on my own without an education."

I sat, digesting. He had extremely valid points. It was kind of crazy how his experience with the army was so opposite of mine.

"I get it." I told him.

"There's two sides to everything, you know?"

I nodded, whispering, "Yeah. Two sides at least." I tilted my head and asked, "Is your mom proud of you now?"

"Oh, of course. She tells everyone at church and anyone who'll listen that her son is a soldier. From my town, it's kind of a big deal." He was shy, now. It was beyond adorable.

"Local celebrity," I teased, leaning into his shoulder.

"Right," he said, smiling. "Not like Austin," he joked as my brother yelled again.

"Ugh, we should go in. I have to remind him that the MPs could come at any time and as far as I know, no one in there is of age except Mendoza," I took my phone out of my pocket and checked the time. It was almost eleven thirty. "Not for another thirty minutes," I teased.

Chapter ✦ Forty-Three

THE PARTY HAD quieted down. The coffee table was littered with beer bottles and plastic cups; the game controller sat idle in front of the TV. Limp bodies covered the couch and a few people had made themselves comfortable on the floor. It was mostly guys (and mostly army, I figured), except for the girl who earlier had been entwined with Austin. She was sitting alone on the floor now, moving slightly to the music, her shoulders doing this chill dance. Basically, she was doing that thing you do when you're all alone at a party and you want to say *it's fine, I'm fine, everything's fine.*

"Do you need another drink?" I asked Kael.

He held up his beer, shaking the empty bottle. "Yeah, please."

We made our way out of the living room, stepping carefully over denim-clad body parts. The kitchen was empty. Estelle's attempts at what she called French Country décor— a dish towel that said *CAFÉ*; a ceramic rooster; a little metal *Boulangerie* sign that Elodie says Estelle pronounces wrong—

were visible among the litter of empty bottles and pizza boxes. Still, seeing Kael here against the backdrop of so many familiar things, feeling him next to me radiating that damn heat ... the kitchen just felt so small. He seemed outsized now, larger than life, and when I scooted past him, I almost elbowed him in the rib cage. He inched further away from me, towards the fridge. Of course I needed to get ice from the tray in the freezer.

"Sorry," he said, nearly tripping over my feet to get out of my way.

"Isss fine," I told him, my words blending together.

He made me feel so ... *nervous*. Maybe that wasn't the right word. I didn't feel tense or panicky, the things that usually come with nerves. It was just that he made me feel as if everything was so much closer to the surface, raw and more alive. When I was around him, my brain processed everything so fast, but everything felt so still, so calm in the cracks of him opening up to me. I felt bright and quick and stable and level all at once.

My heart raced when I glanced over and caught him looking back at me, his long fingers toying with the necklace around his neck. Maybe it was the effect of the vodka, but as I refilled my glass, I could feel Kael's eyes on me, as if he was taking me in, head to toe. He wasn't appraising me in that skeevy way some guys had when they were so obviously checking you out. It wasn't like that at all. When Kael looked at me, it was as if he saw me, *the real me*—who I was, not who I was trying to be. He held my gaze for a moment, then lowered his eyes. My chest fluttered. Forget butterflies, these were blackbirds. Big, glossy blackbirds flapping their wings, making my heart take flight. I took a deep breath to calm myself down. I felt him looking at me and tried to ignore the pang at the bottom of my stomach. I put the bottle back on

the counter and mixed in apple juice. Someone had cleared
out the cranberry.

"What's that going to taste like?" He was standing
right behind me now. Whether he had moved or I had, I
couldn't say. I saw his shadow in the metal sink and hoped
like hell that he couldn't hear the wild beating in my chest.

I turned slowly to face him. He was so close.

"Either great or not." I shrugged.

He took a half-step back. My body didn't calm.

"And you're willing to take that risk?" he asked,
smiling behind his drink. I wanted to tell him that he didn't
need to hide it—his smile, that was. That I really liked it when
he was funny, when he teased me. But I needed a few more
shots to be at that level of bold.

"Yeah. I guess so." I put my nose to the glass and took
a sniff. It wasn't so bad. I took a sip. It wasn't horrible. But
maybe I should microwave it to pretend it was a cider?

"Good?," he asked.

"Yeah," I said. I lifted the cup between us. "Wanna
taste?"

"No, thanks." He shook his head, holding up his beer.

"Do you always drink beer?" I asked him.

"Yeah, mostly. Not in a while, though," he said,
smiling and trying not to. "Because of being gone. Of being
over there," he clarified.

"Ohhh, because you were gone." It took me a second
to catch on regardless of how many times we had repeated the
word "gone".

"Right. Yes. Gone. Over there." I was an idiot,
echoing everything he said. "Wow. Yeah, adjusting must be
so weird."

Every time he reminded me that his life was so
drastically different than mine, I felt shaken. I noticed his

glassy eyes again ... his beautiful brown eyes. Maybe he was just as buzzed as I was. I leaned towards Kael to ask if he was drunk, to ask him if he was okay. That's when Austin barreled in with Mendoza right behind him. Way to kill the moment. "Hey guys! It's awfully quiet in here," he said, clapping his hands together as if he were trying to frighten a small animal.

Kael and I stepped back from each other, as if by instinct.

"My man. You leaving?" Austin asked. When Mendoza nodded, Austin continued, "Thanks for coming. I know it's hard to get out."

"Yeah." Mendoza turned to Austin, then Kael. I felt like something significant was going on in front of me, but I wasn't really able to decipher it.

"Next time bring Gloria," Austin said, reaching for the tequila bottle. And then, "One more before you go?"

Mendoza looked at the thick, white watch strapped to his wrist and shook his head.

"No way, man. I have to go home. Babies get hungry and Gloria's tired. The kid is keeping her up all night."

"I didn't mean you." Austin touched Mendoza's car keys on his belt loop. "But for me?"

Mendoza poured a hefty amount of tequila into Austin's glass. It wasn't my responsibility to worry about my brother. This was his party and I wasn't going to be the house mother. Not tonight.

"It was nice to meet you," I told Mendoza when he said bye to me.

"Take care of my boy," he whispered. Then he hugged Kael and went out the side door, leaving me to wonder what on earth he meant.

Chapter ✦ Forty-Four

"MAN, I LOVE THAT GUY. He's a Grade A fucking guy."

Austin was over-the-top cheerful, even for him. It made me a little nervous. It wasn't that I was worried about him getting into trouble. Not really. It was just hard to see him standing there swaying like that.

"My sister! My beautiful twin." Austin wrapped his arm around me. His movements were fluid and his pale cheeks were red. He was clearly smashed.

"Isn't she beautiful?" he asked Kael. I froze. I hated when Austin talked about my looks.

Kael nodded *yes,* clearly uncomfortable.

"You've really grown up. Buying your own house and shit," he said, squeezing me. "I mean there you are, holding down a steady job and shit. Paying bills—"

"And shit?" I finished for him.

"Essactly," he said.

Something on the bridge of his nose caught my eye. I moved toward him. "Did you actually break your nose?"

I asked, lifting my hand to his face. He jerked away, laughing me off.

"It didn't break. It just, um … it just moved over a little." Then he turned to Kael with a goofy smile plastered on his face. "Be careful with her, bro. I'm not going to be that guy who's like threatening dudes over his sister or anything like that. Nothing like that. I'm just saying, my sister, well … she flips on you and man …" He used his fingers like a knife under his throat.

Kael cast his eyes downward, giving no indication of what he thought about what he'd just heard.

"I'm kidding. She's a peach." He hugged me again. "A real peachy, peach of a sister. Aren't you?"

Oh yeah, totally smashed.

The kitchen was getting busy now with people coming in to refill their drinks, as if shift change had been announced or something. It wasn't until Kael looked at me that I felt like a kid. I probably seemed so immature, borderline wrestling with my brother who was completely out of it. And shit.

"Right. Thanks for the news bulletin," I said, maneuvering out of his arm. "Your new little friend is waiting for you. She looked lonely." I nodded my head toward the living room.

"Did she? She's cute, huh? She's going to school to be a nurse," he told us with pride.

Kael made a face like he was impressed, but I wasn't as drunk as Austin, and I could tell that Kael was humoring him. He mostly hid his mouth behind the dark beer bottle.

"You mean the little girl wants to be a nurse when she gets to be all grown up? After she's out of high school and into the big world?" It was how I was with Austin—teasing him about stuff. It was just part of our twin dynamic. We didn't have that mythical thing where we could read each other's minds or feel each other's pain. Nothing weird like that. Okay, I understood him on a level that I didn't feel with most people. And I felt a closeness to him that I couldn't explain. But a lot of siblings felt that, especially when they'd gone through their parents' divorce and all the mess that came with it. But it had nothing to do with being twins.

So, really, my comment had nothing to do with the girl at all. It was just what we did. Like the comment he made to Kael. (The comment that I swore to myself I wouldn't obsess over until later, when I was alone.)

"She's nineteen, okay? And she's going to actual *nursing school.*" Austin lifted his plastic cup to his mouth, pouring out the last drops of whatever concoction he had been downing the whole night.

"I'm sure she is." I rolled my eyes at Austin. "And the next Barbie will be—"

It took me a moment to register that everyone was looking over my shoulder to something behind me. *MPs*, I thought for a split second. *Damn. We're busted.* I turned around to face the officers, to give them some sort of excuse or attempt some type of negotiation. Only, when I turned around, I saw that it wasn't the MPs at all. It was the girl in the ruffly shirt and she had heard every word I'd said.

Damn. *I was the one who was busted.*

Chapter * Forty-Five

THE GIRL'S FACE FELL. My face fell. We stood there in silence. Caught. Two deer in the headlights.

I had just insulted her, insinuating that not only was she in high school, but that tomorrow night, my brother would be making out with someone else. Which not only made my brother seem like a total douchebag, it was rude as all hell to her.

Her eyes welled up with tears.

"Sorry …" I said. "I'm so sorry … It wasn't anything against you, I just meant—" She looked so young when she pouted like that, her bottom lip quivering. Damn. I didn't want to give her a half-assed apology, or make something up just to make her feel better. But I couldn't tell her that she really did look like she was in high school and I sure as hell couldn't tell her that in all likelihood, my brother really would be making out with someone else—if not tomorrow, then the day after.

I stood in the doorway for a second, not facing the

group, debating apologizing to her again—and thinking of how to smooth things over with Austin, too, even though he wasn't likely to be that annoyed with me. He knew my sense of humor better than anyone. And he gave as good as he got.

But Austin spoke first. "Nice, Kare," he said. "Real nice." He moved toward the girl and put a comforting arm around her. "This here is my sister, Karina," he said, squeezing her shoulder. "Karina, this is—"

She cut him off. "You can call me Barbie," she said through her breaking voice.

The room erupted with laughter. Big, bold, side-splitting laughter. Score one for Barbie. And who could blame her? Certainly not me. I let myself exhale.

Everything would have been okay if we'd stopped there. Awkward moment confronted and dealt with. Move on, folks, nothing to see here. Only Austin had to open his big mouth. "Don't worry about her," he said, throwing his chin in my direction. "She's pissed. She's always pissed," he corrected. The word sounded slippery. Mean. I opened my mouth to say something, but apparently, he wasn't finished yet. "She likes to play the big sister. The only grown-up in the room. Just ignore her."

I felt slapped. Hard. I knew I had hurt the girl's feelings and I really did feel bad about that. But I hadn't done it on purpose. It was a lame joke between a brother and sister and it was just rotten luck and bad timing that it went awry. But what Austin said about me hurt. It really hurt.

I wanted to say something in my defense—anything—but I didn't want to make a scene. If I got upset in front of everyone, it would prove Austin's point and make everyone think I was crazy or that I was *always pissed*. I left the room with a growing ache in my chest. Now it was my turn to cry.

Chapter * Forty-Six

SHIT, AUSTIN. Since when did you think of me as always pissed? Worrying about you wasn't being pissed. Someone had to do it and obviously, you weren't too concerned with your future since you just got out of jail and the first thing you did was throw a party with plenty of booze and underage drinkers. On post. At Dad's house.

Those were the thoughts swirling around in my head as I walked up the stairs to my old room. The air inside the house was thick and getting thicker. I had to get away. I needed a break from Austin. From the vodka. From the party. I wasn't sure if I needed a break from Kael and for a moment, I almost forgot he was even there.

For a moment.

Almost.

There was no way he missed the exchange. He probably thought I was being catty, that I was a bitch. It wasn't true. It really wasn't. I tried not to give other girls a hard time. We had it tough enough. Hormones. Periods.

Underwire bras. Double standards. Douchey guys. We needed to stick together, not stick it to each other. I really believed that. But...there was always a *but*, wasn't there? I just couldn't help that immediate assessment I did of other females. Giving them the once-over, trying to determine who they were, where they figured in our invisible hierarchy. It seemed so mean to put it like that, but it wasn't that I was comparing them to *me*—more like I was comparing myself to *them*.

Ruffly shirt girl was prettier than me. She had beautiful clear skin, slender hips, and long legs. Her hair was amazing. She dressed to flatter herself, to bring out her best features. I dressed in what was clean(ish) or what was on sale. I wasn't competing with Katie, Barbie, or whatever her name was. (Okay, that was bitchy.) I really wasn't. First of all, she was in a totally different league than I was, and second, her target was my brother. That was clear from the get-go. So this comparison thing, this competition ... it wasn't about guys.

If it was, why would I compare myself to the girls on IG or on TV, like I did when Madelaine Petsch looked out at me from the screen? She was flawless. Even with my ultra-high-def TV, she had the smooth skin of a porcelain doll. Not a blemish, not a spot or bump. It almost made me want to go vegan, if that's what it did for you.

I thought about this sort of thing a lot. I tried to figure out where it came from. Where all my insecurities came from. I really didn't care that boys looked at other girls more than they looked at me. It was just that some girls made me feel *less than*. I couldn't explain it, not really, but it was hard to get out of my head. And the thing was, I knew it wasn't just me. I thought about Elodie, beautiful blonde Parisian Elodie with her pretty cheeks and doe eyes. She'd sit with a mirror in her lap, picking at her face, saying how horrible her skin was, that her eyes were uneven and her nose was off-center. Did all women do that?

This was when I missed my mom the most. It would have been nice to be able to talk to her about this sort of thing, to have someone to confide in, to have her listen without judgment. *Has it always been like this*, I'd ask her? And she'd tell me, *No, it was never this bad, social media and selfies and the Kardashians have made everything so much worse.* Or she'd say, *Yes, it really has always been like this. I used to compare myself to Charlie's Angels back in the day.* Then she'd get out her old photo album and we'd laugh at her eighties hair.

Who was I kidding?

That would never have happened.

Chapter ✫ Forty-Seven

MY BEDROOM DOOR WAS CLOSED. Was someone inside? It wouldn't have been unheard of to find a soldier passed out on my bed, or a couple hooking up. Not Austin and Katie, though. They were still in the kitchen, probably talking about me. Katie would be over her hurt by now and, smart girl that she was, she would have turned the situation around to her advantage, used it to get closer to my brother. United against a common enemy and all that. And Austin would have known that he was onto a sure thing, so he'd likely be going on about how annoying I was, how I'd always been so uncool. He had two sides to him, one that fiercely defended me, no matter what. And one that used me as a prop, a pedestal that elevated him to cool guy status. I didn't need three guesses to know which one was down in the kitchen.

No matter how hard I tried, I couldn't rid myself of the habit of imagining what other people were thinking or saying about me. I did it all the time, even though I knew no good would come of it. It was like picking a cuticle, scratching and nipping at it until it started bleeding. I was doing that now, picturing everyone in the kitchen, wondering what they were saying or thinking. Even the ones who didn't know my name, they'd just think of me as that prissy chick who badmouthed sweet Katie. Someone would ask who I was and they'd say, oh, that's Austin's sister, and then they'd remember me as the girl who went around picking up empty bottles and pizza boxes as if she was working the night shift at Friday's.

Ugh.

I hated the way my brain worked. I tried to tell myself that I didn't do anything too horrible, that people would understand I was mostly joking. I never would have talked like that had I known she was there, even if what I said was true.

I was grasping now.

Wasn't it funny how people always demanded the truth, yet mostly couldn't handle it when it came along? In all fairness, I was the same way. Demanding the truth, yet holding onto the lies. They came in handy when you wanted to guard yourself against the truth—lies, that is.

I paused in front of my room. I didn't really think anyone would be inside; this get-together was way calmer than most of the parties Austin had thrown in the past, before he went to stay with our uncle. And I had to admit that Austin seemed a little different now, more stable. Or maybe I just wanted him to have calmed down and thinking this way protected me from seeing the truth.

I knocked, then waited a moment before opening the door into what turned out to be an empty room.

I stood for a moment before entering, just taking everything in. Even the smell. God, the air was like nostalgia, like the scent of my former life. I had been trying so hard to start a new chapter, turn a new page ... whatever it was people did when they tried to move on and stand on their own two feet. I stood there looking at my old bedroom while thinking of my new bedroom. Such a stark difference.

It was the same as it ever was. The same purple bedspread with little white flowers all over it. The same matching curtains with a burn mark on the corner from my one day as a smoker. I got grounded for that. My parents didn't notice the burnt curtain, lucky for me, but they had caught the cigarette smoke as it wafted down the hallway. After that I was forbidden to hang out with Neena Hobbs, the only girl in my grade who was allowed to shave her legs—and who had made me want to smoke like she did.

My dresser was cluttered with the usual teenage girl stuff. Old tubes of glittery lip gloss that had been expired for years. Bundles of headbands and hair elastics. Notes from my best friend, Sammy. Gel pens in every conceivable color. Everything had a memory attached. Some, more than one. I couldn't bring myself to toss a thing. Not the headbands I had worn for years through multiple hair colors and multiple bad haircuts. Not even the sticky lip gloss that my mom snuck me when my dad said I couldn't wear makeup until high school. I picked them up now and rolled them around in my hand. They had names like BERRY BEAUTIFUL, PUCKER PINK, and SWEETER THAN SWEET. Funny though, once you got them on your lips, they all had pretty much the same rosy color, the same sugary and sticky shine that always caught ahold of my hair.

It wasn't that long ago I had moved into my new place, but this room already seemed like a time capsule. I hadn't slept there since the day I moved out. Come to think of it, I hadn't even been in there. Sometimes it felt like I had moved out years ago—other times it felt like days. I wiped my finger in the dust on my dresser. Estelle made sure every room in the house was clean, except this one. What about Austin's room, I wondered. Did she do her Martha Stewart thing in there? Probably. She had different rules for males and females. I realized that I hadn't changed any of the furniture since seventh grade or so. I remembered sitting in that purple beanbag chair when Josh, the guy who thought it was a good idea to give me cornbread for a birthday gift, broke up with me. His mom had told him that he needed to work on his grades, so if he wanted to pursue his supposed football career, he needed to keep his head clear and away from girls. I was fool enough to believe him. But he started dating one of the popular girls the very next day. Word around school was that he had dumped me for her. Seventh grade on really did a great job at progressing my insecurities.

That beanbag chair was the indoor equivalent of the porch swing, full of drama and dreamy memories. I bet there were a lot of teenage tears in that purple fabric.

My nightstand was stacked high with books. My econ textbook from my senior year of high school and the hardcover of *You* by Caroline Kepnes were collecting dust. I had bought another copy of *You* when I realized I'd left my copy at my dad's and didn't want to go back for a few days. Dad and Estelle hadn't been married very long then, and I hated being around the newlyweds—I left every chance I got. That made two copies, three if you counted the audio. I bought that to hear the characters come to life in a voice other than my own. It was one of my favorite books and I always wanted to keep a copy at both houses. It was one of the few stories that my dad and I both loved. I reached for it and cracked open the spine. I could use the distraction.

YOU walk into the bookstore
and you keep your hand on

the door to make sure it
doesn't slam. You smile,
embarrassed to be a nice girl,
and your nails are bare and
your V-neck sweater is beige
and it's impossible to know if
you're wearing a bra but I
don't think that—

When I heard the knock on the door, I nearly jumped out of
my skin.

"Shit!"

"Karina?"

"WHAT?!" I sounded angry, like you do when you're
scared.

"Karina, are you all right?" It was Kael. "Can I come
in?"

"Come in," I said. I nodded too, though he likely
couldn't see me through the crack in the door. He entered
slowly and, once inside, gently closed the door. The little click
sounded so loud. So definite.

"You okay?" he asked as he walked toward me,
stopping a few feet away from the bed.

I sighed. "Yeah," I said, shrugging, closing my book.

"So do you always read at parties?"

When he said that, it reminded me of a book I'd read
last year. I had a love-hate relationship with those books, but
was currently waiting for the next one in the series. So, I was
in love at the moment.

"I just ... I don't know. I got overwhelmed? That
girl—" I raised my hand in the air, holding the book. "She
heard me say that stuff and now Austin's being a dick and she
probably feels like shit."

Kael nodded his head just a little. "You didn't know she was going to walk up."

"Still."

"Try not to worry about it. I know you're going to beat yourself up over it, that's just who you are—"

"You know *what*?!"

Now he was the one who looked caught. It was clear that he hadn't meant to say what he had. Or maybe he'd meant to word it differently. His mouth hung open a little.

"What do you mean *that's just who I am?*" I accused. He better not have meant what I thought he did.

He took a breath. "I just meant that I know you worry about a lot, and you put a lot of pressure on yourself. A lot of blame."

I wanted to stand up, to tell him to get the hell out of my room, but I sat there, holding tight to my book, keeping my legs crossed underneath me.

"And you know that how?" I asked, not really wanting to know what he was going to say. I had already become this girl to him, the one he needed to check in on, maybe take care of. I despised the idea of that.

No way was that going to be me.

No way was that me.

"Come on," he pressed me. He no longer looked unsure about what he had said or would say; he looked annoyed.

"You're acting like you know me. You've been around for what—a week? And half of that time you were MIA."

"So it did bother you when I didn't come back?" he asked.

Why was he talking so much all of the sudden? And how could I get him to stop?

"That doesn't matter. My point is that you don't

know me, so don't say that I'm doing something or being a victim or whatever." My voice sounded screechy and dramatic.

"That's not what I'm doing." He sighed, rubbing his cheeks with both palms. "And I sure as hell didn't say anything about you being a victim."

"You said, 'You put a lot of pressure on yourself.'"

"Never mind," he said, defeated. "Forget I said anything."

I felt so angry, so embarrassed and upset. I didn't know I was directing all my feelings toward Kael. He came up to my room, I assumed, to check on me at the very least. That was a nice thing to do.

"I'm sorry," I said. "I'm just frustrated and I'm taking it out on you. I guess this fits since I'm"—I hooked my fingers into air quotes—"always pissed."

"I don't think you should be too hard on yourself. People do shitty things. It's what we're made for," he told me.

He was trying to change the subject and I was grateful because I felt like crap. Any sort of buzz that I was feeling was basically gone at that point, but Kael still looked different than he had before tonight, even without my vodka glasses.

"Humans are made to do shitty things? That's depressing," I told him. But I kind of liked the way it sounded, cynical as it was.

He sat down next to me on my bed and the metal frame creaked. He was too big for my bed. He looked like a grown man in a dollhouse. I felt like he was going to lecture me about something, maybe ask if I did my homework. His knowing eyes were focused on me, and in a rare occurrence, he didn't look away or stare at the floor.

"That's life," he said. His eyes were still on me.

"Life is depressing?"

"Every life I've come across," he replied.

I couldn't disagree with him, though it made everything feel so heavy.

"Yeah. I guess you're right." I was the first to look away.

"You're the one who told me that when the stars burn out, the good in the world dies." He chuckled softly. "That's the most depressing thing I've heard and I've seen and heard a lotttt." He drew out the end of the word.

I laughed at that and looked into his eyes. He was a good head taller than me sitting down, and his black jeans and dark skin looked so nice against each another.

Kael's hands moved to his leg and my tummy flipped, thinking that they'd move to me next, that he was going to touch me. But instead, he rubbed at the top of his leg.

"What's wrong with your leg?" I asked him.

For all the voices downstairs, I couldn't hear anything except the slowing of Kael's breathing and the sound of the air conditioner vent blowing from the ceiling.

"It's ..." he started to say. I watched the words hesitate on their way out. "It hurts sometimes. It's not a big deal."

"Can I ask about it?" I asked while asking.

I remembered his first massage and how he kept his pants on the entire time, the way I thought I saw him limping, but couldn't be sure.

"You don't have to tell me. I could just ... maybe I could help, you know?" I told him.

He closed his eyes and didn't say anything as the seconds passed.

"You don't—" I started to tell him I was sorry for asking in the first place, but he leaned down and grabbed the bottom of his jeans and started to roll up the fabric.

It was such an intense moment, the air so still between us.

And then the silence was broken by the ringing of a cell phone. Kael's cell phone. I jumped from the suddenness of it. Kael let go of his pants and stood up, pulling the phone from his pocket. His face changed as he stared at the screen, silencing the ringer. My heart was racing, beating inside of me.

"Everything okay?" I said.

His handsome face was distorted into a scowl as he looked at the number. He ignored the call. I thought a text popped up, but I couldn't be sure. "Yeah," he said.

I didn't believe him.

He shoved the phone into his pocket and looked at me. My eyes went immediately to his right leg and he stepped back. Then he scanned the room like he was looking for something he couldn't see.

"I ... I, uhm. I have to go," he stammered.

He moved so quickly, just like a soldier, and he opened my door before I could stop him. His name was stuck in my throat as he turned around to look at me, as if to say something. Our eyes locked for half a second before he seemed to change his mind and turned away from me. I didn't know what to think about what had just happened. We had been so close. I had opened up to him and he was opening up to me ... and then he was gone.

I was so overwhelmed with everything that I didn't even understand why I burst into tears the moment he disappeared from view.

Chapter ☆ Forty-Eight

I WOKE UP with a headache like I'd never had before. My mouth was the inside of a hamster's cage and my hands felt too big for my body. Even my hair hurt. I rolled over and buried my face in my pillow so that I wouldn't have to open my eyes. I rummaged through the bedding to find my phone—when had I climbed into bed and under the covers?—and I felt the cool glass screen against my fingertips. Slowly, I turned over. Even more slowly, I opened my eyes.

Two missed calls and a "where r u?" text from Austin.

But of course, the person I was thinking of was Kael.

Great.

It was bad enough that he was the last person I thought of before I fell asleep. Did he have to be the first person I thought of when I woke up? I could picture him sitting there on the bed next to me. I could almost feel the impression his body made on the bed. And I could see his face as he walked out the door, leaving me behind.

I had to do something about this situation.

I had to keep away from this guy.

Where did he get off thinking that I would be there for him whenever he felt like showing up? Who did he think he was with this on-again, off-again bullshit? This guy was playing me with his *So it did bother you when I didn't come back?* line. Of course it bothered me, Kael. Just like you knew it would.

Last night he had opened up, let down his guard, and let me inside. He talked. He listened. He laughed. And the way he started to roll up his jeans ... We were getting so close, and then he turned back into the stranger Elodie's husband happened to know.

I never wanted to see him again.

I needed to see him.

I didn't want to know where he went last night.

I needed to know.

I should never have let him stay over that night Elodie brought him home. I should never have brought him to my dad's for dinner. And I sure as hell should never have brought him to this party.

I didn't like all this anger and regret. How dare he make me feel this way.

Lesson learned. Remind yourself about that, Karina, as you go about your day.

Shit! My day!

I had to work. I did a quick phone check for the time. It was nine and I had to be at work at ten. It didn't matter that I felt like hell. No way could I get my shift covered on such short notice. Anyway, I needed the hours to pay that last cable bill, so I'd just have to suck it up. I was used to that. At least I didn't have anyone scheduled until after lunch. I'd be the one taking walk-ins. That wouldn't be so bad, though, because most new clients didn't talk much at all during their first treatment. That was something, at least.

Rolling out of bed was the hard part. The first hard part, that was. After I did that—and it was more belly flop than roll—I shimmied into my pants, then my T-shirt. I pulled one of my vintage hair elastics off my dresser and stuck my hair in a ponytail, replaying the events of last night over and over in my head.

I didn't want to admit it, but I was starting to feel that addictive pull. Addicted. There was no other word for it. His beautiful face. His strong body. His confident voice. I loved the way he didn't bother with small talk, as if he knew instinctively what was important. I could tell that the other guys looked up to him. But what else was going on. What was it that made him go from being just another guy at a party with a beer to a soldier, hyper-vigilant and on guard. What had Mendoza been trying to tell me about *his boy?*

Kael's voice in my head was drowned out by the sound of my brother's snores as I passed his room. I was glad he was asleep. I didn't want to talk to him. Or anyone else for that matter. Just a quick pee and I'd—

"Oh crap! Oh … I'm so sorry. I had no idea anyone was in here." I edged my way out of the bathroom, trying to avert my eyes. Did that just happen?

I backed out into the hallway, not knowing if I should leave or if I should wait until she came out. I was trying to figure out what the etiquette was in a situation like that when the bathroom door opened and Katie appeared.

"You sure know how to make an entrance, don't you?" She had a toothbrush in her hand and her hair was brushed neatly to rest just above her shoulders.

"Hey, um, hi." As if this wasn't awkward as hell. "Hey, I'm sorry."

"This is getting to be a habit with us. Me surprising

you. You apologizing to me." She laughed, then. I guess it was kind of funny. "Look, it's okay," she said. "Really. No harm done. I was caught off guard last night. By what you said, I mean."

"Yeah, about that ..."

"No, it's okay. Really. Well, the stuff about me still being in high school wasn't cool at all, but that other stuff, about your brother, you didn't tell me anything I didn't already know."

"Wait. You mean ...?"

"I'm not an idiot, Karina. I've heard a lot about your brother. But, just like you, I don't listen to everything I hear." The look on her face was a knowing one. Her blue eyes honed in on me. She certainly didn't seem like a high school girl now.

I didn't know if it was the hangover or the shock of walking in on her like that, but, what the fuck?

"And that means?"

"Maybe another time, okay? It was a late night." She paused to make an exaggerated stretch, causing the oversized tee shirt she was wearing to ride up high enough to show me that Nurse Katie was overdue for a bikini wax. "I'm tired and I really want to get back to bed. Besides," she added, "it's chilly in here."

And with that she turned on her heels and went back to join my brother.

Chapter * Forty-Nine

ELODIE WASN'T THERE when I got home. I couldn't remember if she had to work or not—I barely remembered that *I* had to work—and I didn't pay attention to whether or not her car was in the driveway.

I took a quick shower, but I still felt like death when I got out. Brien used to keep a hangover kit in his dorm. Extra-strength Tylenol for a headache. Benadryl for puffiness. Pedialyte to replace essential minerals. And Alka-Seltzer to soothe the stomach. He was like a depraved Boy Scout, always prepared. What I wouldn't give for a couple of Tylenol now. Leave the ex-boyfriend, take the meds. That sounded like a good plan. I searched the entire house, but came up empty-handed. I even fumbled through the drawer with the packets of soy sauce and chopsticks, just in case I'd find one of those little individual packets of Tylenol or Advil in there. I wouldn't even have cared if it was expired. No pills of any kind, but I did find an old fortune cookie which I cracked open.

> *You don't need strength to let go.*
> *All you need is understanding.*

Actually, fortune cookie company, I really need some aspirin.

I made a cup of coffee and sat at my kitchen table, staring into space. My mom, my dad, Austin, Kael—every stressor in my life seemed to be weighing on me, hard. Tapping me on the shoulder, pulling the muscles in my back. I wanted to bang my head against the wall, to cry or scream and shout. But I had to leave for work and, as everyone kept reminding me, I was the responsible one.

Just do the next thing, I told myself. Put one foot in front of the other and do what needs doing. That's how you'll get through the day.

With that little pep talk in mind, I made my way out of the house, through the alley to the parlor. The doors were unlocked when I got there, the OPEN sign bright in the window. Mali was behind the desk, checking in a middle-aged man and woman for a couple's massage. I was glad I came in as they were being escorted to the room so that I didn't have to take them. She looked really excited about it. He looked annoyed, as if his wife had dragged him there to work on their relationship or something. You could always tell. That's why couple's massages were my least favorite thing. I'd rather rub a client's thick, callused heels, and I really hated doing that.

"Good morning sweetie," Mali said when she returned. "Or not so much?" she asked, her eyes searching my face. She could see always see right through me.

"Hangover," I offered. I thought it was best to

admit at least half of my problem.

She took in my wet hair, puffy face, and bleary eyes. "Hmm," was all she managed.

It would be a long day if Mali, of all people, was getting on my nerves.

"Is Elodie here?" I asked. I couldn't see the calendar from where we were standing.

"Yes, and on time," Mali told me, nodding her head in approval and maybe making a little dig at me, but for what I couldn't tell. My first client was at one.

"She's not late that—"

"Your client is here," Mali said, looking toward the door.

"I don't have a client until—"

"Not true," she said. "Here. Look at the schedule." She pointed to the name scribbled on the little blue line that said ten o'clock.

"Did someone move their appointment? I can't read this," I said to Mali.

The bell dinged behind me and Mali turned to address the customer in her sweetest voice.

"Mikael? For an hour deep tissue at ten? That you?"

I nearly choked on the air when I turned around and saw Kael.

Sure enough, there he was wearing a gray T-shirt and joggers. They were black, tight on his legs, with a big Nike swoosh on the thigh. He looked exhausted, or hungover. Like I was.

"Kael," I said, like I had to tell myself that he was actually standing there.

"Hey," he replied.

Hey?

Was he here to talk to me? Or to get a massage?

Both?

It was all too much.

He waited patiently while I collected myself and checked his name off of the schedule. I stared at Mali until she walked away—reluctantly—a smirk imprinted on her face. I looked at Kael and felt the tape of the last twenty-four hours unwind.

I didn't like him, I told myself. That addiction stuff was nonsense. It was just that it had been a while since I'd been in close contact with the male species, so of course he was getting inside my head. I was lonely, that was all. Everybody got lonely. It was only natural.

"Right this way." My voice was cool, professional. He wasn't the only one who could be aloof. I pulled the curtain back to enter my room, and as I did, Elodie popped up around the corner, a little French jack-in-the-box. "Hello!" she said, her voice high and cheery. She scared the hell out of me and I jumped away from Kael.

"I left before you woke up. I had—" She stopped talking when she saw who was with me.

"Kael? Hello!" She double-kissed his cheeks and I moved out of their way. In fact, I leaned my back against the wall. An appropriate metaphor, I thought.

"Elodie. How's it going?"

They talked for a moment, good-natured casual conversation. But when he put his hands on her elbows—a friendly and completely appropriate gesture—I felt a wave of anger swell. That's when I knew I had completely lost my mind.

"I'm really hungry all the time. I can't seem to gobble down enough food." She laughed as she said this. Kael smiled at her and I found myself glad he didn't laugh with her. Yep. Mind was lost. She looked at me and I avoided her eyes. She had to be wondering what was going on.

How could I tell her if I didn't know myself?

"Well, I'll see you around," Elodie said, and made her way back to Mali.

I walked into the room without even looking at Kael. I was usually much politer to clients; I would never turn my back on them. But I did now. Let him follow behind me. Let him feel what it's like to see someone's back disappear through a door.

Chapter ✱ Fifty

THE ROOM WAS DARK so I lit a few candles. It was one of those small tasks that helped me ease into the day. Almost a ritual. Mali had a couple of those Bic automatic lighters in each room, but I preferred matches. I loved the scratch as you ran the match head over the striking surface, the tiny little explosion that brought the flame to life. So much better than the nervous *click, click, click* of those lighters.

I was aware of Kael, standing just inside the doorway. He might have been evaluating his escape route or maybe even considering a quick getaway. Who knew? I ignored him as I lit the candles. Almond, from Bath and Body Works.

"I'll come back in a couple of minutes, give you some time to undress," I said, but he pulled his shirt off as I made to leave, so I didn't get a chance. I exhaled a small harrumph to express my displeasure, then turned around to face the wall. I could sense the tight movements of his shoulder muscles as he lifted his shirt over his head.

"I could have gone out."

"I just need to take my shoes and shirt off," he told me. He was still a client, regardless of whatever had or hadn't happened between us. Regardless of what I felt. As if I knew what that was. I didn't want to even come close to being inappropriate with him in my work place. Outside this building I might have slapped his face. But here . . . well, my job was to heal, not hurt.

I stared at my dark purple wall and tried to imagine it navy. I was still undecided on what color to paint it, but Mali had given me her approval yesterday, so that was a win for this crazy week. The clean, masculine aroma of the candle was working its way through the room and I felt my breathing slow. I stared into the flame until I heard the table creak and the soft pull of the sheet. I counted to ten once he stopped moving.

"Same pressure as before?" I asked. He was lying there on the table face up, his stomach exposed. The thin blanket and sheet were pulled up only to his hips.

He nodded. Great. Back to this. His eyes were open, following me around the room.

"Usually I start with the back, which means that the client lies on his stomach," I told him.

"The client," he said. "Right. That's me." Kael turned over and rested his head in the face cradle. I grabbed a hot towel from the warming cabinet and tried to think about him as simply my ten a.m. appointment—an impossibility, really. Was he playing some kind of game with me? It sure felt like it.

I placed a hot towel on his back. The moist heat would help relax his muscles and make the massage more effective. I took another hot towel and wiped his arms and feet. In silence, I focused on his soft skin, taking in his scent: cedar and campfire, I think. And definitely bar soap. Kael was not the body wash type.

I started to pump peppermint oil into my open palm,

but stopped when I remembered he had refused it on his first session—that curt *no* being one of the first of his monosyllables. I rubbed my hands together to warm them, although I would have loved to surprise him with icy fingers on his warm skin. A little bit of payback for the merry-go-round he's got me on.

I was getting myself worked up again. In fact, I was about two minutes away from telling him to get off the table and get the hell out, or at least explain what his deal was. I was already regretting opening up to him. All that stuff he knew about my mom, my dad . . . about me. I turned the music up on my phone. Banks. Let him tell Kael that I was tired of his waiting game. I made sure that the music was loud enough for him to hear the words, but not loud enough to disturb any other patrons. See—still professional.

Kael's sweatpants were faded and the hem at the bottom was almost purple from being washed so many times. Black cotton can do that, turn the color of eggplant. Great. Now I was back to last night—to the party, my bedroom, my purple bedspread. Again, the flash of us alone together. Kael dropping his emotional armor. Leaving those invisible bodyguards outside.

I looked around the room and saw the purple glow of everything. Why was I surrounded by purple? In that moment, I felt fortunate to have seven brains in my head, all thinking different things at the exact same time. It was my own little streaming service and thank goodness I could switch between channels so that the next fifty-five minutes wouldn't be awkward, for either of us.

Comedy? Drama? Home improvement?

Take your pick, Karina.

It was good for me to think about other things while I rubbed the balls of his feet, while I ran my palms up his calves. Tylenol. I'd drop by the drugstore after work and pick up some Tylenol. What else did I need—shampoo? I tried to push the leg of his pants up a little, but they were tight at the bottom. They wouldn't give. He was pulling at his pants and his phone rang but he didn't answer. I couldn't bring myself to be nosy enough to ask who it was.

I was about to tell him that most clients prefer to turn off their phones, that they find the interruptions jarring. But who was I kidding. Kael wasn't like most clients.

I moved up the back of his thigh, gliding my hands along his bare back. I tried to think of what movie I'd watch when I flopped down on the couch after work, but it was hard to think of anything other than the muscles along his shoulders, so prominent under his soft, dark, skin. Right under his shoulder blade, there was a spot that had to be giving him some kind of pain when I pressed into it.

"Does this hurt?" I asked him.

"Yes," he replied.

"Like all the time or right now?"

"Aren't those the same thing?"

"No." I pushed the side of my thumbs into his muscle.

"Oh, yeah. That hurts all the time."

"You didn't say anything before?" I didn't remember feeling it, but there was no way it got like that in a week.

"Why would I?" he asked. I wished I could see his eyes as he spoke.

"Because it hurts?" I pressed harder than normal and he groaned. The tissue separated under the pressure of my touch. "Because I asked you?"

"Everything hurts," he said. "All my body. All the time."

Chapter ✷ Fifty-One

I LOVED MY JOB. But I didn't love the stereotypes. I had worked hard to become a massage therapist, taking classes in anatomy, bodywork, physiology, even psychology and ethical business methods. I practiced countless hours, passed my Massage & Bodywork Exam, got my license. All that and I still had to endure those classy jokes about Happy Endings.

I remember the first time someone implied that I was a sex worker in scrubs. He got a gleam in his eye when I told him that I worked in a massage parlor. I had been sitting in a coffee shop, enjoying a latte and a book when this older guy sat next to me and asked me what I was reading. We chatted for a bit—he seemed nice enough. Until, that is, the conversation came round to what each of us did for a living. He told me that he was a lawyer at this prestigious law firm. I could tell that he was trying to impress me by name dropping some big clients and talking about billable hours. =

I told him that I was a newly qualified massage therapist and that I was really happy to be starting my career,

I was going on about health and wellness, about the whole mind-body connection and how massage therapy was a growing industry when he raised his eyebrows, leaned in close to me and said, "Oh, you're a . . . *massage therapist.*" His meaning was clear, and so were his intensions. Even outside of creeps with gross offerings, I got the usual jokes from friends and family- those may be worse.

Most clients were respectful and seemed to understand that very few sex workers hid under the title of massage therapist. There had been a recent bust of a little parlor on the other side of town and that shook us up a bit. I had applied for a job there before Mali hired me, and I got the creeps just thinking about it. It also made me appreciate Mali even more, if that was possible. The way she ran a tight ship, looking out for our best interests.

I loved my job, being able to relieve pain and soothe people using my hands. Healing people, offering them relief, both mental and physical. My career was my passion and I hated that the industry I loved so much took such a hit because of just a few. I wouldn't ever be one of those people who took risks, who stepped over the line of what was appropriate, whether for money or desire. So I tried hard to focus on the treatment I was providing, without so much as a gratuitous glance at Kael's body, no matter how hard it was.

He was on his back, now, arms at his side. I took a deep breath. I wouldn't look at his bare skin.

I had never thought about a client in this way before and I wasn't going to start. Well, it had already started, but it wasn't going to continue. I tried to distract myself with physiology, by naming all the chest muscles. Pectoralis major. Pectoralis minor. Serratus anterior. I remember learning in class that women are biologically wired to prefer men who have strong chests and shoulders, something about testosterone levels. So really, I wasn't being inappropriate. It was biology.

"I like this music." Kael's voice cut through the dark, surprising me.

"Thanks," I said. I wanted to tell him that Kings of Leon were one of my favorite bands of all time and that their first album was the closest thing to a masterpiece my ears had ever heard. But I was done opening up to him.

When I finished working on the top of his thigh over his pants, I moved up to the top of the table where his head rested. My fingertips trickled down his scalp, pressing firmly against the soft tissue of his neck. His eyes, which had been closed when I worked on his legs, opened slowly.

Did he see me staring at his strong features, at the deep curve of his lips? I refused to be the one to break the ice today. He left me so suddenly last night, without warning or any explanation whatsoever. He had the nerve to prance in here and act like nothing had happened?

Maybe that was why I was so upset. Because nothing had happened.

I skated my fingers down his chest, circling around the span of him. The way his tight muscles felt breaking up under my fingertips. I could almost feel the tension releasing from his pores.

"You're quiet today," Kael said.

My hands stopped moving.

"You haven't said anything," I countered.

"I just said I like the music."

I rolled my eyes, pursing my lips together.

"You want to say something, I can tell."

"Oh, you can tell," I said. "Right. I forgot. You know me so well." Sarcasm is a girl's best friend. "Why are you even here?"

"You knew I was coming."

"You told me you wanted a massage. You didn't say when. You didn't give me a time," I explained. "Or anything."

He was quiet for a few beats of the song.

"Yeah, thought so," I said under my breath.

Kael's hand shot up from under the blanket, his fingers wrapping around my wrist. His eyes were deep pools and I couldn't look away from them. I didn't move an inch. Everything stopped. Even my breath. Intense didn't begin to cover it.

"Why don't you just tell me what's going on inside that head of yours, Karina?"

I didn't think before I spoke. "There's too much." I stood at his side, my hips aligned with his chest. "Too . . ." I couldn't finish.

His fingers were so warm, pressed against my pulse. It had to be pounding under his fingerprint.

"Just let go," he told me in barely a whisper. His pupils were so black in the candlelight, probing me, searching for my words. My insecurities told me he was searching for more, searching for a weak spot.

"So you can leave?" I bit at him.

His eyes closed, thick lashes dusting over his cheeks. I couldn't believe there was a time when I saw him and didn't see what he actually looked like.

"I deserve that," he said. He still hadn't let go of my hand. "I deserve that and more." He opened his eyes. "So give it to me."

I sighed, pulling my hand away. He gripped a little tighter, but I still pulled away.

"What are we doing?" I asked him.

I had so many things to say. So many things to ask.

But my thoughts were tripping over my words. I didn't have a clue of what he had locked away in that head of his. I didn't know where to begin.

"We're talking. Well, you were about to."

I stepped away from the table and he sat up, turning to me.

"I'm serious. Why did you come here?"

He stared at me. No words, just that look.

"Now you're back to this." I spoke loud enough so he could hear me over the music, but not so loud that anyone outside of the room could hear.

"Look." He straightened his back. His hand lifted up like he wanted to reach for mine, but dropped it before I could decide what I would have done.

"I'm sorry that I left last night. Something . . . my friend had something come up and I had to go. I shouldn't have just left like that, but I—" He spoke like the words were being ripped from him. "I can't. But I had to be there."

"If your friend needed you, why wouldn't you just say that? I would have understood."

His brow raised. "I don't know. I just panicked I guess?"

He looked down at his hands.

"I'm uhm, not the best at this." Kael stumbled over his words.

"Neither am I." I was pacing around the small room now. A vain attempt to get away from him. "And I'm not asking if we're dating or whatever, I just don't have the space for this type of thing in my life right now," I rambled. "You come and you go, and I've had enough of that in my entire life. I don't need another second of it."

"I wasn't trying to come and go."

"What is it exactly you're trying to do then?"

His shoulders slid down in defeat. "I wish I knew. Honestly, Karina, I barely even know what day it is, so I'm confused too. Meeting someone was literally the last thing on my mind."

"Is that what I am? *Someone you met?*"

He shrugged. "I don't know what it is either. But what I do know is that I drove around the block four times, telling myself not to come in here." He looked at me. "But here I am."

For once, I was the silent one.

Chapter · Fifty-Two

THERE ARE TIMES when you don't need to say anything. Times when everything is easy and you can share a room or a moment without having to fill the space with words, when everything just falls into place. This wasn't one of them.

You could cut the air with a knife.

Kael must have felt it too. "I've been spending a lot of money on massages," he said, his first attempt at small talk.

"Self-care," I said.

We both laughed, then, and relief poured through me. The way his laughter mixed with mine was like music. It was one of those moments I wished I could just bottle up and keep in a vial around my neck, the way Angelina Jolie had saved her lover's blood.

Okay, now that was a weird thought. Why did my mind ricochet like that?

"If it makes it any better," Kael said, "I regret it."

"Leaving last night?" I clarified.

He nodded, swinging his long muscular legs over the

side of the table. I was surprised they didn't touch the floor.

"I wanted to be there with you, in that room, listening to you tell your stories. I love it when you tell stories . . . I could listen to you for hours," he said.

I turned the music up a notch to drown out our voices. "The Hills" was taunting both of us. Raspy and suspenseful, the song fit perfectly between us, filling our silence.

I love it when . . .

"Then, why didn't you?" I finally asked.

"It was a friend thing—" Kael's expression changed.

"Friend?" I asked and it clicked. "Oh, you have a—"

"Not that kind of friend," he said. He wanted to reassure me and that was thrilling. A line of electricity charged through me. "One of my buddies is having a rough time right now. It, uh . . . his wife called and I had to go over there." Kael's expression was stone.

I was confused. He was opening up, but I needed more. "So, again, if you were going to help a friend, why couldn't you tell me? I would have understood if you told me—"

He cut me off. "Mendoza's business isn't mine to tell."

"Mendoza?" I moved across the room, stopping directly in front of Kael.

He sighed. He bit down on his lip. "It's not my place, Karina. I'm not talking about it."

I appreciated his loyalty to his friend. Really, I did, but wasn't I his friend too? Wasn't I someone? Apparently not. "And that's so far from the norm. You not talking about it." I meant for my words to burn him, or at least make him sweat. They did neither.

He looked at me like he was taking a lie detector test and I had just asked his name and if the sky was blue. Complacent. Assured. Calm as fuck.

Chapter ⋆ Fifty-Three

IT WASN'T EVEN NOON and I was ready for the day to be over. How dare he come here and complicate my life like this. All I wanted was a normal life. A nice job. A nice house. A nice guy. Other people had these things. Why not me?

I took a breath and tried to soften a little. But I was careful not to melt. Not in front of him. Not anymore.

"Are we done here?" I asked. He shrugged his shoulders.

"I still have ten minutes left." He held up his phone as if to prove it.

"Fine. But you need to act like a regular client. This is my job and unlike you, I can get fired."

Kael looked away from me and at the wall behind my head, focusing on the shelf where I kept my speaker and clean towels. Next to the towels, in a little wooden frame, was a picture of me, Austin, and Sammy. It was homecoming of freshman year and Sammy and Austin went together, their second try at being a couple. I went without a date.

Sammy and I were all dolled up for the evening. Her dress was a shimmery red with a scoop back. Mine, was purple, come to think of it. Purple *ombré. The neckline was a pale color, almost mauve, but the color changed as the dress draped my body, moving from light to dark until the bottom looked like it had been dipped in ink.* We got our dresses at JC Penny, but kept the tags on so that we could return them the next day.

"Fine. Regular client. I get it," he said. He was trying to crack my shell, but I wasn't having any of it. He shrugged his shoulders and lay back down on his back. This time I did what I usually did with new clients or walk-ins and draped a soft towel over his eyes.

I lowered the volume on the music and lifted his right arm. I bent it gently at the elbow, then pulled softly, and as I did the thick muscles in his back shifted in response. I worked my way down his biceps. They weren't beefy in that artificial way, jacked up on supplements and daily visits to the gym. He was solid under my hands, and I knew it came from hard physical work. Army work.

I used my forearm to apply pressure to the knot just under his bicep where he had a scar that looked like an unfinished *M.* The pink tinted skin was puffy and soft. It took everything in me not to run my finger over it again. I tried not to think about the pain he must have felt when it happened, whatever it was that cut at his body.

The scar was deep, like from the lashing of a serrated knife. It made my heart ache for him. I slid my fingers down his forearm, the part of his body that was the deepest in pigment. He had a soldier's tan, which was like a farmer's tan, but worse because they were in the desert getting baked by the sun. I lifted his hand into mine and pressed my thumb against the base of his palm and held it there. I felt his fingers go slack and moved the pressure along the palm of his hand.

Was it only the night before that we sat together, side by side on my childhood bed?

I started to think about Mendoza, wondering if he was okay. He hadn't been gone very long when Kael got the phone call. It had to have been only twenty minutes before Kael left, and if he lived on base near my dad he couldn't have been home for longer than fifteen. I hoped he didn't drive.

"That feels so good," Kael said to me when I bent his wrists, pressing against the sides, slightly pulling at the same time.

"I just learned it," I told him.

"Really?"

"Yeah, I saw a YouTube video and tried it on myself first. It felt so good. Especially for people who use their hands a lot."

"Wait, you learned it on YouTube?" he asked me, lifting his head a little. I pulled the towel back over his eyes and gently pressed my palm against his forehead to lay him back down.

"Yes. It's helpful."

"You're such a millennial."

"So are you." I laid his arm back to his side and moved to the other side.

"Technically, yes. At least tell me you have an actual license and didn't learn everything on YouTube?"

"Ha. Ha." I rolled my eyes back. "Of course I have a license." I remembered it was his birthday. "Happy Birthday by the way."

"Thanks."

I quietly slid back into the treatment and even gave him an extra ten minutes. When we were finished, he thanked me, paid, tipped well, and mumbled a shallow goodbye like a good client.

The fact that he had given me what I asked for and I hated it, burned like bad coffee.

Chapter * Fifty-Four

I WAS NEVER so relieved to be done with customers for the day. Mali had asked me to take a walk-in after that awful session with Kael. I don't know if it was the mood I was in or if it was the client, but nothing I did was good enough for her. The pressure was too light, then it was too heavy. The room was cold, could she have two blankets, then her feet were hot under the blankets, could I take one away? And could I please blow out the candle because the fragrance was giving her a headache.

I made every accommodation and even tried to reason with myself over her. She felt like a test from the universe whether Kael could ruin my day or not. Somehow everything linked back to him and my imagination started to take her on, creating her life where she's overworked or in a shitty marriage. Maybe I was the only person in her life that she could take her anger out on. Better me than her kids, or family, or even herself. I started feeling for her, everyone has a bad day. Even when she said my nails needed to be clipped

… and then she left without giving me a tip. I may have flipped her off as she walked out of the door.

My one o'clock was okay, thank goodness. The walk-in after that was fine, too—a pretty young woman from the yoga studio the next block over. She fell asleep almost as soon as she lay down and her skin was soft, no tense muscles to work out.

Still, I was happy to call it a day and to be heading home. Thank God. Mali had given me some Ibuprofen, and that helped turn down the volume in my throbbing head. But I still felt like complete crap. I was anxious and annoyed and nothing was helping.

All I could think of was flopping down in bed with the blinds drawn and the covers over my head. I wanted darkness and quiet. But then I rounded the corner to my little house and saw him waiting for me on the porch.

My biggest problem and biggest relief wrapped up and delivered directly to my front door.

Kael.

He looked nervous, sitting there with headphones on, a faraway look in his eyes. He was so distracted he almost didn't see me approach.

"Did you come for a refund?" I asked, trying to keep it light. I wasn't at all bothered that he was there. I wasn't nervous. No, I wasn't. Nope. Not at all. I was cool. I hadn't let him get to me, not the way he thought he did. Not me.

"No refund," he said, shaking his head. "I think we should finish our conversation."

"Oh? And which conversation is that?" I was playing it coy and he knew it. Cat and mouse. You know, how adults foreplay.

"About meeting someone. You know, whether or not we're dating, or not."

"We're definitely not dating," I said through a forced, fake laugh.

"Well, what are we doing then?"

"You didn't know earlier," I reminded him.

"Neither did you," he flipped it back to me.

Kael held an orange in his hand. It was a big orange, but small in his hand, with the little SUNKIST sticker still on it. He was massaging it gently with his thumb, but hadn't broken into the peel yet.

"I want to know more about you. That's all I'm asking, okay?" With a face like his, I doubted he ever had to ask that question. Who wouldn't want to say yes without even thinking? I was the only idiot who would confuse things. How could I have such a strong attraction to this guy and still be so unsure of how I felt. Of how he felt.

I took him in. I couldn't help it, but I ran my eyes up and down his strong body. He was wearing a gray Army T-shirt and black sweats. It was unfair how hot he looked in everything he wore.

"How do you plan on doing that?" I asked.

I seemed to be responding the way he had hoped. He was pleased with that, as if that was his plan all along. I liked that he had one. The idea of a plan made me feel important. He made me feel important.

"By asking you questions about yourself. How else?" He was being so playful, so unlike the composed man I'd come to know over the last few days.

"Okay." I was skeptical. "Go ahead."

He gestured to the empty spot next to him. "At least sit down with me. What kind of a date is this?"

"It's not a date. We're just hanging out, getting to know each other. That's it."

That was meant more for myself than for him, but

Kael didn't need to know that. I sat down at the top of the porch and let my legs dangle over the lower steps.

"You keep saying we don't know each other, so I'm going to get to know you if it's the last thing I do," he assured me. He was so confident. In his words, his smile. Even the way he leaned back on the concrete steps conveyed his confidence. I felt that familiar pull move from the bottom of my tummy down toward my legs.

"Okay, okay. Enough small talk, ask something." I needed to be distracted from the way Kael's mouth made me ache as he licked his lips while peeling the skin off of the orange.

"I only brought one, but we can share," he said. I loved this playful version of him.

"Some date," I joked and he shook his head.

"Nope, you said it wasn't a date."

"Touché. Now questions or I'm ending this not-date prematurely," I threatened. We both knew it was an empty threat. "Anyway, you're the one who doesn't tell me anything about himself."

"You go first then," he offered. I thought about what I wanted to know about him. There was just so much.

Music. That's what popped into my head first. I'd ask about music! "What's your favorite band that no one really knows?"

He turned to me, his eyes wide, happy.

"So many, I love unknown bands. It's most of what I listen to. What about Muna. I just found them. They're great."

"Muna isn't unknown, they went on tour with Harry Styles." I told him how I loved their music and how Elodie and I tried to get tickets to the concert but they sold out so quickly, so I'd need to pick up a few more clients before I could afford resell tickets.

"Harry Styles, huh? If you could go to any concert, ever, who would it be?" he asked me.

I nodded a solid yes to Harry Styles, and thought about what concert I would choose if I could see anyone. Alanis Morissette had always been my go-to answer, but with Kael, I chose what I actually thought of first. It felt freeing, to be honest in this way. I liked how he brought me out of myself. I didn't give him the answer I thought he wanted. I gave him the truth.

"Shawn Mendes," I told him.

"Shawn Mendes?" he repeated. I could practically hear the joke coming, so I tried to move the conversation along.

"And you?" I asked.

"Me, well, I would probably say either Amy Winehouse, before she …" He paused. It was lovely, a mark of respect somehow. I smiled, urging him to continue. "Or Kings of Leon on their first tour. Back when they were virtually unknown."

"I'm going to make a list of unknown bands before our next … hangout session or whatever we're calling this," I said.

"Our next not-a-date," he said. I think we were both relieved to hear the word "next."

"Right," I said, feeling both relieved and excited.

"So," Kael said. "Here's another question for you. If you could describe Austin in one word, what would it be?"

"Hmm." I tapped my nose, thinking of just one word to describe my twin. "Well-intended?" I finally answered. But I was unsure. It wasn't the word I was going for. Not exactly.

"That's two words," he said.

"Actually, it's hyphenated, so that counts as one

word." He liked that. I could tell. "He has good intentions," I continued. "He just makes bad choices to go along with them."

"I get that," he said. And I really felt that he did.

"My turn," I said. "What about you? What about your little sister?" His expression hardened for a moment, almost as if I imagined it. Then just as quickly, it went back to normal.

He thought for a moment, considering not answering. I saw it on his face, but he came up with, "Powerhouse."

"Powerhouse?" I repeated. What a lovely way to be viewed by someone, especially by someone in your own family.

He nodded. "Yeah, she's brilliant. And doesn't let anything stop her. Her high school, it's one of those fancy private schools where they only teach the thing the students are good at. Science is her thing. She tested high enough to get into the school back when she was nine, but my mom can't drive and wouldn't let her ride the city bus alone until she turned fourteen. Now she takes the bus alone, across town, every morning, and every afternoon."

"Wow," was all I could manage. Of course Kael's sister was a science prodigy. It was impressive and humorous to compare this teenaged prodigy riding a bus across town to get to her gifted school to my brother who got himself in trouble even when he stayed home.

"Next?" it was Kael's turn to change the subject.

I asked a basic question. "What do you like to do in your spare time?"

"Get massages," he smiled at me, "and work on my house. I bought a duplex while I was deployed. Remember when you took me to the parking lot to get my keys? They were supposed to be there. Anyway, I bought this run down duplex and I'm fixing up the empty side now, and slowly working on my side so I can rent it out and then move into another one and repeat the cycle. Maybe spread out toward Atlanta when I can."

"I bought my house for the same reason," I told him. He took a bite of the peeled orange. I could smell the sweetness from where I sat. My mouth watered.

"Well, the remodeling part. I couldn't stand living with my dad and his wife anymore, so I found this little house online and have been slowly, I mean, s l o w l y fixing it up." I dragged out the word for emphasis.

He laughed, inching closer to me. "I noticed."

"Don't you think I'm doing a good job?" I asked. "Didn't you see the shower tiles?" I bet he cringed at the number of unfinished projects scattered around the house.

He was close to me, so close that I could smell the fruit on his breath. I didn't know if it was me, or if it was Kael, but one of us was inching closer to the other. By the time Kael and I had asked each other random questions like how long we could hold our breath and what noise could he listen to all day, every day without being annoyed, we were inches away from each other.

It was a magnetic pull. An irresistible attraction.

"I could listen to you talk all day," he said, surprising me. "It's become one of my favorite things to do."

His eyes were on my mouth.

My heart was beating out of my chest.

"I wish I could hear you talk all day," I confessed to him. We felt so close there, huddled together on my porch, not noticing the cars or any of the people passing us.

"One day you'll regret saying that." Kael's breath covered my cheeks, my wet, needy lips.

His lips were so close to mine. Was he going to kiss

me, here, now, out of the blue, with the dew of orange on his lips?

My mouth begged for his to inch closer, to touch mine. I had never wanted something more than I wanted him to kiss me, there on my porch.

Was he going to kiss me?

His lips soon answered my question. He leaned over and put his soft mouth on mine. Everything went quiet then. The traffic. The sound of the birds. Even the noisy station inside my head. I had no words. No thoughts. Just him.

He was timid at first, gentle ... until I pushed my tongue between his lips and tasted him. From that taste, my addiction flared up and I knew I would never get enough of him. I would need every hit and I would take every chance to get it.

That first kiss turned into countless more as we toed the line between causal and committed. I knew the danger. If my own history had taught me nothing, at least I could heed the lesson of nearly every issue of *Cosmopolitan* and every romantic comedy from the past two decades. This was never, ever going to work.

But I had to risk it.

No matter what the cost, I had to risk it.

Chapter *Fifty-Five*

KAEL WAS PARKED in the back of the spa when I got off work the next day, his huge Bronco dripping water from its massive body. He was wearing a long-sleeved shirt with his company's name printed on the front and blue jeans with frayed bottoms, as if he had worn them for years. I wanted to touch the soft, worn denim and feel the thread of the fabric against my fingerprints.

"What are you doing here? How did you know when I would be finished?" I was surprised to see him at my work, waiting with a freshly washed car and new shoes on his feet. Thrilled, but surprised.

"A little birdie told me," he said, pulling his sunglasses off his eyes, opening the passenger door for me.

"Does that little birdie happen to have an adorable French accent?" I asked.

He shrugged. "That's confidential," he said with a straight face. I could see a little gleam in his eye. How was it possible that I missed him overnight when he had stayed on my porch with me until almost midnight, and here he was again.

"What are you doing here?" I asked again. I wasn't going to just climb in the car without making him work for it.

"I came to hopefully get you to go on a date with me."

"A date? I thought we said we weren't going on dates, that we were just hanging out, seeing where this goes?"

He shoved his hands into his pockets and stood there, next to the open door.

"We don't have to call it a date then. But would you like to hang out with me tonight since you're off work until tomorrow at noon."

I said yes without even pretending to have to think about it. There was no point. We both knew I would go anywhere he asked me to. He held me by my elbow as I climbed inside and he shut the door behind me. The fact that he opened doors for me was so polite. He was a gentleman without even trying. I couldn't wait to meet the woman responsible for raising him and his science prodigy of a sister.

"I have something planned for you. I put together some music," he paused, sheepishly, "and I want to take you to my favorite food spot in this whole city."

I was getting more excited by the minute.

"I found like five bands I think you've never heard of. One is called Chevelle. I once knew this guy in basic training who would scream their lyrics over and over. They were from his hometown and by the time we graduated, I knew almost all of their songs by heart. I don't know if you'll like them now, but if you had listened to them before you fell for Shawn Mendes, it might have been a different story."

I loved the way Kael's tongue wrapped words up to sound so much more impressive, more pleasurable to listen to, when he spoke them.

He was lighthearted and heavy, both home and away. Biting whiskey and smooth wine. I loved the way he contradicted everything about himself. He was a fascinating man and I couldn't wait to learn more about him.

"Leave Shawn out of this," I told him with a smile.

"I saw that poster in your room at your dads. I didn't think about it then, but I remember it now."

Kael turned onto the highway as daylight was disappearing from the sky.

"He's the John Mayor of our generation," I argued.

Kael snorted. "John Mayer is the John Mayer of our generation."

A few minutes later, he was quiet and I was happy as we listened to music and drove down a long, curvy road I had never been on before. I would always remember the way the sun and moon danced in the sky that night and what a sense of calm his silence had started to bring over my body.

I listened to his voice when he asked me random questions like he had on our first "date" on my porch. It would forever remain the best first non-date of my life.

"How many siblings do you wish you had?"

"Which is your favorite character on *Friends*?"

"How many times have you watched *The Lion King*?"

I was starting to get too comfortable with him, there in the front seat of his Bronco. And yet I could almost feel the chaos brewing somewhere nearby. Everything was going too well. I was starting to feel too much for this guy.

My brother's name popped up on my cell phone screen and I thought about ignoring it, but decided against it. Music boomed through his side of the line and his slurred words were tumbling through, becoming inaudible.

"Kareeee, come get me. Please, Katie. Fuck Katie.

Fuck Katie and her ex-boyfriend and her fucking phone ..."
Austin slurred his words. "Kare, please come get me."

Chaos. No longer brewing.

I couldn't say no. I asked Kael to drive me to the address that Austin gave me and we went straight there. By the time we arrived, two guys were rolling around in the middle of the street, a red T-shirt and a black T-shirt were all I could make out of the bodies.

"Get off him!" I recognized Katie's voice before I saw her.

"Come on, Nielson, fuck him up!" Someone said in the background. A couple more lines of toxic encouragement were thrown out before I realized it was Austin in the red shirt. He looked like he had the guy in a head lock and he didn't seem to plan on letting up anytime soon.

"Stop it!" Katie yelled again. I ran over to where she was standing, her face streaked with mascara tears.

"What happened?" I asked, grabbing her by the shoulders. Kael was yelling Austin's name, trying to break up the fight.

"My ex, and Austin—" She started crying hysterically and couldn't tell me anymore than I could see in front of me.

Sirens whirled through the air as Austin let up on the choke hold so he could punch the guy in the black shirt in his ribs. They looked like little boys wrestling in their WWE themed bedrooms, but they were adults, and the police were pulling up.

I yelled Austin's name and Kael tried to pull at Austin's shirt to get him off the guy. If he got arrested again, he would be fucked. The siren cut off and the voices got louder. There were only maybe five people outside, but when all of the voices were yelling at once, it was complete chaos.

Everything happened so fast.

The MPs rushed out of their car, heading straight for Kael. I screamed, running to him when Austin's body hit the ground, knocking me into the man he was fighting, whose elbow or fist was flying toward my face. I lifted my hands up to block my face and heard Kael scream. Not just a scream, but a guttural groan of pain. It was animal like in its intensity and it shot straight through me. I turned to him, no longer thinking about shielding myself. The only thing on my mind when I saw the MP draw his black baton into the air was that Kael was on the ground, his right leg in the line of direction for the officer's assault.

Another scream rang through the air. Maybe it was Katie. Maybe it was me. I'd never know. What I did know was that while Austin crept through chaos and found the Bronco, he managed somehow to lift his drunk ass up inside and lie down.

Kael and I were questioned by the MPs.

"Where were you two headed?

"Are you sure you weren't drinking at the party?"

"Let me see some ID, soldier."

I glared at the cops long after Kael stopped shivering on the parking block. The other guy involved in the fight walked away too, yet it was Kael's identification they had asked to scan.

When I told Kael it wasn't fair that he was being treated this way when he wasn't even fighting anyone, he told me not to question authority, that it wasn't safe. Give a man power, and he'll ruin the world, my mother always told me.

She was proving to be more right every day.

An hour later we finally made it back to the car. Austin woke up, we were almost to my dad's house. My brother was out of it all right, asking for Katie, for our mom, for a peanut butter sandwich.

"I think he's more than drunk," Kael told me after he helped Austin into my dad's house and up the stairs. Kael practically tucked Austin into his bed, yet my dad had the nerve to text me and ask if Kael was drinking and driving a few minutes after we pulled away. I wondered why my dad was up so late on a weekday, but I didn't respond. There was only so much I could take.

"What does that mean?" I looked at Kael with harsh eyes. It wasn't the time to throw out unreasonable accusations. Like my brother was on drugs, he could barely afford to get his haircut, let alone buy drugs and keep up with his love of alcohol and Chipotle.

"Nothing, I'm just thinking out loud," Kael told me.

"Well don't." I was defensive and Austin was my twin. He wasn't on drugs, he just drank way more than he ever should have.

"I think it's best if neither of us talk," I said, just to try to get a rise out of him, which was completely unfair, especially given the altercation with the police. I still couldn't believe the way they behaved toward Kael. It was like they had something against him personally. The MP nearly took a night stick to his already injured leg. The sight of it had been horrifying and the memory of it was a hundred times worse.

"I'm sorry, I really am," I told Kael, reaching for his hand to calm me. His fingers, warm and familiar, threaded through mine and I felt grounded again.

"I'm sorry for all of this. You standing up for Austin and getting attacked by those fucking MPs, having to nurse my brother, ugh, I'm sorry for all the complicating of your life I've been doing lately."

Kael sighed in the quiet car and pulled my fingers up to his lips. "You are worth every single complication you bring along." He leaned in to kiss me. "I hope you'll always feel that way about me," he said to me, cradling my face between his large hands.

"Always, huh?"

"Well maybe not always, wouldn't want to scare you off," he said.

"Almost always?"

Kael nodded, smiled and pullied me close to him. Even inside of the eye of a storm, he could make me feel like I was safely planted. It was all about perception, and mine could have used a dose or two of reality. But instead of searching for the ground, I was floating in the sky with the brightest star of all. My mom's voice echoed in my head as I kissed Kael again: *The brightest stars burn the fastest, so we must love them while we can.* She only told me that once, but all these years later I still remembered it. I guess now that she was gone I couldn't afford to forget all her wisdoms and wives' tales she collected over the years.

"Let's go home?" I asked Kael, knowing he would know I meant my house.

He nodded and we drove home in the most peaceful silence and my mother's words faded from my mind as we merged onto the highway.

Chapter ✦ Fifty-Six

I DON'T KNOW what I'd do without my job. It wasn't only about paying bills—although God knows there was that. It was about turning the key in the front door, switching on the lights, making sure we had fresh towels and were stocked with oils. Each little task took me out of myself and helped me connect to the world around me. I was sure of my skills as a massage therapist, proud of what I could do to help people disentangle the knots of their own lives. I needed that more than ever today, as I tried to disentangle the mess of my own life.

Mali understood why I was late. She had urged me to take the day off when I called to tell her what had happened, but I couldn't bring myself to do that. Kael had appointments on post all day and I needed the distraction. I thought about going with him, but I was afraid to be mistaken for his young wife. Even more afraid that I would like it. I did hate being away from him, and even called him while I walked to work.

I was grateful for the work, but I had put in an almost

full day and was ready to be going home, especially since Kael said he'd come over after my shift. I was scheduled to work until four, but I would slip out an hour early if I didn't have a walk-in by three.

I was tired, worn out from our date night from hell the night before. The way Kael had tried to come to Austin's aid with the MPs, the way he kissed my forehead when I cried in his arms on the way home. Austin didn't remember any of it. Of course, he didn't. He was beyond recollection. I knew it wasn't just alcohol—although that was bad enough. (Our mom should have been a warning to us both.) But it was more than booze, that much was made obvious by his big, black pupils. He was disoriented and sloppy, like someone who had been left blindfolded in a forest and was trying to make his way out. When he called my name he couldn't even form the first few letters. All I heard was a strangled "K." Was Kael right? Was it more than alcohol controlling his body, clouding his mind.

I wanted nothing more than to clear my own head of the events of last night and I sure as hell didn't want to experience something so frightening ever again. Everyone was saying that I wasn't as shaken as I should have been. I'm not sure what they meant by that. Was it supposed to be a compliment? Elodie made tea and sat up with Kael and me while I talked and cried, trying to make sense of everything. Trying to punch my way out of the darkness. When I could talk no more he lifted me under my knees and back, and carried me to my bed. To be held like that. To be picked up like that ... it was the closest I'd come to being rescued.

I was exhausted. My body melted to the mattress until noon.

Kael wasn't fazed by the incident, other than being angry. I supposed it would take a hell of a lot more than a dickhead MP who had probably been bullied in high school and was now taking it out on every person of color he came across. I watched the news; it was an epidemic across the country. Kael didn't want to *pull the race card* as he called it, but I wanted to. I wanted to pull the whole damn deck. The least I could do was try to use my privilege for something meaningful. But you don't realize how powerless you are until you try to do something meaningful.

I saw it. Every dirty moment of bias and racism. I loved my brother and no way would I want him to get hurt, but man … no matter how fucked up he was, Austin was treated like an upstanding citizen. The way the cop protected Austin's head as he helped him get into the squad car for the two minutes he actually had to stay in it. Even Austin was taunting the cop, or trying to anyway. He could only spew out little bits of words from his slanted mouth. It would have been funny if it wasn't so tragic.

It was awful to watch him look so much like our mother.

I still didn't fully grasp what happened, it all went down so fast. I was yelling for Austin, then Kael, then black sticks were pulled from belts, I was shielding Kael's leg … I shivered. Okay, maybe it still bothered me a little. I just felt like it didn't make sense how fast they came, how quickly they went from nearly attacking Kael to telling me to get my brother back into the Bronco they had pulled him out of. Even when they questioned us, they were harsh and biting, but retreated so quickly. Little bits and pieces of the incident

I was halfway done with the day when Kael texted me. He was leaving post and would come over after he had stopped by his duplex to drop off some paint. I told him to use the key under my Hello welcome mat. It was worn down and the letters weren't so clear as they once were, but it was fine for key hiding purposes.

I'll keep the bed warm, he texted me.

I sighed, pressing the phone against my chest. I felt that sense of relief you feel when you slip into a warm bath or a warm bed. Bed. When I thought about Kael waiting for me in my bed … He had a way of making everything seem manageable.

I sent him a kiss emoji and he sent me one back. I missed him so much that I could physically feel the emptiness of his missed presence. At three p.m., there were no walk-ins. Not a single one. It was Tuesday. I needed to squeeze in every minute of my time with Kael before going to my dad's house for dinner . I thought about bringing Kael, but I didn't want anything to poke at our happy little bubble, especially not my dad. I couldn't imagine Austin telling him about the incident, so it was very possible he didn't know. I was counting on that.

I wanted to skate through dinner without any complications or drama. I didn't want to go, I wanted to stay in my bed with Kael. I was completely addicted to him and it terrified and thrilled me at once.

Chapter ✶ Fifty-Seven

THERE WERE SO MANY THINGS I wanted to do, and they all involved Kael. There was only one thing I had to do—dinner at my dad's.

I could still taste myself on Kael's lips when I kissed him again. I was wrapped around his body, stuck to his side. He was so warm, his skin and body were so beautiful, like he was sculpted directly from the soil that nourishes and feeds the earth itself.

I licked his skin, just to taste him. I didn't even worry about anything at all, except him and the way he groaned when I sucked at his skin. I never really thought about this kind of dating before I knew him. Brien and I started dating without ever saying we were dating too. I didn't know we were a couple until he told me that I shouldn't wear such short shorts in front of his friends. He didn't protect me in any other ways, only when he wanted to act macho in front of his friends. Toxic masculinity at its finest.

I didn't even know dating or whatever it was we were

doing could be like this. Brien and I made out a lot in the beginning. I'm not sure what happened, but our physical attraction turned in to something else. That something else was comfortable ... and destructive too. It wasn't good for either of us. Well, it wasn't good for me. I only wish I'd had the sense to know that at the time. Anyway, we started out hungry and hot, but we grew tired of our anxious and inexpert fumbling. Then our time together seemed to be spent going to the movies and the mall. After that we broke up a few times and hooked up again. Because we were lonely, or bored, or whatever excuse I told myself as I drove to his place those last few times.

I didn't feel the way I do now, with Kael. I didn't try to count the number of times he breathed in a minute. I didn't try to hear his heart beating inside his chest.

I kissed Kael again and his hands moved from my back down my body, and his hands squeezed my ass.

"God." He groaned into my neck, kissing me. "It was like you were sculpted just for me." He moved his hands to the front of my panties. He rubbed gently, brushing over me. I tried to stay quiet, it just felt so good. I didn't want him to stop and I also didn't want to make a big deal of it. So as my hips moved and lifted gently, and my breath caught in my throat, I swallowed his name as my eyes closed. My body tensed and released and I clung to his body as I came.

I kept my eyes closed as I came down from my blissful state, only to enter another one. I hoped with everything in me he wouldn't be like Brien and ask how it was. It instantly made everything about him. I didn't think Kael was like that and he proved me right as I laid my head on his chest and the silence sat comfortably between us.

"I want to show you these new windows that came in for my place," Kael told me out of the blue, while he drew circles over my bare hip.

"Is that what you think about after you make girls come?"

"Just you. My two favorite things, my renovation projects and you." He looked shy when he said it and that made me giggle.

"I'm just ready for you to finish that duplex so you can work on my house," I joked. I did love the idea of Kael tearing out the cabinets in my kitchen, without a shirt. Wasn't that every girl's fantasy, a devoted guy hard at work—for her.

I buried my head into his chest like he could hear my thoughts.

"Mhmm, I can't wait to work on your house so I can sleep here every night, in this bed." He squeezed me tighter.

"I love when you're off work. You need more days off. Imagine if we had an entire day to ourselves," he said into my hair. I loved the way his thick fingers wrapped around my dark strands, gently twisting between and around them. It made me think of him rubbing at my skin, making me orgasm without taking my panties off.

I nodded against him, so content and warm. I felt tired all of a sudden, and I realized that I could actually sleep if I wanted to. That was a first for me to be so relaxed during the day that I could fall asleep. I suspected it had everything to do with the company.

Kael was humming a song, telling me about this little band he found in a bar in Kentucky after he graduated basic training and how he heard their song on the radio. I loved when he was tired and his voice was even deeper than it always was.

"I'm so relaxed, you would think that I came too," he said.

I leaned up, lifting my face to where he could see it.

"Do you want to?" I kissed his chin.

He smiled. "Is that a rhetorical question?"

I shook my head.

I started to kiss down his chin, around his collarbone and shoulders. His skin was so soft under my lips, I kissed the scar across his shoulder twice.

He started to talk to me, to encourage me, tell me how hard I made him, when his phone started to ring on the nightstand. He grabbed it, eyes reading the screen.

"It's Mendoza," he said, showing me the phone.

I nodded, telling him to answer.

"Hey, you—" Kael started to speak, but he was cut off by shouting.

"Hey, hey man, slow down. Everything's okay." Kael's voice was different again, back to Sergeant Martin he was.

It astounded and impressed me. He had such great empathy, his soul glowed from the inside. I thought maybe our empathy would one day be our destruction because it seemed neither of us could control it. But for now, we were both alive and he was showing me what a thoughtful man looked like. Beautiful brown skin, sympathetic eyes, and a considerate heart. That's exactly what it looked like.

"No, no. We're okay, bud. Let's talk about where you are? And I'll come meet you, we'll grab a beer, shoot some darts, whatever." Kael was out of my bed, sliding his pants up his legs before his friend responded.

I didn't know what to do so I just sat there on the bed as Kael moved around me, in full-on mission mode. His eyes touched me every few seconds to remind me that he knew I was still there, but he was so focused on Mendoza on the other line that it was impressive and chilling.

"Just me. I won't tell Gloria where you are. I don't

want Karina to know either." Kael looked at me. *I don't mean what I'm saying,* his eyes told me. I knew that.

Kael's shoes were on and he told Mendoza he was on his way. "Look, look, go back inside and order us some beers. Hell, I'll drink tequila with you, but don't leave, wait there for me."

Was he going to hurt himself? I got out of the bed and moved toward Kael. He held his finger up to tell me to keep quiet.

"I'll be there soon, everything's fine. Don't talk to anyone else until I get there," Kael instructed.

"Is everything okay?" I asked him. He nodded.

"Mendoza, he's drunk and started saying these guys were spying on him. It's paranoia from having to watch your back all the time. From seeing your buddies get blown up. I get it," he said. His words rattled me.

"I'm sorry I have to go again." He kissed my forehead, then my cheeks, then my mouth. "I'll be back as soon as I'm done there."

"Don't drink tequila and drive," I told him. "Actually, let me drive you?"

He shook his head. "I'm sorry, Kare, but if he sees you after I told him you weren't coming, he won't trust me. I'm not going to drink tequila there, and neither is he. I'm going to convince him to go to Steak and Shake with me. Milkshakes only," he told me.

"I have to go to my dad's, but I'll have my phone on me. I really don't want to. I'm so tired," I told him, leaning against his chest for one more touch before he left.

"Don't go then? It's just one night. You've been working your ass off lately and wasting all your free time entertaining me." He hugged me. "You hate going there anyway. Why not just take a week off?" I couldn't see Kael's face, but his voice was convincing enough. He was right, why was I so willing to put myself through the inconvenience of going to these scheduled dinners every week just so I wouldn't upset my dad and his *Stepford* wife. At least when Rory and Loralie are forced to go to Rory's grandma's house, they miss when something comes up. I could do that. I was an adult, I could miss it.

"I l—" Kael started to say when he pulled away.

I pretended not to hear it. I didn't want anything to ruin our happy little bubble and if he started saying he loved me when we had only known each other a week, I would never forgive him.

"Be safe and text me when you get there to let me know everything's okay, please?" I asked of him. He nodded, kissed me again and walked to the bedroom door.

"What are you going to do about tonight?" Kael asked.

I made up my mind. "Tonight, I'm going to nap until you're back."

A smile spread across his face but it didn't quite reach his eyes.

"He's okay, right?" I asked him.

He nodded. "Yeah, Kare. He's going to be okay," he reassured me.

I fell into bed thinking about how many soldiers across the globe had demons chasing them long after they had left the battlefield. Home wasn't such a safe place for them. I drifted off to sleep wondering how strong the demons chasing my soldier were.

Kael was asleep in my bed when I got home from the store. I texted my dad, only saying sorry I can't make it, and took a three hour nap and then went to the grocery store. I called him back while I walked through the freezer aisles and told him that I didn't feel like coming. That was it. He didn't like my answer, but let me get off the phone when Austin called his other line. Elodie was at another FRG gig, a cookout this time. She seemed happy to be out socializing, especially since she found a couple of wives who were actually nice to her. They were new at the post and didn't want anything to do with the catty assholes who thought it was fun to target Elodie. Being outsiders themselves, they could see the situation for what it was, a pack of mean girls who hadn't quite grown up who somehow thought it was okay to let jealousy guide every action. Elodie's new friends just wanted to drink wine and watch Netflix so, minus the wine, it was perfect for Elodie.

Kael was shirtless, wearing boxer briefs that accentuated his muscly thighs. I thought back to the first day I saw him in the lobby, when he refused to take off his sweats or let me touch his right leg. It wasn't that long ago that the stranger with the strange name was lying on my massage table, and here he was, lying on my bed, his arm dangling over the side.

I lifted his hand and held it in mine, brought it to my lips and kissed him gently. He didn't stir. Holding his hand like this … touching each of his fingers, tracing the little creases around his knuckles … just his hand in mine was the best remedy. I loved his hands—how big they were, how strong. I thought of how they held me, touched me, brought me to the brink and beyond. I gently dropped his arm, slid my shoes and pants off, and climbed into bed with him. He woke up as soon as I wrapped my body around his, clinging to him like he was life support.

Life support. That's what he was starting to feel like for me. I should have been worried about that, but I wasn't. I'd never been the needy type, never played the damsel in distress. It's just not my style. And yet … there he was, this knight sprawled out and cozy in my bed.

I should have remembered that not all fairy tales end in *happily-ever-after.*

When Kael's eyes open, confusion filled them for a few seconds. I saw the moment he came back to reality. "Hey." He curled his body into mine. We were trying to crawl inside of each other, anything less … well, nothing would feel close enough unless that was possible.

"How was the store? Do you need help carrying bags in?" he asked.

"It was good, I—"

He cut me off before I could finish. "Why are you still dressed?" he whined, though I was pantless.

Having this man want me gave me a high I never could have dreamed of. I'd never felt like this before. Not once. I knew what a cliché it was, and I didn't care. All I cared about was right in front of me, moving closer.

Kael lifted himself up on his elbow, leaning over me, positioning himself to gaze down at me. The angles of his face continued to surprise me, as if each time he looked at me from a different viewpoint I saw a new side of him. The way he took me in … he swallowed hard, wanting to devour me. It was a small movement, almost imperceptible, and yet an act so intense I had to close my eyes to keep from falling.

I could feel the heat of his face moving closer to mine, his lips moving closer to mine. His fingers were warm when he inched my shirt up above my belly button, up my torso, until I shimmied enough for him to pull it over my head. I felt cool air on my skin, but the goose bumps, the electricity coursing through my body came from Kael.

"I missed your mouth." He spoke slowly, each word

betraying his want, each breath revealing his need. He touched his fingertips to my lips, tracing them. I licked them, running my tongue under his soft skin, over his hard nails. I nipped him playfully and he reacted first by licking his lips, then biting them. He was trying to slow himself down. I could hear it in his breath, see it in his face. He wanted me.

"Kael," I said, taking big gulps of air. "This moment. Now—"

"The words, your words—" Kael's voice was raspy, his dark eyes smoky. "The way they taste." He bent down to kiss them. "They taste even better than they sound." He pulled away and then dipped down to kiss me again.

It was more than a kiss. It was a touch and a kiss, and something that I couldn't begin to explain and it pulsed through my body as pure arousal. He slid his tongue between my lips, separating them to have more of me.

My body had come alive. I was closest to the purest human form when under his spell. When he was touching me, I could feel my mind opening up. Vast spaces were cleared, every move he made pushed aside the chaos inside my head, put me at ease.

"Every part of you," he kissed my jawline, making my eyes close, "tastes so good."

He was so hard. I could feel him pressing against me, my body reacting to him before my mind could. I reached between us to touch him, but he grabbed my wrist, pinning it above my head.

"In a hurry?" Kael dipped his head down again, this time sucking at the flesh spilling over my bra. I shuddered.

"I've been thinking about your tits all day. How they would feel in my hands." He reached up and covered my entire breast with his large hand. My eyes rolled back in my head and I swear I could feel myself moving in and out of consciousness. He sucked at me until I felt the sweet sting of the blood breaking over my skin. He was marking me. Branding me. Making me his.

I ached between my thighs.

"How they taste." He bit me gently, dipping his tongue beneath the lacey cup of my bra.

"I missed you," I managed to say through the moans slipping from my lips. He was sucking at my nipple now, biting gently. The pain mixed with pleasure sent a tantalizing surge through my entire body.

"Oh, I missed you so much."

"I want …" I gasped. I was no longer capable of breathing.

"What, Karina? What do you want?" he asked. He was teasing me. Taunting me.

I swallowed sand, my mouth was so dry. All of the wetness had moved elsewhere on my body. Never in my life had I known why people liked sex so much, why sex made them do crazy things. Yet, if Kael asked me to rob a bank with him right at that moment, while he gently sucked and pulled at my nipple, I would have happily said yes. Not being with him. Not feeling his hands on mine, his mouth on me … that would be the real crime.

"More, Kael. I need more—" I had barely gotten the last word out before his hand pushed under my body and he lifted me, carefully flipping our bodies so that I was on top of him. I could feel the pool of arousal soaking through my panties as he throbbed against me, pressing against my pulsing sex.

I wanted to tell him to fuck me. I didn't care if it hurt. I wanted him to plow into me. To take me until there was nothing left to take. I wanted to slide my panties off and lower my body onto his.

Like he was reading my mind, his fingers went from digging into my hips, to slipping inside my panties. I moaned, my head dropping in relief, then thrown back in arousal. I was throbbing from him at the core of my body.

Kael's thick finger teased me, tracing up and down, all over the sticky wetness, but not where I needed him the most. He knew just where to touch, I could tell by the way he handled my body, the confident way he talked me through it. I moved my hips, sliding myself up so his finger slid against my clit. I groaned and suddenly two fingers were inside my panties, spreading me open. I felt a small pinch and then a wave of extreme pleasure.

"I want to lick you, suck on you, taste you, tease you." Each word was breathed, rather than spoken. His eyes were blazing now. Another pinch.

"Fuck." I moved my hips again, rubbing his cock against my aching core. It was the switchboard for my body and Kael was testing all the circuits. He took his fingers from my flesh and brought them to his mouth, tasting me. I looked down at him, feeling like a goddess, feeding a starving man. He sucked at his finger, eyes closing.

"Come here," he said, his hands gripping my waist. He lifted me up, bringing me to his mouth.

"I—Are you—" I started to ask questions but his tongue gave the answer as it licked circles on my body. I wanted to pull away, to tell him ... to apologize for not shaving all the way. All of my insecurities bubbled to the surface, battling with the pain of pleasure building inside of my body.

I don't know how it was possible, but for once, the pleasure won the war inside my head, and I thought only of Kael's hands on the top of my thighs, just below my waist. The way he held me in place, over his tongue. When my body started to shake above him and inaudible words fell from my lips, he used his finger to help his magical tongue and I came so hard that I collapsed on his warm, solid body.

He held me, his arms wrapped tightly around my back, pressing my body to his. While my body danced and glowed in post orgasm bliss, I wondered if other boys knew the female body the way Kael did and it made me start thinking about the girls Kael had touched before, kissed, and made moan his name as they came.

"You're so beautiful when you come," he said into my ear, tracing his fingers down my back.

I wanted to punish myself, remind myself that this is all most likely too good to be true, but the way he lifted my face with both his hands on my cheeks, and kissed me, made me forget about all the doubts swirling inside of me. He had that power, it both terrified and electrified me.

Chapter ☆ Fifty-Eight

MY SHIFT THE NEXT MORNING was so long that I could barely keep my eyes open. It was toward the end of Stewart's treatment and she was telling me about her upcoming move to Hawaii. It was a big deal for her—the promotion she'd been angling for had finally come through. Stewart was talking a mile a minute about her partner, about how optimistic she was about moving her small business to Hawaii. She designed these cute floral dresses and sold them online and in a few local boutiques, so her business was portable. Actually, she'd most likely do better in a beach town than here near the border of Georgia and Alabama, almost five hours away from the coast.

I was a little distracted while Stewart was talking. Every time I moved, I felt Kael coursing through my body. Twelve hours after that explosive moment and I could still remember every moment and every touch. I had barely landed back on earth.

"She's going to set up one of those little shops right

on the beach. She's convinced she's made for beach life," Stewart winced as I applied my harshest pressure. She was always full of knots, but she could handle the pain better than most.

I laughed a little while she continued talking. Her head was in the cradle and her voice was muffled a bit, but that's something you get used to. "I reminded her that we're going to be living *by* the post, since we can't live *on* post," she said. The military needed to catch up with the times. It blew my mind that she could serve her country the same way as a straight woman, but she couldn't tap into the same benefits for her family that a straight soldier could. Seemed like *don't ask, don't tell* was replaced by *don't care, won't pay*.

Kael once told me that he knew a gay woman who was on her deathbed in Germany from war related injuries and the Army never called her partner. Just her homophobic parents who left her to die alone. They hid behind regulation to get away with their horrendous negligence.

"I heard the on-post housing is really nice, but we did find a cute little house only a few miles from post. It has a small garden for the dogs. Speaking of dogs, it's next to impossible to bring them to Hawaii with us. People are telling me that their animals were quarantined for months before they would release them. That's a headache we're still trying to navigate."

I listened to Stewart talk for the rest of our session, but underneath every word, there was Kael. His calloused hands grazing my thighs, his mouth between them, spreading me open. Being exposed like that didn't frighten me. The way he touched me, the way he looked at me, it was as if he found something inside of me, made it blossom. I begged for his mouth to suck at my skin, pleaded for him to hook his fingers inside of me.

My tummy ached, my body missed his. After last night, I didn't feel so afraid of what was going to happen next with us. We didn't have a plan, but we didn't need one. We had time to go at our own pace and tailor this ... relationship to exactly what we wanted it to be. Right now that meant spending each and every waking moment questioning the world together.

I found myself counting down to the end of Stewart's treatment so that I could at least check my phone. I wanted to connect with him in any way I could. I needed to feel closer to him. Even just to see his name on my phone screen. To reread the texts he had sent this morning. I wanted to see the picture I took of us, lying in my bed with his arm draped lazily across my lap. His eyes were closed, a big smile on his face. Three more minutes. That seemed excruciatingly long. I didn't think Stewart would even notice since I was already just doing a sort of cool down on her, gently moving my hands over her skin to relax her after the deep tissue massage.

I waited it out for one more minute and ended her session with two minutes to go. I felt a little guilty, but a little rush too. I grabbed my phone from the shelf the moment my hands left her body.

No new messages, but I did have a missed call from my dad. Well, that could wait. I didn't feel like talking to him. The only thing on my mind was how Kael's mouth tasted like his cherry ChapStick and how hard he laughed when I tripped over a piece of tile in my bathroom. We had moved from my bedroom to my bathroom, still not able to let go, to stop touching, stop exploring one another.

"Karina?" Stewart's voice made me jump. My phone dropped to the floor, the picture of Kael and me open on the screen.

"Oh my God, sorry!" I hid my face under my hair as

I bent down to grab it. "I'll let you get dressed. See you in the lobby," I told her, leaving her in privacy.

When I stepped into the hallway, I had to bite my lips to stop myself from laughing. Typically, I would fret over something like that. Even something as small as that. Was Stewart uncomfortable or thinking that I lost my mind? This time, my brain didn't go there the way it normally did, until I forced it to. It naturally thought about how obsessed I was becoming with Kael and how big his smile would be when I told him about my phone mishap in front of Stewart.

What I felt for Kael was something between sweet infatuation and total annihilation. It was powerful and raw. He was fierce as an animal, and yet so kind and gentle. He was a bundle of contradictions. Every conflict there was. He had an animalistic nature. It was more secure and calm than the chaos of being on the verge of commitment. I was terrified because no matter how thrilling it was to immerse myself in Kael and the stillness he brought to my life, until last night my fears had made me fight against everything, even my own desire. As he slept on my chest, and again when he woke up in the middle of the night asking for someone named Nielson, then shouting Phillip's name, I made a promise to myself and to Kael that I would confront my fears, that I would stop letting the terrible unknown control everything. I deserved to let go and live—really live. And he deserved the version of me who didn't need to know where everything would fit.

And I was living, now that my doubts and insecurities had been lifted just enough enough to feel the buzz inside me turn from panic to excitement.

Was this what happiness was like?

Chapter * Fifty-Nine

"IT'S SO GOOD TO SEE YOU like this," Stewart told me. squeezing my hand as I handed her a pen and her receipt.

I smiled, shaking my head. "What? I've always been like this."

We both laughed and I felt that I was sharing something with her. Yes, this must be what happiness was like.

"See you next week," she said.

I was pleased for Stewart and the change ahead, but I was going to miss her so much.

I cleaned up my room as fast as I could while still being thorough. I threw towels in the laundry and checked the bathroom to make sure it was clean and that the scented wax burner inside didn't need another cube.

I didn't wait for Elodie to finish her client, just shouted a general *bye* in Mali's direction and left. Every day that passed I loved my house more and was thankful I only had to walk five minutes. I texted Kael to make sure he was still at my house.

* On my way. I missed you. I hope you're still in my bed ☺ *

I stared at the phone as I walked outside, turning into the alley. It was cool, the clouds blocking the sun. I thought, feeling only slightly ridiculous, that when I saw Kael, even the sky would shine brighter. A few more minutes. The texting bubble popped up, three little gray dots were there, then they weren't.

I looked up from my phone and down the alley. I could see Kael's Bronco parked on the street right in front of my house. *Curb appeal of a different sort*, I thought. But when I got to the end of the street and went to cross, my eyes landed on a black Buick parked in my driveway. I hadn't noticed it until now. I didn't need to see the US ARMY sticker on the bumper to know it was my dad's.

I felt as if someone had poured a bucket of cold water over me. I was nervous, now. Unsettled. I almost wanted to turn back around and hide behind the line of dumpsters in the alley while I text Kael and tell him to get rid of my dad. Honestly, I would have, and should have, but my dad's voice boomed through the yard and across the street to me.

The screen door was open and as I walked faster I could see the shape of my dad, his back turned to me. He was standing just inside my little house and his hands were raised like he was yelling. Kael's voice was next.

"You don't have a fucking clue!" he shouted. Chills ran from the tips of my fingers to the tips of my toes and something in my brain, some minuscule detail of a buried memory, told me to stop there, right before I reached the porch.

I stayed in the cover of the alley while they were going at it. And they were going at it hard, each word a blow.

Afghanistan. Cover-up. How dare you come here. Criminal. My family. My daughter. My daughter.

I hugged the wall and crouched down small, a vain attempt to protect myself from what I was hearing. But of course I didn't know what I was hearing. I couldn't make sense of it other than to understand that my dream of happily-ever-after had just ended. And a nightmare had begun.

Chapter * Sixty

"DON'T THINK I DIDN'T recognize you the moment you walked into my house," my dad said. He was angry. The last time I saw him this mad was when he saw "DIVORCE LAWYERS" in my mom's search history on the family computer. Yeah, my dad was the kind of guy who checked up on his wife's search history.

"Why didn't you say something then? If you were so worried about my intentions with your daughter?" Kael's words stuck to me.

What was this? What was happening?

I felt like I was in a fun house, mirrors cut in weird shapes, bent to confuse you with a distorted vision of reality. What you *thought* was reality. Everything around me was warped, I could barely feel my feet on the grass.

"I wasn't sure at first. Then I asked Mendoza if it was you. You've grown up a lot since then."

"Because I was a child. A few months out of high school."

"You're still a child. Going around asking questions, sticking your nose where it doesn't belong."

"They came to me. I got pulled in for questioning because he tried to blow his fucking head off, okay?" Kael was trying to tame himself. I could tell by the way his breath pushed through his words.

"That was unfortunate, I'll grant you. But this can't get out." My dad's voice was lower to the ground now. He was menacing. More than a little scared, too. "We'll all be fucked! Do you not realize that, boy?"

"Don't call me boy! I'm not your fucking boy."

I stood up, not caring now if they saw me.

I knew I needed to go inside, for my dad's sake. I couldn't let this escalate, but I knew that I couldn't trust either of them to tell me the whole truth when I got there. I hated that.

"We'll all be fucked. I'm retiring, you're so close to that medical discharge you want," he told Kael. "Mendoza—he's getting the help he needs and can stay enlisted. We can't have people snooping around."

"Snooping around? Innocent people died and you fucking knew and hid it!" Kael shouted at my father as I opened the door. When he saw me his anger turned to panic.

With a slower reflex, my dad turned around to see what had Kael's attention.

"Karina, I told you about him." My dad pointed from Kael to me. He was always quick at trying to slap a Band-Aid on a problem. "I told you he was trouble and you didn't take me seriously."

"What the hell is going on?" My heart was pounding. Kael looked different, like a stranger again. It made my blood run cold.

"Tell me what you're talking about!" I yelled, and when neither of them spoke, I screamed, "Now!"

Kael reached for me but I jerked away. "I can tell you what's going on, your dad's a crooked son of a bitch and has—"

"Bullshit!" my dad tried to interrupt.

"Let him speak!" I snapped at my dad. My hands were shaking. My whole body was shaking.

"It's him, Karina. He's a senile narcissist who has convinced himself of some plot that I'm with you because of him. It's not true, he's the cause of all of this!" Kael's veil of composure was slipping. I wanted to comfort him. I wanted to run away.

I stood there between them as their truths swirled around me, trying to stick.

"Mendoza ... the MP who fucking came at us! He's behind all of it. My dad balled his hands into fists. "Speaking of military careers, did he tell you he's on the verge of getting himself a dishonorable discharge?"

I could feel my face changing colors. The blood was rising to the surface as my chest throbbed under my work top.

I tried to read Kael, but I couldn't. I couldn't pull back the screen to see the Kael I was falling for.

"At this point you don't even care, do you, Martin? You have your bags all packed to move up to Atlanta. Word travels fast. You bought a house there, right? Another project for you to destroy." My dad's golf shirt was pulling, untucking from his jeans and his skin was red, all blotchy. Like a liar, or an innocent man on trial. I couldn't tell.

"You bought a place in Atlanta?" I turned to Kael. A lump in my throat.

He was speechless. I wasn't having it.

"Did you?" I pushed hard at his chest, but he didn't move. He was in his uniform. The green and tan had always been an omen to the bad shit in my life. Looks like that hasn't changed.

I pushed him again and he latched onto my wrists. "It's not like that. He's twisting everything, Karina. He is. This is me." He tapped his fingers against his chest.

"He falsified a report, don't let him fool you. He signed that paper knowing damn well what happened. Are you denying it, Martin?" My dad was goading him. I knew the tone. I had despised it ever since I had learned to decipher it.

"Are you denying that you came into my office, shivering, your leg all bandaged, and signed your name on the bottom of that page? You signed it. Mendoza signed it. Lawson signed it. All of you! And now you decide, almost two years later to come back and dig up old bones?"

My dad was in full-on officer mode. I listened obediently. So did Kael. It was sickening to watch the way my dad knew just how to warp the tone of his voice to whip soldiers into submission—anyone, really.

"His friend died, Kare—"

"Don't call me that," I managed. My stomach turned. My dad's ashy skin fell in loose folds around his jaw. That, combined with his shock of white hair made him look like a villain. Kael looked wounded and hurt, more hero than antihero. But looks can be deceiving. I knew that. I wanted both of them to disappear. The façade of a normal life … this stability I had convinced myself that I had with Kael was shattered. Shattered into tiny little shards too dangerous even to attempt to pick up.

"His friend was shot in the firefight when Mendoza murdered those innocents. Do you know how much investigating goes into those types of claims? You are children." Now he was talking to both of us. "I was helping them! I saw their faces when they returned. You." He pointed an accusing finger at Kael. "I watched you pull his body into camp, barely able to walk yourself."

"You were protecting your own ass!" Kael snarled at my dad. "You didn't give a fuck about us or our lives!"

My dad was talking over him. My head was spinning.

"Tell your daughter how you use the lives of young men and women to get promotions and medals. Tell her that because of you damn near threatening us, my fucking friend is losing his mind over the guilt and he can't even talk to anyone about it because he ..." Kael stepped toward my dad. I gave up trying to stand between them. "Tell her that Mendoza begged you to let him turn himself in. Those victims haunt him and you're keeping him from healing so your retirement won't be at stake!"

"Those victims haunt him? Are you hearing yourself, Martin? You're a soldier. I'm a soldier. We've seen and done things most people can't dream of." My dad was talking to Kael in his own language. I could hear the words, but unlike them, I couldn't call up images of death and destruction like they could.

"You know what will haunt him? If he can't feed his family and his wife is left alone with those kids and no paycheck. That's haunting. You need to man up. You and him. This isn't some fucking video game. This is grown man shit and if you can't handle it, you're a waste of a soldier. Either you want to protect your friend and his family, or you want him to heal. You don't get both in the real world."

My dad always invoked "the real world" when he

wanted to make a point, the point being that he was a grown-up and everyone else—me or Austin, or in this case Kael—were not.

"Going about this by sleeping with my daughter isn't the way to resolve this, unless you want to get yourself in more trouble." My dad was threatening Kael, openly. Then he turned to me. "He's trying to strip my rank before my retirement and I won't allow it. I'm sorry, honey." My dad was working hard to compose himself, shifting now to the dad costume he's so quick to throw on and off. It was eerie how he could change his voice, his stature, to match the role he was playing. At the moment, it was concerned parent.

"This goes way beyond you and whatever feelings you have. He's putting people in danger, including himself by trying to shine a light on a closed case that not one of us need to open up. This will bring attention to you too. Did you think of that?" I couldn't tell if he was talking to me or Kael.

"All I did was ask Lawson if it was you." Kael turned to me. "I didn't know, Karina. I would never lie about that. I didn't tell you the rest because—"

"Because he knew it was better for everyone." My dad interrupted.

I stared at Kael while he tried to explain himself. I tried to find my footing, my center of gravity. I needed to process everything but it was beyond me. I looked at Kael. I searched his eyes but I couldn't find what I was looking for. He was blank, shutting down, taking my silence as doubt.

"I didn't even recognize your dad at first, I swear." Kael reached for my hands. The oven timer went off randomly and I thought it was pretty ironic the way it was beeping and beeping, almost as if my house was trying to help me escape the chaos.

My dad started in on me next. "He was using you to get back at me, Karina. Trying to take you away from me. I had your picture on my desk, everyone saw it. Think about it, how distant you've been lately. The missed dinner. Not returning my calls. He put that in your head, didn't he?"

I thought about it. I thought about it hard. I thought about how easy it was for my dad to twist the truth. He was so good at it. He should have been a politician.

And yet, Kael had told me that my dad was complicated, but I had shrugged it off. And he had told me that I should give myself a break by not going over to my dad's for dinner. I had shrugged that off too. And what about Kael and the discharge and the house in Atlanta. What about the sudden change in his behavior, how he went from being flaky and unpredictable to constantly at my side. What about the way he told me I could trust him? He peppered my face with gentle kisses after he'd had his way with me. I could throw up just thinking about it.

"Karina, you're my daughter. I have no reason to lie to you."

At that, I laughed. "That in itself is a lie."

"You barely know him. Think about it." My dad was talking to me like I was a child. Like he was on the verge of telling me that I was overreacting, *kids your age are so emotional.*

"How easily you're influenced scares me and he's irresponsible, Karina. Risking his career to ask questions about something that's over, done with."

"I wasn't asking questions of anyone except Lawson," Kael said at the same time that I said, "How easily

I'm influenced?"

"You brought Mendoza to mental health. Did you not? I have eyes and ears all over this post. Did you forget that?" My dad had given up being the concerned parent. He was pure wolf now.

"He was in his front yard, waving a gun around in the air. He told me he didn't deserve to live." The words tore through Kael. I could feel it. I felt everything he felt on top of my own emotions. My back was close to breaking from the weight of it all.

"He told me he was a monster. A monster. Gabriel Mendoza thinks he's a monster? If he is, we're all fucking Satan himself." Kael's voice was creeping into the darkness that made me split in two. Half of me was terrified that this was going to swallow him whole. He needed me to pull him out of this quicksand, but how could I when I didn't know who or what to believe. I knew both of them were pulling at me, using me as a pawn to hurt the other. Even if it wasn't premeditated on Kael's part—and I honestly couldn't imagine it being true—I couldn't completely dismiss it either. There were still lies. Lots of lies.

"Karina, honey. You know right from wrong. You may not think I've been the best father to you and your brother, but you know that I would do anything for you and for the soldiers under my command. I've dedicated my life to serving this country. I meant no harm when I tried to help them. Tell him that, Karina, if he doesn't want a dishonorable discharge." My dad held his hands up like he was praying.

I had only seen him do that once before when my mom was packing her bags, the first time. He followed her around the living room, telling her all the reasons their life was *fine*. Not good, but fine.

You'll be fine, he told her.

Everything will be fine.

Between his begging hands and the almost believable devastation in his eyes now as he looked at me, I could see a flicker of what my mom saw in him all those years ago.

"Come on, Karina. You don't want that for him. It will ruin his future."

Kael was slipping away from my little living room. He was leaning against the drywall that he had patched up after I tried to hang up a clock and ripped half the wall down. My house, like my personal life, was becoming too much for me to repair.

"He can't look at his kid's face without seeing their faces. You know that? It's eating him up. He's not right in the head over it. None of us are." Kael had torn me open, devoured my body and mind in such a short time. I would have done anything to heal his pain any other time since I met him, but not then, when everything was foggy.

"We're all like that. We all have demons that keep us up at night. He can go in for PTSD if he needs to, but you have to stop poking a sleeping dragon. That's the last warning. You're putting us all in danger, even her." He pointed at me, using me to chip away at Kael.

If my dad thought Kael was deceiving me, why would he think he cared that he was putting me in danger? My dad was a liar. The good kind. Not good for anyone but himself, but still the very, very good kind. My mom told tales about the man she met her senior year of high school and how he wooed her when she served him a stack of pancakes every Tuesday. That's where the Fischer family tradition stemmed from.

The man she fell in love with had soft eyes and a

thoughtful heart. Supposedly, he even called her sunshine, like she used to call me. That man had slowly disappeared, dissolving into a manipulative piece of havoc that I had stumbled in to.

"Think about it, Martin. Don't jeopardize your future. I'll make sure that medical discharge goes smoothly as long as you can promise me the same about my retirement."

There he was scheming in front of me. Asking Kael to ignore the pain of his friend and make a selfish choice to appease my father.

"You're disgusting," I told my dad before Kael could agree or disagree to his deal.

"Stay out of this." He brushed me off. There he was, diminishing my intelligence, my strength to make my own choices. He was feeding off of my insecurities. Was Kael too?

I looked at Kael, then my dad. "Both of you, get out." My voice was shaky in its delivery, but the words made it to their ears.

"Martin, don't be a fool and get yourself tied up in something you can't handle. There will be no more lifelines after this," my dad continued despite my very blatant request.

"Get out of my house," I said, louder this time.

Kael begged with his eyes and my dad with his voice. "Get out. Now," I said as Elodie stepped into the house. She took in the scene in front of her.

"Should I—" she began to ask.

"No. You stay. They were just leaving," I told her.

My dad was the first to give. To not break character in front of Elodie, I was sure. I didn't care what it was, only that he walked out of my living room and the door shut behind him.

Kael was harder. He was shaking. I could see his shoulders shaking under his ACUs and it took every last drop of ability within me to repeat it to him.

"Get out of my house," I said with as much conviction as a broken voice and heart could manage.

"Karina, please listen to me."

I held up my hand. "If you want me to ever speak to you again, get out of my house and let me breathe." I refused to raise my eyes to him. I knew better.

I only had a few breaths left in me until I would collapse in his arms, healing us both. I could see the pain burning bright in his eyes as he turned and finally walked out of the door.

Chapter ⭐ Sixty-One

WHEN I WOKE UP the next morning, my head was throbbing. My body ached. My heart was broken. It all came flooding back to me.

Kael.

My dad.

Their history.

My dad's accusation that Kael was using me as a pawn in some revenge plot for what happened in Afghanistan. What they did there. What Kael had to go through. What Kael had covered up.

Part of me thought my dad was completely delusional, obsessively creating this entire thing in his head. It was a just a coincidence that Kael and my dad had ever known each another. A coincidence, like bumping into an old friend at the movies, or thinking about someone you haven't heard from in a while and then seeing their name pop up next to a text. The fact that my dad and Kael were in the same Company was like that. A very extraordinary circumstance. But that they had actual contact while overseas at the same time. And the way Elodie's husband just happened to be Kael's close friend. That was pushing it even for someone who wanted to believe. The pain of it made me want to torment myself just to distract from the agony I was already feeling.

This was exactly what I had been avoiding with Kael.

I knew that, sooner or later, he would reveal himself to be exactly what he was, what we all are, the most selfish of creatures. I shouldn't have ignored that little voice inside that told me we were headed for nowhere fast and running out of gas. I felt it, the way he withdrew from me the moment we were close. It was fucked up the way he cracked me open, turned me into a freaking Blossom Family maple tree, my deepest private thoughts pouring out of me and into him. He soaked them up, but kept the tap closed when it came to himself.

I got a line here or there, a little image of his former self lying in my bed in the middle of the night, wrapped in each other. Everything was different now, even if I did believe that our relationship wasn't premeditated. He promised me, over and over, that he wanted to try this, whatever it was.

Was, was, was, I reminded myself.

While I got dressed I tried to think about something, anything other than Kael. Other his brilliant deep mind. I could spend days inside, picking around his light. He was everything a man was supposed to be, the first one I had ever loved, and he turned out to be just another factory model.

Even so, my body clung to the hot flash that he was in my life. And then I thought about my own advice to

Sammy after she and Austin broke up again, that he was only a teen tiny little part of her life, that in a year he wouldn't matter. In five years, he'd barely exist in her memory. She said she'd never forget him because she'd always be around me, and that where I was, Austin wasn't far behind, but things change. Obviously. I walked around my room and with each step I felt my body ache from last night. Every ounce of pain was felt through my entire body.

Even so, my body didn't get the memo that we hated Kael now.

I wanted his touch. I needed to feel him, skin against skin. I couldn't get him out of my mind, he had gotten so comfortable there. My fingers ached for him as I dug through my drawers for something thin and comfortable. I cancelled work for the day, ignoring the questions in Mali's voice. I hung up before I started to cry. I focused on getting dressed. Of course today would have been a short day at work, and of course Kael and I had plans to drive as far away from this town as we could. We were preparing questions for each other, gathering music. Just the night before, Kael was making plans to thread our lives together.

Or so I thought.

Maybe he was just making plans to avenge whatever the fuck happened during that deployment.

How had everything shattered so quickly?

I thought that if I cleaned myself up, if I had a shower and brushed my teeth, I might feel a little more like myself. A little less than a zombie, anyway. But when I got to the bathroom and saw his tube of cinnamon toothpaste, rolled up at the end, I nearly choked. I hated the way this felt. This was bad. This was almost worse than the good had been good. I wasn't sure if any of it was worth it. I never wanted to feel this again. Right then and there I decided that I wasn't ever going to allow myself to step inside this danger zone.

I grabbed his gross toothpaste and tossed it into the trashcan. When I missed, it cracked against the drywall and a black line spread across at least five inches. I was starting to despise this house and it knew. That's why it was falling apart right along with me.

Chapter * Sixty-Two

THE SHOWER HAD HELPED a little, but I still looked like hell. I threw on black leggings and a T-shirt and towel dried my hair and sprayed a little salt spray throughout. It was a lifesaver on my thick hair. I wanted the day to go fast, that's all I wanted. I pinched my cheeks to bring a little color to the surface.

I heard Elodie's voice as soon as I stepped into the hallway. It sounded like she was hushing someone, but she was alone with her laptop. Phillips voice was coming through the speaker.

"Don't lie to me," he said.

I thought I heard him wrong, but he said it again. "Don't lie to me, Elodie. Cooper's wife told me that you were over there. His wife tells him everything, unlike mine."

Elodie was crying. I had to hold onto the doorjamb in the hallway to stop myself from getting into her business. I didn't know what Philip was talking about, but I knew I didn't like the sound of his voice. I had never seen that side of him, or heard it. I couldn't tell if his wife was used to it or not.

"I'm not lying. We stopped there for an hour at most. We went to the meetings, then to that house. There weren't any men there," she told him.

I tapped my fingers against the wall to let Elodie know I was coming. She perked up and wiped at her tears as I knew she would.

"Phillip, Karina is here," she said. To warn him, I guess.

I didn't know what was going on between them, but I knew I didn't like the way he was speaking to my friend, who was swollen with his child.

"Hey, Karina," Phillip said, his voice nice and friendly, opposite of what it just was.

I threw him a bland "hey," and walked into the kitchen. Dishes were piling up in the sink. The laundry in the corner of the kitchen was overflowing in the basket. I couldn't even blame the mess on my emotional despair, because the breakup had happened barely twelve hours ago. I managed to take one bite of an orange before he surrounded me again, the taste of his lips on mine the first time he kissed me. I felt the warmth of him, tasted the sweet citrus that clung to him the first time he kissed me and I tossed the orange in the trashcan.

This was getting to be a habit, tossing things into the trashcan.

Elodie signed off Skype and met me in the kitchen. Her eyes were bloodshot; the tip of her nose was red as fire.

"Everything okay?" I asked, licking the last of the orange juice off of my lips.

She nodded and sat down across from me at the kitchen table.

I didn't want to press her, but she was obviously not okay.

"Elodie, you know you can talk to me?"

"You have enough problems." She tried to smile, to be strong.

"Elodie, we can talk about anything. I have time for you."

She shook her head. "No, no. I'm fine. Really, it's just drama from the other soldiers. Why is there so much drama? Don't they have anything better to do?" she asked me, sniffling and rubbing her nose.

"How are *you*?" she asked, reaching for me. I pretended not to notice as I lowered my hands onto my lap.

"I'm fine. Just tired," I lied.

If she could lie to my face, I could do the same.

Chapter * *Sixty-Three*

I SPENT MY DAY READING. Elodie was working and going straight from there to one of the other wives' houses. Instead of worrying about her, I tried to do the things I liked to do before I met Kael. It wasn't so long ago. That meant reading an entire poetry book, the new hipster style of poems with black covers and catchy titles. I'm a sucker for good marketing, so I ordered three more from Amazon. Every time I ordered something online I felt like I was receiving some sort of adult points for having enough money in my checking account to be able to afford it. After I scanned Amazon for too long and talked myself out of buying a pressure washer that I would most definitely never use—the one I was eyeing was called The Clean Machine—I got on Facebook. A quick scroll would clear my head. I mean, it was so much easier to focus on everyone else's problems than my own.

I felt .better—shamefully so—when I saw that Melanie Pierson was getting divorced. Melanie was in the grade above me and slept with Austin her senior year. She pretended to like me, no doubt to get closer to my brother. Until one day we were swimming and she saw the little white lines on the tops of my thighs. I hadn't noticed them, didn't even know what stretch marks were, until she made her hand look like a paw and called me "tiger." Just another person who tried to boost her own poor self-image by making fun of someone else.

Melanie no doubt thought that she would escape this town by marrying a soldier, and look at her now. Coming home with her tail between her legs. She updates everyone on everything she does, so I knew that she was moving back one week to the day. Literally.

I moved on from her to my uncle who had posted pictures of rocks that look like people. Boredom and lack of motivation will do that to a man. I wondered how people would respond if I posted a broken heart emoji. Or a lengthy paragraph about my heartbreak and how it was eating me up from the inside out, and how I probably deserve to feel every bit of this agony for being so desperate for attention that I lost control of myself and my life.

I wondered if Melanie would have the same reaction to my misfortune as I had to hers. Did she see me as Austin's bitchy sister who was always tagging along, the girl who wore a bathing suit that showed too much, things she found repulsive enough to pick at in front of everyone we knew. I wondered about Sammy too, and if she would see my post and feel bad for her best friend, or whatever we were supposed to be. We barely talked anymore, but I still considered her my best friend. At least when anyone asked. Not that anyone did. A habit, I guess.

I closed out of Facebook before I could follow through with my social experiment. I moved on to the porch. It was the perfect temperature outside, warm enough not to have to

wear a jacket, but not too warm as to be hot and sticky. I took
the poetry book and a beer that Kael left in my fridge and
spent the next hour outside in the fresh air. I had one drink
of the dark amber beer and all I could taste was Kael.

He was everywhere. He had become everything. I
turned the pages in my book and felt like every single poem
was read in Kael's voice, I skipped from page to page.

Your skin is dark

As the velvet night

Your starred eyes

Are tenants in the constellations

I closed the book and tossed it, watching as it went
skidding across the porch. *The Chaos of Longing* is exactly
what I felt and I wanted the collection as far away from me as
they could get. I kicked the little pink book and watched as it
disappeared into the patch of weeds next to my porch.

Then I felt guilty. It wasn't the poet's fault that my
first love only lasted a week. I crawled over to grab it and
dug my hand into the stringy weeds. They were too long,
too unmanageable, growing into unpredictable vegetation
overgrowing my yard. This little house was the only thing
that wasn't going to turn out to be something that it wasn't.
I knew what I was getting when I signed the dotted line for
the basically abandoned house at the end of a strip mall
covered street. The house was exactly what I knew it was.
Sure, it was falling apart and unkempt, but that's what I had
signed up for. I was working my way back to making it
beautiful. My house. For me. And yet, it had become
another thing that reminded me of Kael. I began to pull at
the weeds in the yard. I needed a distraction and had the rest
of the day to do as I pleased, as long as Mali didn't drive past
my house and see me out here yanking the weeds from the
yard. Minutes went by and I moved on from the weeds to

sweep the gravel back into my driveway. It had started to take over my yard.

I thought about Kael and his remodel plans for his duplex. He had a talent for home design and I hated that he told me I should pave my driveway and now every time I see the gray stone gravel, I'm would think about him.

Don't even think about that, I told myself. Possibly out loud, but at that point I couldn't be sure. *Don't let him make you turn on this house. It's all you have.*

Chapter * Sixty-Four

AT FIRST, I THOUGHT the white Bronco pulling up to my house was a mirage. The sun was setting so I had to have been out there for at least two hours. My mind was obviously playing tricks on me. I stood up and stared, watching unwavering as he pulled up.

When he got out of his truck, it hit me. He was at my house and I was letting him walk toward me.

"Karina." His voice danced around me, hypnotizing me.

I opened my mouth to speak and heard my dad's voice in my head, followed my Kael's, then my dad's again. I didn't have enough time to figure out what I felt, or what I was going to do.

"You can't be here. I need time, Kael," I told him just as he reached the grass. My back hurt as I stood there with one hand on my hip and one blocking my eyes from the burning sun.

"The yard looks good." He looked and pointed past

me, ignoring what I said.

"Kael. You can't be here."

"Karina, please," he pleaded. I only caught a tiny glimpse of his face, the sadness in his eyes as he used them to steer me back to him. I moved my hand down, like a coward so I couldn't see his face.

"I need time. I'm not the kind of girl who likes to be chased, Kael. I won't tell you again," I said the same thing to him as I did to Estelle when she called to try and butter me up. At that point the only people who I could trust were Austin and Elodie. And with the way my luck was with people, they were probably going to betray me too.

Kael was staring at me, I could feel it. He was registering everything I was feeling, absorbing it, the way we both do when it comes to people.

"Let me fall in love with you, Karina."

His voice was so soft that I was skeptical whether I heard him correctly, or not.

"What?"

He stepped closer and I walked backward, putting even more distance between us.

"I'm so close, Karina. Let me fall in love with you. You know me." He touched his chest and I shook my head profusely.

How dare he throw that word around like it's nothing, like I was going to just forgive him because he used that word.

"Don't you dare use that against me," I spit into the night air between us.

The trees shook as my anger grew. I told myself it was Mother Nature helping me out, giving me strength for this.

"I'm not, Kare," he said, coming closer again. I dug my nails into my closed palm until I was close to breaking skin.

"Don't you call me that," I warned him. "That house in Atlanta? You were going to move without telling me!" I didn't care how loud my voice was or who heard it. "I don't know you at all," I said, mimicking his signature flat tone. I wanted him to hear it and feel the sting of it. He must have found something in my expression when my eyes finally met his that told him to back off, because he put his hands in the air and turned around and walked away.

I collapsed in the grass after he pulled away and stayed there until the stars dried my tears and moon glared at me to go to my own bed and leave hers.

Chapter ✳ Sixty-Five

MALI WAS OKAY with me the next day. I thought that maybe she'd give me a hard time, but she knew something was up and gave me the space I needed. I concentrated on my clients, on making them whole. They didn't need to feel as broken as I did. My shift passed uneventfully. Slow, but uneventfully. The short walk home was hard. I kept thinking of the last time I had taken the same steps, how I had started out in joy and ended in despair.

Life went on like that for a couple of days. I worked. I slept. I may have watched a couple of movies with Elodie. I can't be sure. Really, everything was a blur. I'm not sure when it was, how many days post breakup, that I had come home from work to find Austin waiting for me.

His face was red and his hair was a mess. His hands were rigid, white fingers shaking. There were no cars in the driveway or parked on the street, so I couldn't figure out how he got there.

"What's wrong? Are you okay?" I asked, mildly

panicked. He'd only been to visit once since he got back.

He shook his head. "Me and Dad got into it."

I sat down next to him on the cold cement. "Into it yelling? Or into it, fighting?"

"Both. I swung on him."

"Austin!"

"He charged at me though. He made me lose it, Kare. You know how he is. He sits there like he's high and mighty. *Do this. Don't do that. When I was your age ...*"

"I know, I know. I've had my share of lectures, believe me."

Austin continued his rant as if he hadn't even heard me. "You know, he doesn't care about her. He doesn't give a fuck about her. When I asked if she'd been in touch or anything he just laughed. I swear Kare, he fucking laughed. Right in front of Estelle. You don't think he's heard from her, right? You still haven't?"

I shook my head. I was used to shaking my head when it came to my mother. *She. Her. My mother.* I knew exactly who he was talking about.

"No." My insides were scalding.

"She's close though. I know she is. I can feel it."

"Austin." I reached for his hand. We were never a touchy family, except for our mother. When we were little she would hug me for the smallest thing, like a happy face sticker on a book report, or cleaning my room without being asked. Even when I got older she would run her hands down my back almost every night before bed. Sometimes she'd trace words over my pajama top with her long nails.

Nite nite.

Love you.

Kare bear.

"You can't worry about her, Austin. She's an adult.

She's made her own choices. You'll drive yourself crazy if you obsess over her." I was such a hypocrite.

I couldn't stop thinking about my mother, no matter how hard I tried. I'd see her in line at the grocery store. I'd hear her voice in my head as I washed the dishes. I'd climb into bed at night and cry myself to sleep. She was everywhere. She was nowhere. And I was so Goddamned pissed at her and the world. How could she take off like that? How could she leave and not get in touch with us? How could she have this relentless hold on us?

"I'm tired of this place, Karina. I just want to go somewhere else. Not back to Rudy's, just … somewhere else. Don't you feel the itch anymore?"

Wow. The itch. That brought me back.

It felt so long ago, those days when we'd plan our escape. We plotted everything right down to the last detail. I'd wait tables and he'd change tires and pump gas, depending on where we'd land. I'd find a nice restaurant with gingham table cloths, and a sassy older waitress named Phyllis who would call me "kid" and take me under her wing. Austin would work hard and stay out of trouble. He'd be early for his shift most days. The proprietor of the gas station would notice what a good employee he was and after a while would show him how to fix cars. Austin would be good at that, fixing cars. If only he'd put his mind to solving problems, instead of creating them.

We came up with so many adventures back then, hanging out on the futon in Austin's room, an hour past bedtime. We knew they wouldn't notice. They never came in to check on us anymore. We were just kids and already we thought of our parents as *they*. As *them and us*.

I told Austin that they didn't come in to check on us because we were older—almost twelve, then thirteen and fourteen. He was fifteen when he stopped asking why. We'd talk for hours, dreaming of our future travels, the small town where we'd make our home. We'd learn to fit in, be whoever we wanted to be. He'd be that mechanic. I'd be that waitress. Or maybe he'd be a musician and I'd be a painter. Or a glassblower.

I wanted Austin to believe more than I wanted it myself. I spun the words tightly around him, pulling him in closer until I could tell he had accepted the possibility of a better future. And when I could feel him attach to the dream we were drawing for ourselves, I'd relax my own breathing and sometimes even I could believe in that glorious future. I spoke in a loud whisper those nights, cupping my hands over Austin's ears to distract him from the waves of misery coming from our parents' bedroom down the hall.

"Where is there to go?" I asked him.

"Arizona. Barcelona. Anywhere. Hell, I'd go live with our grand—"

"Do you even know where your passport is?" I asked.

"Yes. And yours. They're both at Dad's, in the drawer."

Before our orders to Georgia, my dad told us we were going to be sent to Germany. My mom was as close to happy as I'd seen her in a very long time. She had always wanted to visit Munich; apparently one of her friends had moved there after high school.

We rushed to get our passports. Mom spent her time mapping out trains across Europe and learning basic words in German. It was *guten morgen,* when she woke us each morning, and *guten tag* when we returned from school in the afternoon.

"Kare," she said to me one day. "Listen to this: '*Schönes wetter heute, nicht wahr?*'" She was beaming from ear to ear. "I just said, 'It's lovely weather today, isn't it?'"

"Mom," I kidded her. "It's raining.

"Oh, don't be so literal," she said, laughing. How about this one: "*Das sind meine kinder, Karina und Austin. Ja, sie sind sehr gut erzogen. Vielen dank.*"

Austin ran into the room when he heard his name. Mom beamed at him. "I just said 'These are my children, Karina and Austin. Yes, they are very well behaved. Thank you.'"

"You just said that Austin is well-behaved? Mom! You're hilarious. You can't deceive those poor Germans like that. I give Austin three days before he's breaking some international law or something."

"Ha. Ha. Ha. Karina," Austin said.

We laughed and my mom made homemade spaghetti that night.

It was easy to remember that happy time. There were so few of them.

Chapter ∗ Sixty-Six

MOM WAS BACK. She was lively without being manic. Clear and in charge without being hyper-focused. Understanding and forgiving, she was like those TV moms who always seem to know the right thing to say. She spent her time cleaning and sorting, boxing up all our stuff. Her collectable dishes and vintage jewelry. Our toys and clothes. The TV hadn't had a break like that since before she started to fade.

"They'll be worth something someday," Mom said, going through her old magazines. "Once the printed word is completely extinct." She liked to warn us about the future almost as much as she liked us to know how well-prepared she was for it.

I was sitting at the kitchen table that afternoon; Mom was standing behind me, pulling my hair through a sadistic highlighting cap. I suffered through it gladly, though, just to have hair like the girls named Ashley and Tiffany. Our house was packed up well before the movers were scheduled to pack everything for us. Mom kept her vinyls out though, and even started singing along again when Alanis Morrissette was at her feistiest.

"It only takes two hours from Paris to London. Can you believe that?" she asked. She was dancing around me wearing those weird plastic gloves. When "You Oughta Know" came on she punched her hands through the air like it was her fight song. I remember how she looked that day. She was wearing eyeliner and had decorated her long brown hair with little braids randomly scattered. She was beautiful, happy.

"Karina, we are going to have so much fun. Imagine the people we will meet. Everyone is different there, mixed around, and no one cares like they do here. People won't judge us. It's going to be incredible, Kare," she promised.

Why is it that happiness is always so short-lived when despair seems to stick around like an unwanted guest?

It was the next day while Austin and I were at school that my dad broke the news. We were no longer going to Europe. A change of command meant that we would be stationed in Georgia, just two states away. My dad said it was better for his chances of promotion. My mom said it was worse for what was left of her soul.

The next morning, I found an empty bottle of gin in the bathroom. I bagged it up and carried it outside to the big trash can, helping her hide the evidence. Enabling, I think they call it. At that point with my mom, it wasn't the empty bottle that worried me, it was the fact that since it was gin, it meant she must have run out of vodka.

Chapter ☆ Sixty-Seven

"DO YOU WANT to stay here for a little bit?" I looked at Austin and for a second, I could see her in him, something around the eyes, about the shape of his mouth. We'd always be a mash up of our parents and that horrified me.

"No," he sighed. "I don't know. I need to figure my shit out. I can't do that from your couch."

"It's cheaper than Barcelona," I joked.

"I was thinking about staying with Martin." His words punched me. A sucker punch.

"Martin?"

I was going to make him say his name.

"Kael."

"Since when are you two friends like that?" I couldn't even hide the hurt in my voice.

"I don't know, a week or so." He laughed. I couldn't breathe. "He's been at Mendoza's a lot."

"Seriously?"

I couldn't believe him.

"Look, I know something happened between you two and I know it ended. And that's all I know. You told me it was nothing serious, that the shit with Dad was a mix-up, right?" he looked me straight in the eyes. Daring me to be honest.

That was a dare I wouldn't take.

"So unless there's more to it, more that you want to share with me, I don't see the problem with me crashing with him. He's the only one beside Mendoza who just chills at home and doesn't bring chicks home every night. He doesn't get in trouble."

I wanted to throw up. I was relieved and devastated. It was a wretched combination.

"I'm not saying not to be friends with him." I let out a breath of frustration. "I just …" I couldn't think of a valid reason to tell Austin not to stay with Kael unless I wanted to tell him everything and that just wasn't possible. He would hate all of them, maybe even Mendoza too.

It was enough that I hated them.

"If you don't want me to, just say it. Just know that I can't stay at Dad's anymore, Kare. I can't do it."

I nodded. I understood needing to get away from our dad's. He should stay at Kael's house. Or Martin's house. I liked to think of him as Martin, as the soldier who was just doing what he was told, who had offered to help my brother when he needed it. Not the man who I fell for, the man I fell too deeply and foolishly for.

I hadn't seen him for a while, except when I scrolled through my Instagram, looking at the row of pictures of us.

He had changed me so much in such a short amount of time. The captions seemed so clever then, "Atlanta refuses to see us now," I wrote under a picture of us in the car, a copy of *Fifty Shades of Grey* on the dashboard. Preparing for the upcoming movie, I was doing a reread, and it was even more exciting when I had a man who liked to get bossy in my bed when I closed the book. My tire blew right as we were leaving for our trip to Atlanta, the trip that never happened.

I had to shake it off, to actually shake my head, to stop the thought of Kael invading my mind. My hands were trembling. I thought I was over this.

"Dad's calling me again," Austin said, changing the subject.

"Are you going to answer?"

"No."

A car drove by, a little boy in the backseat waved at us. Austin waved back, even smiling for the child.

"I got a job, too," Austin told me a minute or so later. The sun was going down and the sky was changing colors around us.

"Really?" I pepped up for him. "That's great news," I told him. I meant it. He hadn't had a job since he got fired from the drive-in. "Where is it?"

He hesitated. "It's with Martin."

"Of course it is." I hung my head between my knees.

"He's flipping that duplex, you know? The one he lives in. He's paying me, Lawson, everyone to help him. I'm going to get more hours in than everyone else since they all have to work during the week. It's just like tearing up carpet, shit like that."

I needed to be happy for my brother, even if he was wrapping his life around the one person I was trying to detangle mine from.

"You two are a lot alike, you know that?" he said, a smile on his face. It was the first time he looked even close to happy since I walked up.

I shook my head. "That's so not true."

"Whatever you say, Karina."

"How's Katie?" I asked, flipping the attention back to him. I knew they were back together, I saw it on his Facebook. I guess her ex-boyfriend was out of the picture for now.

"Good. She's good for me. She keeps me in line. And she wakes up early for school, so I go out less, you know?" He sounded so proud of himself and I let him be. We were two totally different humans even if we shared a womb.

"That's good. I'm happy for you," I said to him. I laid back on the porch, resting my head close to his. We were almost kids again.

"Thanks. I won't bring him around if you don't want me to, but he's really helping me out."

I stared at the sky, begging for the stars to come out and play. I wanted to know that I could count on them. I wanted to be certain of something.

"It's fine. I'm seeing someone anyway." The words slid from my tongue, devious as the lie itself.

"You are?" he asked.

"Yeah. I don't want to talk about it," I told Austin, knowing he would shy away from anything complicated when given the chance.

"Okay," he agreed. "So you can't be mad that he's picking me up here like any minute." He said the words fast, as if it would change their meaning.

"Austin," I whined his name, twisted it around my tongue. "Fine. I'm going inside. You really need to get a car."

"I will, now that I have a job." He beamed, easing my pain a little.

"I'm proud of you, really. And see, you didn't have to join the Army after all," I joked. I knew he wouldn't have gone through with it, no matter how much our dad tried to force it on him.

I heard the roar of Kael's truck before I saw it. My body reacted at the same lightning speed as my mind and I had to actively force myself to go inside the house before he turned on my street.

Go, I told my feet.

Now, I told them.

But he was out of the truck and walking up the grass before I had moved even an inch. His eyes were hooded. He wore a baseball cap. I saw the confusion flashing across his face when I didn't run.

I wish he knew I couldn't help it. I wanted to move. I desperately wanted to move and run inside and hide under my covers and pretend it never happened.

"Karina." Kael's voice was punishment wrapped in silk.

I couldn't speak through the lump in my throat. My tongue felt so heavy.

He looked the same and it surprised me. How had it only been a week since I had touched him? It didn't seem possible. My body was a traitor, reminiscing over his warmth as he stood in the yard, too far away from me.

My brother stood up, covering my view of Kael for a second. Just what I needed to help me snap out of it.

"See you later," I said to Austin, as casually as I could manage without looking at Kael. I deserved an Academy Award. I grabbed the screen door handle and didn't look back again. Once inside, once I heard the click of the lock, I pressed my body against the front door. It was an attempt to stabilize myself, to keep myself upright. It didn't work. I cried so hard that I slid down onto the floor. That's where I stayed until Elodie came home from work and lured me up with pictures of her sonogram. Her little avocado was now the length of a banana. She was so happy that I cried again.

Chapter ⁕ Sixty-Eight

I WAS FINE CLOSING for Elodie since she was having back pain. And I was fine when Mali left early to let her dogs out because her husband's poker game bled over and he wouldn't be home in time. But being in the spa alone? I hated it.

My imagination was the problem, the way it loved to travel to extremes—and quickly. I was starting to get creeped out, like I used to when I was left alone in my parent's house and still do sometimes in my own place. I was thinking of all those urban legends that everyone thought were so funny. *The call is coming from inside the house!* I never got the joke, myself. And the one about the man hiding under the girl's bed, licking her fingers so that she'd think it was her dog? Yeah … I was freaking myself out.

I didn't have long to go. There were no clients on the schedule sheet and I doubted anyone would be walking down the strip mall within the next twenty minutes, so I closed down my room for the night and got stuff ready for the morning. The cleaning company had been in the night before and everything was in pretty good shape. I just had to straighten up a few things and make sure all the candles were out. That kind of thing. I turned the lights off, one by one, before locking the back door—padlock too—and shutting off the office light.

I practically ran to the lobby where the lights were still on, and switched off the overhead lighting. I turned on the flashlight on my phone and walked to the front corner window to turn on the floor lamp. We always kept one dim light on, to prevent break-ins. Mali told me that schools did this too, and for the same reason. Just the mention of a break-in plucked at my nerves.

Freaking yourself out much, Karina?

I was laughing a little at myself then, telling myself what a wimp I was. It was like all those *CSI* scenarios I made up for people. And *Law & Order*? Too many *Law & Order SVU* marathons had obviously done a number on my head.

And then I saw a shadow approach the door and practically jumped out of my skin. I think I may have screamed a little, too. I stood still, trying to catch my breath and slow my heart rate. The shadow moved closer into view and that's when I saw that it was a man—a young one, but not a boy. Maybe a soldier given the haircut. It was a little late for someone to just pass by. Plus I didn't recognize him, and that made me a little uneasy.

I had never been alone in the spa at night before and I would surely never do it again. And I wished to God I had listened to Kael when he told me to start carrying mace again. I looked at the now empty pink stick dangling from my purse. Wasn't it funny how it was pink? Like it just had to be "cute and girly" so I could protect myself from men at night.

The man tugged at the door and I stepped into view, flicking the other lamp back on. I turned the flashlight off on my phone and kept a little distance from the door.

"Hey, sorry are you closed?" He was calm. His voice was friendly enough.

"Yeah, well, in ten minutes." I sounded like a terrified church mouse. I felt like one too, and I hated that. Courage, Karina.

"Oh, sorry. I think I did something to my back during PT and was hoping you guys would still be open." He sounded genuine enough, but I couldn't see his face.

"We could see you in the morning? I could come in early?" I offered, assuming he would have to work, but feeling sort of guilty knowing he was a soldier and in pain.

"I think I can get out of PT in the morning, can I come in and put my name down?" he asked. I looked up at the little red light of the camera hanging on the wall and unlocked the door. My mind flashed back to *Law & Order* and how Mali would react when she discovered my body in the morning.

The man stepped inside and looked into my eyes. It was a little off-putting, but honest too, in a strange sort of way. He followed me to the desk and I grabbed the paper version of the schedule since I had already shut the computer down. I looked at my day tomorrow.

"I have a ten o'clock opening and a twelve, but I could come in at nine or eight thirty for you since you came all this way tonight," I told him.

I didn't know where he came from, but I was trying to recite some of the typical customer service lines I've used from job to job. Inconveniencing yourself for the unhappy customer or client usually does the trick, unless the customer is a real jerk. Then they're on their own.

"Let's do nine thirty so it will be extra quiet in here."

He looked behind him to the hours of operation painted on the front door in clear white letters.

"Okay." I swallowed. "Nine thirty it is. Can I have your name please?"

"Nielson," he told me. I wrote it down. It sounded familiar, but I knew I had never seen his face before. I knew faces.

"Are you the one who ... you know, gives the special kind of massage?" His voice crawled over me like tiny little spiders.

My stomach dropped. "What did you just say?" I asked. Accused was more like it. I looked at the camera again, this time in a real obvious way. This time he noticed.

"Um, er ... yeah. Well ... I heard there's one of you here who does," he slithered. "You know. *Special massages ...* "

I wanted to throw up. I wanted to run. But I reached deep for my courage and held my ground.

"I'm going to ask you to leave," I said, as firmly as possible. Then I reached for the land line and lifted it halfway to my ear.

He held up his hands in mock surrender, smirking. I thought I saw a flash of metal in the back of his jaw when he laughed. "Sure, okay, okay. I'm teasing. Sorry, sorry." He held his hands up. "No harm done. No need to get defensive."

I stared at him, silently, not lowering the phone and hoping he couldn't see my hand shaking or the way my knuckles were stretched and white, holding onto the phone as tightly as I could. After the longest few seconds of my life, he retreated, walking backward toward the front door.

He kept his eyes on me though. Those icy blue eyes and taut pale skin were much sinister now that he was scaring the shit out of me. I couldn't let him see that he was though, so I held my lips in a tight line and kept the phone up so that he could see.

Just before he backed out of the door, the stranger smiled again. "You're Fischer's daughter, right?" An alarm sounded in my head. Who was this guy?

The bell dinged when he pressed his back against the door. My heart was pounding out of my chest. Please leave, I silently begged him. Please go. He turned around and hovered in the doorway. And in that moment, just as the door was slowly pulling closed, Kael appeared on the sidewalk. I thought I was going to pass out at the sight of him there.

Kael. In the flesh. I wasn't alone anymore.

Chapter ✳ Sixty-Nine

KAEL OPENED THE DOOR and I climbed into his truck. I tried not to think about how much was left unresolved between us or how much I wanted to move next to him and hold onto his warm body.

Old-school Kings of Leon was playing low through the speakers.

"Seatbelt," Kael reminded me, as usual.

"You're in no position to be bossy," I told him. He smiled. "I'm starting the clock now," I said. "Twenty minutes." And I did too. I set my iPhone timer.

He smiled again. I hated that my guard was slipping and slipping fast, but the burst of relief I felt when he looked at me, head titled and lips parted … well, I didn't hate that.

"What?" I asked him, tucking my chin into my shoulder to hide my mouth.

"It feels good to breathe again," he responded, eyes locked onto mine. That was it. Addiction. Relapse. I couldn't help it if I wanted to.

"Mhmm," I teased him. "Ask me stuff," I said to break the intensity. It was either that or give into my body and touch his shoulders, his neck, his lips.

All of the pain from the last week felt worth it just to be sitting here beside him. As I said. Addiction.

He turned the radio down.

"Are you sure you're okay? You looked spooked. You know, by that guy who was walking out of your work." He sounded concerned. I wanted him to be concerned, even if I wouldn't ever admit it to him.

I nodded. "Yeah, I'm fine. Really." It would hit me later on. I knew that. When I was alone, without the safety of Kael's body next to me, without the protection his presence offered, it would hit me what happened, that some creepy guy came in and made a disgusting joke and knew my dad by name. I rolled down the passenger window to get some fresh air. It smelled a little like fresh rain and earthworms. It helped calm me. The wind blowing, Kael driving, the loud thrum of the engine in this beast of a truck he drives. It all helped calm me.

"Okay, as long as you're sure?" He waited for my response.

I nodded.

"How old were you when you lost your first tooth?" he asked.

I thought about it for a second. "Six? I think. My mom said I used to eat them. Like literally I would swallow them before she caught me so the tooth fairy missed me twice."

He bit his lip, trying not to laugh.

His next question was, "Okay, how many tickets have you gotten? In your life?"

I tilted my head. "Traffic or concert?" I clarified.

"Traffic."

"Three."

"Three? You've only been driving, what, four years tops?" he teased me. "Well, if you're going for one a year you're a little behind. You know that don't you?"

I nodded.

He continued. "How many pets have you had over the span of your life?"

"Only one. His name was Moby." I explained how I loved that furry little fella until he ran away for the fortieth time and never came back.

"Like the whale or the singer?" Kael asked.

I bit down my laugh, but missed a little of it. "Neither. We just liked the name."

He was wearing a gray T-shirt with a navy bomber jacket over it. The jacket was tight on his arms and his jeans were black, with rips in the knees, my favorite jeans. Ever created really.

"What does the taste of macaroni and cheese remind you of?" he asked me as he turned on to the highway.

"Where do you come up with these questions?" I was laughing now.

He shrugged. "Why, did I stump you?"

I shook my head. "Mac and cheese reminds me of my mom." I leaned forward, covering my face. "That's always my answer." I uncovered my face and pushed my wild hair back away from my cheeks. "But she makes … *made*, the best macaroni and cheese ever. From scratch. Except the noodles, of course. She doesn't make the noodles," I told him.

"She always told me that when I get married she'd

teach me the recipe. Which is weird." I half laughed.

"And outdated," he added.

"Totally outdated," I agreed.

"I have a few more questions," he said. The turn signal clicked as we waited at a red light in front of Kroger. It was across the street from a car wash, the one where Brien and I broke up while he was vacuuming his car. He was obsessed with vacuuming his car.

"Go on." I encouraged him to keep going so I could wash Brien from my brain.

"When did you realize that you're different from everyone else around you?" he asked. Our eyes met, just then. It was so dark in the car, he had one hand on his steering wheel and one hand on his lap. I wanted so desperately to touch his fingers. All of the will power I summoned up over the last week had evaporated so quickly. I moved a little closer to Kael and moved his leather book bag out from between us. A small stack of papers fell out of the unzipped top; I sat them on the empty space next to me.

"What kind of car do you imagine you'll drive in five years?"

"Hmm, probably the same one? I don't know, I don't care about cars," I told him.

"What's your biggest fear?" Kael asked me.

I answered that one without even thinking about it. "Something happening to Austin."

Kael looked over at me and without a word, told me that he felt my worry for my brother. Kael was the first person to ever just get me so effortlessly, it was so refreshing to be around him again. So much so that it overpowered the doubt that had been clouding my mind since I had seen him last.

"My turn." I was quiet for the last couple of questions. I didn't have an answer for the first question he asked because I had never seen a Marvel movie.

"Do you feel like you know me now?" he asked. I shook my head.

"I said, *my* turn." I was nearly next to him in the front cab now and he looked down between us.

"Put your seatbelt on, then it's your turn." No sooner were the words out of his mouth then a flash of light illuminated the windshield.

He had swerved into another lane. A horn blared as Kael jerked the wheel to straighten the car and I caught my breath.

I moved back to my seat at the other side of the cab and buckled in. Kael was looking straight ahead, his hands strangling the steering wheel.

"Are you okay?" I asked him.

A couple seconds passed and he swallowed. "Are you?" he asked me without looking at me.

"Yeah. You were so worried about my seat belt that you almost killed us." I reached for his hand and realized just how hard he was gripping the wheel.

"Kael," I said his name softly, like I did when he woke up in the morning, confused as to what continent he was on. I saw the same look on his face now.

"Kael, it's okay. I'm okay. We're okay. Do you want to pull over?"

He was silent. I reached across the pile of papers and the book bag and put my hand on his leg. I gently stroked his skin over his jeans.

"Pull over." It wasn't a question. I could see that he still hadn't snapped out of it. "Kael." I lifted my hand into the air. "I'm going to touch your face," I warned him, not knowing how he would react. My body was going to give up on me if I kept going through rush after rush of fear like this. He nodded slowly and I gently placed my open palm on the side of his cheek, pressing softly into his warm skin. I kept it still and slowly rubbed my thumb across the light stubble on his jawline.

He pulled to the side of the road before I had to say his name again. His breath came in heavy puffs, thick blasts of panic. I was so happy to be there with him, so close and forgetting the pep talks I had given myself every morning and night while trying to keep my distance. I should have known that it would be impossible to stay away from him.

"It's okay," I said again, hugging his waist.

"Karina." His breath came hard and fast, like he had run up a flight of stairs.

I leaned over and knelt on the cushion, my body turned toward him.

"We're okay. Look." I nudged his nose with mine and his eyes regained their focus. He looked like a little boy, not a war veteran. Not a man. It melted my heart. It made me want to tell him that I was falling for him, that all he needed to do was explain what had happened without any lies or bending of the truth. We had so much to talk about.

Right now, I just wanted to comfort him. He was coming down from it—wherever *it* was. He was coming back to me.

I moved my body closer to his.

"I'm just going to move these papers," I said as I stacked them neatly. There was an Army folder on top with the typical Army star. Kael stilled next to me. I felt the shift in the space around us as I realized what the packet said. Cars passed us on the freeway, but I didn't care. I wanted him to be calm, to be able to breath.

"Who's enlistment packet is this?" I asked, curious as always. "Thought you were trying to get out?" I couldn't stop myself. I opened the folder. That's when Kael reached over, trying to grab it from me. "I can't believe you're going to re-enlist, after all you—"

And then I read the name on the first page.
AUSTIN TYLER FISCHER

Chapter ★ Seventy

NOW IT WAS KAEL'S TURN to call my name. Kael's turn to bring me back to earth.

"Karina. Karina," he said. "Listen to me, Karina. There's an explan—" His words were gibberish. I could make out my name, but that was it. I could barely feel my body.

"What is this, Kael," I managed at last. The truck was parked on the soft shoulder, but felt like it was dangling over the edge of a steep cliff.

When he didn't answer me, I screamed. I didn't have time to waste on his cons and excuses. I was reading the evidence.

"WHY IS THIS ... WHY IS THIS IN YOUR CAR?" I slammed the folder down onto the empty space on the seat between us. A semi honked at us and Kael shifted into drive.

"Do not move this fucking car until you tell me what this is and why it's in your car!" I was every emotion: fear, anger, disgust, contempt. He was a marble statue—beautiful, but cold.

The alarm on my phone went off. His twenty minutes was up. Had it only been twenty minutes? Had Austin really joined the Army? And Kael knew? More to the point … what was his part in it?

"Answer me or never speak to me again," I told him as I dug in my purse for my phone. I had a missed call from a local number that I didn't recognize, but nothing else. I searched Austin's name and my head was spinning so fast that everything was blurry when I tried to type a text to him. I called him, he didn't pick up.

"You made him, didn't you?" I spat at Kael. "You did this to hurt me!" I screamed at him.

"I did this because he needs structure. I did this because he needs to stop fucking up his life."

"Oh my God! You're unbelievable! This is how far you're willing to take this thing against my dad? Shipping his only son off to the war?"

I was going to be sick. I tried to roll the window down but couldn't find it. I reached for the door handle and Kael tried to reach for me.

I jerked away. "Don't you dare! Don't you fucking dare touch me!" I nearly fell out of the Bronco. "Get away from here. Get the fuck away." Tears soaked my face and my hair stuck to my wet cheeks.

"Go!" I screamed, not caring that it was dark out or that I would be alone on the side of the road. I just wanted to be as far away from him as humanly possible.

And of course, because the universe hated me, the moment my shoes touched the ground and I yelled at him again to drive away, the sky started to cry, covering me with thick tears of rain from head to toe.

To be continued...

Stay tuned for part two of
Karina and Kael's story,
coming in 2019.

Title to be announced.

Acknowledgements

This is that awkward part of a book where I pretend I just won an Oscar and name the first people that come to mind, so bear with me as I try to give these humans a tiny bit of what they deserve,

Flavia Viotti, agent extraordinaire - You are such a bad ass, hard working woman and one of the best momma's I know. I'm so honored to know you and I can't wait for the future with you. You worked your ass off on this book and it means the world to me.

Erin Gross - You complete me. Literally. Thank you for being my right and left hand, brain, arms, etc etc. You're the best and we are taking over the world together. You're so innovative and literally work through your sleep. I heart you so hard.

Jen Watson aka Jenny from the block - You! You're a road dog for life and we have had so many adventures together, work and mostly not lol. I can't wait for more.

Ruth Clampett - You're our own meditation app. Your grace and kindness is something I have come to not be able to live without.

Erika - You're the ultimate supporter of me and I literally wouldn't have a career without your influence on my life and words. Thank you for being such a great mentor and woman for me to look up to.

Kristen Dwyer - This is our tenth book together! Whattttt. You're the bomb and I can't wait for eleven, twelve, ninety-nine.

Brenda Copeland - What a freaking trooper you are! I'm so glad you're a part of this team and you rocked the first chaotic book, get ready for the next <3

To all my publishers around the world, the editors, the sales team, the cover designers, everyone who spends any of their precious time trying to help my dreams come true, thank you!! Your time and dedication doesn't go unnoticed.